LOVE AND DREAMS

A Beach Reads Billionaire Tycoon Contemporary Romance

~ *Book II* ~
The Summer Sisters Tame the Billionaires
~ *Book Club Edition* ~

Jean Oram

This is a work of fiction and all characters, organizations, places, events, and incidents appearing in this novel are products of the author's active imagination or are used in a fictitious manner—unless stated in the book's front matter. Any resemblance to actual people, alive or dead, as well as any resemblance to events or locales is coincidental (unless noted) and, truly, a little bit cool.

Love and Dreams: A Beach Reads Billionaire Tycoon Contemporary Romance Copyright © 2014 by Jean Oram

All rights reserved, including the right to reproduce this book or portions thereof in any form whatsoever, unless written permission has been granted by the author, with the exception of brief quotations for use in a review of this work. For more information contact Jean Oram at JeanOramBooks@gmail.com. www.JeanOram.com

Printed in the United States of America unless otherwise stated on the last page of this book. Published by Oram Productions Alberta, Canada.

LIBRARY OF CONGRESS CATALOGING-IN-PUBLICATION DATA

Oram, Jean.
    Love and Dreams: A Beach Reads Billionaire Tycoon Contemporary Romance / Jean Oram.—1st. ed.
    p. cm.
    ISBN 978-1-928198-00-0 (paperback)
    Ebook ISBN 978-1-928198-01-7
1. Romance fiction. 2. Sisters—Fiction. 3. Businessmen—Fiction. 4. Romance fiction—Small towns. 5. Love stories, Canadian. 6. Small towns—Fiction. 7. Muskoka (Ont.)—Fiction. 8. Interpersonal relations—Fiction. I. Title.

Summary: Business grad Maya Summer believes her life is about to take off in a big way when business tycoon Connor MacKenzie hires her to be his personal assistant during a two week stay at her Muskoka cottage. Sparks fly for the couple as they butt heads about work, life, and more.

First Oram Productions Edition: April 2015

Cover design by Jean Oram

Dedication

To my grandmothers. For helping me rediscover Muskoka each summer.

A Note on Muskoka

Muskoka is a real place in Ontario, Canada, however, I have taken artistic license with the area. While the issues presented in this book (such as water shed, endangered animals, heritage preservation, shoreline erosion, taxation, etc.) as well as the towns are real, to my knowledge, there is no Baby Horseshoe Island nor is there a Nymph Island, or even a company called Rubicore Developments. The people and businesses are fictional, with the exception of The Kee to Bala and Jenni Walker—you can read about how she ended up visiting Muskoka in the acknowledgements.

Muskoka is a wonderful area where movie stars and other celebrities do vacation. Yet, having spent many summers in the area during my youth and adulthood, I have yet to see a single celebrity—though a man I presume to be Kurt Browning's (a famous Canadian figure skating Olympian) father did offer to help me when the outboard fritzed out on me once. Damn outboard.

You can discover more about Muskoka online at www.discovermuskoka.ca/

Acknowledgements

Thank you to Lurie Twist, a member of my fan group/street team on Facebook, for naming Connor MacKenzie's business, CM Enterprises. If you'd like to join in such fun and games as naming characters and more (as well as get incredibly rich and famous—hey, it could happen—by being mentioned in one of my books) join us at www.facebook.com/groups/jeanoramfans.

I would also like to thank my critique partners who, as always, do their best to keep me in line. As well, thank you to Emily and Erin for cruising the book for errors that slipped past me after making the corrections suggested by my editor, Margaret.

LOVE AND DREAMS

To the Sylvan Lake Library, Aug 2017

A beach reads for a beach town!

xo

Jean Cram

Chapter One

Maya Summer shifted shifted from foot to foot in the tall grass and squinted up at the sky. Where was that plane? She was more than ready for her future to land, and now it was delayed. She checked her watch and hurried into the private airstrip's terminal, a small shack, to use their washroom again.

"I shouldn't have had that extra cup of coffee," she muttered. She was wired, jittery, and so nervous she wasn't sure whether to throw up or break into delirious laughter.

"Meeting someone important, dear?" asked a woman as Maya hurried into the washroom's one stall.

"Connor MacKenzie. I'm picking up Connor MacKenzie." She grinned as she flushed the toilet, and refrained from giving a little happy dance there in the cramped enclosure. Connor MacKenzie was coming to see *her*. Live with *her*.

"*The* Connor MacKenzie?" the woman asked, surprise evident in her voice, as she made room for Maya at the sink.

Maya nodded and adjusted her suit jacket in the mirror. It was kind of boxy, not as fitted as she'd been looking for, but it was all she'd been able to find at the local Salvation Army, and it went with her flared dress pants. She was going to spend the summer with Connor. Okay, okay, two weeks—only two weeks. *Oh, man. Breathe.* She had two weeks to convince Mr. MacKenzie that she was worth taking back to his Toronto office, where she'd be employed as his right-hand woman. His personal assistant, Stella

Bijania, had on-the-spot hired her less than twenty-four hours ago to take care of her boss during his impromptu retreat and to do whatever was needed to ensure he got the downtime he was paying for. It was also her job to prevent him from falling too behind while in Muskoka.

She could do it. And she would do it well. In less than a month she'd be in the city, settling into a penthouse off Yonge Street, wearing Prada, because the devil wore Prada, and she was going to be the devil of the business world. Plus, she was about to learn the best strategies straight from the man who'd invented most of them as he went from MBA student to the new king of Bay Street as well as the city in less than a decade. He was barely older than she was, and he was already worth billions. The next two weeks were going to rock.

"He's going to change my life," Maya declared as she touched up her lipstick. He'd quickly see that she wasn't just another university grad with no experience. It was as her hero, the entrepreneurial Arlene Dickinson, said, "You have to surround yourself with people who are more talented than you are." And Maya was ready to surround herself with all things Connor MacKenzie. The man was a walking business bible she was eager to speed-read.

"Connor MacKenzie?" the woman repeated. "He's coming to Bracebridge?"

"The one and only. And no, he's coming to stay at my cottage. On an island." She barely held in a sigh of longing. He was smart, rich, and business-minded. Don't forget hot. Man, what she wouldn't give to wrap his expensive silk tie around her fist and pull his sweet lips against hers when she got the chance. That guy had a checkmark beside all the things a woman wanted in a man. Plus some.

"Are you his…?"

"Business associate." Maya followed the woman out of the washroom. Okay, she was going to be his assistant and, well, maid, while he took a business retreat at her family cottage for the next two weeks, but still. She was working *with* him. One on one. Discussing business things, creating presentations, drafting emails to all the bigwigs he associated with. She was going to be the sexy, smart, witty woman in high heels and power suits nodding beside him, pointing out things he hadn't thought of, while he enjoyed his retreat from the city's stifling summer heat. He'd turn to her with respect brimming in his gaze, and ask how he'd ever got along without her. His lips would be just a whisper away from hers when he'd say…

"Is that him?" The woman pointed out the dusty window.

Maya staggered on her heels before catching herself. "He's waiting. I've left Connor MacKenzie waiting!" She scrambled out the door, before catching herself and adopting her best no-nonsense stride. Several feet away, she extended her hand for a shake. Too early. She hurried her pace, hoping he wouldn't notice.

"Mr. MacKenzie!"

He turned to her, all sexy five o'clock shadow and Gucci shades, ball cap parked low on his forehead.

"Mr. MacKenzie!" Maya reached to shake his hand, and he thrust a heavy duffel at her. The bag dropped, wrenching her shoulder. "Oomph!"

The man packed like a girl, with everything in one ginormous bag that was nearly impossible to lift without seeing a chiropractor afterward.

"Do you have other bags?" she asked, looking around for a laptop. He had to have a briefcase. Maybe two. "On the plane, perhaps?"

"That's all."

Where were his computer and business papers? Surely not in

the duffel, getting crushed. Crushed like the disks in her spine, one by one, the longer she stood clinging to the bag's handles. She readjusted her grip and leaned back so she wouldn't be tempted to allow gravity take over and cause her to kiss the tarmac.

"Good flight?"

She could barely believe how *human* he seemed in person. Not at all the bouncing, vibrant machine whose mouth could barely keep up with his ideas during his TED talk two years ago. Watched: 73 times. University essays written about or referencing that talk: 13.

But this man here in front of her? He wasn't exactly exuding power and energy. No overflowing enthusiasm. He was mellow. Really mellow.

It kind of bummed her out, actually. But at the same time, there was something irresistibly intriguing about his quietness.

Connor stared at her and, with a quick inhalation, she launched into her rehearsed introduction. "My name is Maya Summer. I'll be your everything this summer."

An eyebrow appeared over the frame of Connor's sunglasses, beneath his sun-faded hat. "Everything?" he asked, his voice thick and rough, its tenor low.

Sweat pricked Maya's back, and she knew it wasn't caused by the heat of the July sunshine radiating off the cracked tarmac. It was the way his tone hinted at something less businesslike.

"Just about." She shot him a playful smile.

Some women might think her ambitious to a fault, but she'd sleep her way out of a starting position in the mailroom if she had to. And with this man, it would not be a hardship. Give her half an excuse and she'd run her hands over those broad shoulders, down his chest and lower. Her eyes drifted where her imagination was going, before she caught herself.

Right. He was her boss. No need to make him feel similar to a piece of man meat. Not yet, anyway.

"You'll be staying at my cottage for the next two weeks," she said. "A quiet, rustic business retreat. And I will be available as your personal assistant—um, business executive. Are you sure you don't have another bag?"

He gave a small shake of his head.

"Okay, great. So, I will be your liaison with…with, uh, everyone you require while you enjoy your retreat. Whatever you need, I can take care of it. And, uh…" Damn, where had all her lines gone? She'd imagined a much brighter meeting. For example, one where he talked and shook her hand. One where he asked about her, or at least her qualifications, so she could tell him she'd graduated with distinction, made the dean's list, won a scholarship from TD Mutual, and all that other stuff that made businessmen get a hard-on when discussing the pillageable assets they could get for pennies on the dollar in their overeager assistants.

And okay, so things weren't unrolling the way she'd expected, but she was already learning things from him. For instance, when it came right down to choosing the proper power outfit, a short skirt was always the way to go.

MAYA UNLOCKED THE TRUNK of her car and perched her sunglasses on her head as she hoisted Connor's bag into the trunk of her old Honda, her high heels sinking into the grass parking lot. Peering around the side of the car, she hoped Connor wouldn't notice the car's rust spots and its general lack of va-va-voom. She paused when he climbed into the backseat. Did she look as though she ran a car service? Why wouldn't he ride up front with her?

She clutched the wheel and promised herself that it was only jet lag making him seem different than she'd expected. Soon he'd perk up, fill her brain with valuable business tips, and the formal, boss-assistant line would become blurred.

The only problem with her jet lag theory was the flight from Toronto was supershort. Maybe he'd been in France. Or up all night hashing out a deal. Maybe he trusted her, and that was why he was so quiet. Maybe this was the real Connor MacKenzie.

Yes, that was likely it. He could tell she was someone he could be himself around and that she wouldn't judge him. He'd be spilling his secrets and insecurities in a matter of hours, wondering how he'd ever managed to get by not sharing his burdens with someone like her.

"I thought you were my assistant?" he said as she started the engine.

"I *am* your assistant."

"How are you going to do that if you're driving taxi? This job has a very demanding schedule."

"Oh! The door? It's from the wreckers. Mrs. Star accidentally backed into it and the only door I could find was off one of Alvin's old taxis—it hit a moose. Anyway, Mrs. Star is on a pension and it didn't feel right for her to shell out for a proper door that matched. Especially since I'll be buying a new car in the fall. Why have either of us spend money painting over *Alvin's Taxi* on this old clunker, right? Plus it's kind of fun. Sometimes I pick up fares to help pay for gas. Alvin doesn't mind as long as I charge reasonable rates and buy him a coffee every once in a while."

Silence.

Okay. Making the best out of a crappy old car didn't amuse him. Good to know.

Maya drove through the rocky terrain of the Canadian shield's

Love and Dreams 7

countryside, forcing herself to not give excuses for her car's lack of newness, and parked at the docks where the family's old boat waited for them. She tried to surreptitiously fan herself with her suit jacket, hating the fact that Connor was comfortable in a faded T-shirt, shorts and a ball cap, while she was dying from the heat. But it was worth making a favorable impression, right?

"What are we doing?" Connor asked as she got out of the car.

"Taking a boat."

"A boat?"

Oh, thank the heavens for the breeze off the lake. She could stand here for hours.

Connor's voice sounded thick, slow. It was as if he was struggling his way through molasses. Was he on drugs? Was he on this retreat to try and get clean in private? Because she was *so* not the merry maid type and was not going to nurse him back to health. Play-acting nursemaid for a man as sexy as him? Hell, yeah. But cleaning up other people's vomit in a century-old cottage sounded like her idea of Hell with a capital H. Because, seriously, that stuff was not going to come out of the plain oak floorboards, and she'd rather go back to her crappy old service jobs if that was the way this was going to go down. Her family might need Connor's money in order to save their cottage, but a girl had to draw the line somewhere. Even for him.

"You're staying on an island," she informed him. "With me." A secret little jump of glee partied in her belly.

"An island?" He sat back in the seat as though stunned by the revelation, even though his tone remained flat and lifeless.

"Yes. It said as much in the ad."

"Oh." He waved, as though she should proceed to drive the car onto a ferry. "Very well then. Carry on. And please tune the radio to Met Opera Radio. Channel seventy-four."

Maya stared at him for a moment. "Um, first of all, does this car seem like… Never mind, you have to get out of the car to take the boat."

He paused, then slowly reached for the handle, fumbling with it before heaving the door open as though it was made of lead.

This was not good. Seriously not good. She popped the trunk and hauled his bag to the simple motorboat. The forty-year-old Boston Whaler was great for hauling stuff out to the island, but was definitely not a yacht, nor the kind of boat where someone could hide from the wind or any splashing she might intentionally cause in order to wake up her passenger.

"This is it. We'll head across Lake Rosseau to my private island, where you will be staying." Damn if that didn't sound good. "It has one building—the cottage, Trixie Hollow." No need to mention the leaning boathouse along the rocky shore. "It's rustic. Private. Quiet." Well, it was when Rubicore Developments wasn't blasting into the Canadian shield to demolish the point on nearby Baby Horseshoe Island. The company's representative, Aaron Bloomwood, better have swept the debris off her dock as she'd asked when she left a few hours ago. Come to think of it, she still had his offer to purchase in the boat's seat pocket. Once she got Connor settled she'd have to pull it out and read it over to see if they were offering a solution to all her problems. She almost laughed at the thought. Money couldn't solve everything, but it sure could help when you were pushed against the wall like she was.

Maya boated across the lake, resisting the urge to make small talk with Connor. She had to rethink everything if he was going to be out of it the whole time.

She moored the Boston Whaler on Nymph Island and moments later Connor stood on the dock, stretching his back.

"It's really quiet here," he said.

Maya nodded and chucked his bag in the ancient lift she'd

tinkered into working again. It ran from the dock up the hill to the cottage, since there was no road to drive up heavy items. She swung its rusted door shut, latching it before sending the bag up with motorized grunts and groans.

"We don't get to take that?" Connor was eyeing the lift as though it was a glass of water in a desert.

"We take the path." She pointed to the dirt trail edged with large rocks. Trees overhung it, creating shade at all times of the day. It got a tad steep at the top, where it curved around a massive rock to meet up with the steps that led to the cottage's veranda, but it wasn't anything someone their age couldn't easily manage.

"I'd prefer the lift."

"My hundred-pound mother is the only one who takes it, and even then it's pretty rough going." Maya studied Connor's frame. He'd lost weight since the last time she'd seen him speak—a conference she'd snuck into last fall. He was still hot, and still a broad man, just a little leaner than she preferred. She'd have to see what she could do about that. But even with him slimmer than usual, he wasn't going up in the lift.

Maya led him up the path to the cottage, trying not to be obvious about how she was slowing her pace to match his. A man his age—only about seven years older than her—shouldn't be working this hard. She racked her mind for any recent news stories that mentioned anything about his health. Nothing. They were all about his golden touch, fabulous mergers and net worth. Or sometimes about his still-single status.

She guided Connor up the steps to the veranda, dreading how run-down the place looked despite the hours of hard work she and her sisters had put into it. Even this morning Hailey and her new movie star boyfriend, Finian Alexander, had been out helping put last minute touches on the place. And yet it still appeared neglected.

Maya flashed Connor a bright smile, hoping he wouldn't step on the rotten board third from the top. The last thing she'd need was him to fall through the steps, injure himself and sue them.

"We have a lovely new chimney thanks to Finian Alexander's generosity. Do you know his movies? He left just this morning." No need to tell Connor the man had been part of a frantic working bee, and not here as a guest. "So, anytime you want a fire in the fireplace—you'll notice it's gorgeous flagstone from the Parry Sound quarry—we can set you up."

Connor's glazed eyes took in the veranda as it came into view as though he was seeking a place to collapse. "It's hot."

"You'll find we get a lovely breeze here on the veranda. It's often seven degrees cooler here than in port." Maya tried to keep smiling as she stepped off the stairs. There wasn't enough breeze to whisper the feathers on a hummingbird.

"Is there air conditioning? My assistant said…" He frowned as though trying to recall a conversation, his mouth curving into a perfect, kissable arc.

Maya clasped her hands to pull her mind back to business before it filled with fantasies involving Connor laid out in the nude. "Um, no air conditioning. This is pretty rustic, as the ad mentioned. Back to basics, you know?" She swallowed hard. She knew the kinds of places Connor MacKenzie normally stayed. Five star hotels with valet, personal concierge and a penthouse suite. Not…this. Hadn't his assistant filled him in?

Maya could so totally replace someone like that in a heartbeat.

"Quaint." He tumbled into a wicker chair, reminding her of a long distance runner whose legs had turned to jelly. "I'll have to remember to thank Stella."

"Yes, quaint," Maya said in a rush. She pointed to a clearing just off the veranda. "This over here used to be the ice shed, and there was an outdoor kitchen, as well. The cottage was built one hundred and ten years ago and has been in the family for—"

He patted his pockets as though seeking a phone. "Does WiFi come with a rustic retreat?"

"Yes, of course. We're not *that* rustic. The password is *Trixie Hollow*. Zeros for Os. That's the name of the cottage. If you don't see the network, let me know and I'll switch on the generator—sometimes the battery doesn't hold its charge." She was talking too much about things he didn't care about. She'd turned into one of those annoying, nervous, buzzing women she despised.

"I have internet." He frowned when he failed to find his phone.

"We don't get cell signal in the cottage. Sorry." She tugged down her suit jacket. "This way," she called, opening the wood-framed screen door. "I'll show you around."

"No cell signal?"

He was going to ask for her to take him back to shore. She could feel it. Why had she thought this was a good idea? Why had she allowed herself to get excited?

Or maybe someone needed to bring back the real Connor MacKenzie, because this couldn't possibly be him. She didn't know who this guy was, but he was *not* the man she'd planned the next two weeks of her life around. Truth be told, it didn't really matter if he didn't talk to her for the next fourteen days, as working for him would be better than being the fill-in gopher girl at the local dealership, where there was absolutely no chance of advancement. And missing a few shifts at the Bar 'n' Grill wouldn't exactly kill her, either.

But still, this version of Connor was... Well, she couldn't quite put her finger on what it was. It was more a case of who he *wasn't*.

"You can get a decent signal on the dock, or if you take a nice little hike to the top of the hill out back."

"Landline?"

She shook her head and he let out a disgruntled sound.

"We can Skype or VoIP, though. Unlimited data. You wanted rustic and no interruptions, and that's what we offer." She turned to face him, standing close enough to be perceived as challenging. "That's what you booked, that's what you get."

The screen door slammed behind Connor as he moved a few inches closer. For a moment she feared being alone with him on an island. So far away from everyone, and with a version of her hero that she hadn't anticipated. And he was tall. Taller than she'd realized. He filled the wide door frame and created a shadow over her.

"My room?"

Maya let out a soft breath of relief.

"Right. You'll be staying in Daphne's—the Daphne Room. Very nice. View of the water." She hurried across the open plan living room and pushed on the door to her youngest sister's room. The white-painted, antique bedroom set looked cozy and inviting. "Upstairs is a conference room slash large office. Can I do anything for you as your executive assistant?" She stood in the doorway to his room, uncertain.

He said nothing as he walked past her and fell onto the bed, splayed out, facedown.

From her position on the threshold, she leaned closer. Should she be checking for a pulse? Taking off his shoes so they didn't mark Daphne's white bedspread?

"Um, Mr. MacKenzie?"

She didn't expect being his personal assistant to be so... *personal*. She'd expected him to remain formal and for her to be hurrying around after him, scrawling ideas in a notebook.

"Maybe we should discuss my tasks later. Right now all you need to know is that the bathroom is down the hall. Kitchen, the opposite end. I'll be around the whole time, so if you need anything let me know."

A sound came from the bed and she took a tentative step closer. The sound came again. It was a snore.

Feeling strangely rejected, Maya left the room and closed the door. She'd go take a shower and change into something more casual, then reread the notes from Stella, his Toronto assistant. Just because he was sleeping didn't mean she had time to twiddle her thumbs.

CONNOR STOOD OUTSIDE the bathroom and smiled as he listened to the shower run. Stella had done well, bringing this temporary assistant up to speed so quickly. Thank the stars and lucky paperweights that his new woman—even though she was a babbling, nervous wreck—was the type to stay on top of details. Otherwise there would be no way he could get through the next two and a half days of being disconnected.

He rested a hand on the doorknob, turning it to go in. This woman knew what he wanted after an afternoon of travel and a nap. She might even be better than Stella, if she caught on to his needs this quickly. And that's what he needed, if he was going to use the next few days to prove to his doctor that he wasn't on the brink of a stress-related heart attack, or a life-changing collapse due to exhaustion. A man such as Connor MacKenzie didn't need two weeks off work—a few days would suffice.

He stepped into the misty, warm bathroom. It was exactly the way he liked it. Good old Stella. He needed to give her a raise, even though it was her fault he was stuck here for the weekend. Leave it to her to threaten to quit if he didn't listen to the doctor and take a few days to see if he could decompress. And as much as he liked to think that his secretary, Em, could fill Stella's shoes until he found a new assistant, he knew Stella was simply irreplaceable.

Shaking his head, he tossed his sunglasses on the sink counter and inspected his black eye. Yep, it still looked awful—just like the rest of him. Glancing away from his pale reflection, he peeled off his shirt, doffed his shorts and underwear. He picked up the shorts and inspected them. He hadn't realized he still owned any that weren't a form of businesswear. He didn't even wear shorts on the golf course. Where had these come from?

Smiling at the towel laid out for him beside folded casual clothes, he shook his head in wonder. How had Stella managed to find time to go shopping for him? She was amazing. Knowing her, the new clothes probably fit perfectly, even though his waistline had decreased over the past few months.

He pulled back the curtain on the old-fashioned claw-foot tub, eager to let the water wash over him.

"Oh."

His temp assistant scrambled to cover herself, but then, with a change of mind that surprised him, turned to face him. Full on. Nude. Water cascading over her curves as though she was a nymph, ultra feminine and seductively wet.

"This shower is obviously in use," she said.

"So it seems." She was sexier without her clothes on. Definitely. She had round hips and a narrow, high waist that had been hidden under the suit jacket she'd been wearing earlier. It had hinted at her shape, but this was so much better, he decided, eyeing her small belly button. He liked that she worked out and took care of herself, but still had curves and an irresistible softness. Her skin was taut, breasts round and delicious in a way that would make any man with testosterone in his veins stand up and say hallelujah. And heavens above, those shoulders… especially with water tumbling over them like floods off a mountain.

She was a mermaid. No, a siren. A siren for sure.

"Enjoy what you see?" She placed her hands on her hips. Her new position changed the way the water poured, making it head for the gully between her breasts, creating a waterfall off her pubis.

Mmm. She was gorgeous. And sassy. He liked sassy.

He didn't need to glance down to know his exhausted body wasn't reacting to her *Playboy*-worthy physique in a way she rightly deserved. He wasn't sure if it was betraying him or saving him in this situation, but his pride was leaning toward betrayal. Although the silver lining of not waving an engorged, throbbing penis at her naked form was that maybe she'd be less likely to beat him out of the room with a back scrubber.

"What does your name mean?" Shifting his hands to cover himself, he met her eyes. They sparked with daring, and something within him tugged, drawing him closer, even though he hadn't moved a muscle. "You're interesting."

Most women would have rammed him in the nuts and had him strung up on sexual harassment charges by now. He'd stared for too long at something an honorable man would have looked away from. He should have apologized, left the room. Not gawked, analyzed and then started an asinine conversation about her name.

The city had wrecked him and destroyed the man he'd once been.

How had he not noticed?

"A mermaid? Siren? Greek goddess?" he probed.

The woman was assessing him as much as he was her. Her dark blue eyes were flecked with yellow. Pretty. Unfortunately, she didn't seem to think much of what she saw. Maybe it was his lack of physical response. That had to be insulting. A relief for sure, but also insulting.

Her earlier admiration had dried up. There was no cloud of excitement swirling around her, only brewing storms.

"A nymph," she replied finally.

"That's it. Right." He turned away.

"You know..."

He turned back, head quirked in question.

"You know..." Her voice shook as she repeated the phrase. Her cheeks had pink splotches. Uh-oh. "If we're going to be living together we need to set some ground rules. Namely, if the shower is running—which you can hear from outside the bathroom—don't come in."

"And you could learn to lock the door."

"It's broken." Her voice was hard.

Everything around here was broken, including himself. Connor didn't know whether to make himself comfortable or to run away. He pushed his fingers through his hair, then, remembering he'd tossed aside his sunglasses, grabbed them and put them on.

Maya's voice rose. "And if you happen to barge into the bathroom while I am showering, leave. Don't open the curtain and stare at me like a pervert. I'm not an object you purchased with your rental."

Oh, boy.

"Hon, everything was laid out."

"Don't call me hon."

"Towel." He pointed to the fluffy object folded on the small bench. "Shampoo. Toothbrush. Clothes."

"I am not your personal butler. This is not the Hilton."

"I know. The Hilton doesn't make it a habit of leaving mouse turds on my pillowcase. They prefer chocolate mints."

"I'll take care of that." Her chin lifted in a way that he could have sworn made her breasts perkier. Was that possible? He wanted to see it again. "In the meantime, eyes up here." She pointed to her own eyes, and despite everything, he wanted to kiss her. Kiss her for being strong while being exposed.

Damn, he liked her already.

But most of all, he wanted to kiss her for reminding him that there were still people left in his world who would stand up to him. That right there was worth every penny in his bank account.

"I should explain that my assistant does these things for me in the city. I like a shower after flying and I prefer the bathroom steamy." He swept a hand toward the laid-out toiletries.

Oh. Was that lavender shirt there before? The white lace bra folded on top? Pink razor? Damn. He wasn't just losing it, it was *gone*. He placed a thumb and index finger over his eyelids and then pinched the bridge of his nose. "I'm a bit exhausted and not myself. I apologize. If it isn't within your job description to make my life easy, then fine. You can take care of…faxes."

He left the bathroom and slammed the door, laughing to himself. Fax machine. Nobody sent faxes anymore. And this place didn't even have a phone.

Chapter Two

Connor had been hoping to find a wet bar after leaving his assistant to finish washing the conditioner out of her shoulder-length hair, but the only liquor he could find was a bottle of vodka stashed in the fridge freezer. He sat on one of the veranda's wicker chairs and sipped the cold drink from a short glass.

Much better.

He stared at the swaying trees, then closed his eyes. There was the breeze his spitfire nymph had promised. It was nice. Strong enough to brush away any mosquitoes, but not so much he needed a sweater. His vision blurred and spun slightly as he looked out at the maples and oaks again, but it wasn't the vodka. It was his new friend, fatigue. For weeks he'd found himself struggling to focus on conversations, unable to recall basic facts such as his phone number, and once, even his company's name, which was his own damn initials—CM Enterprises, Ltd. But two days ago—or was it only yesterday morning?—he'd woken up, his vision blotchy, his head unable to retain a thought for longer than five seconds. He'd had to concentrate incredibly hard just to pretend to be alive. When he'd walked into his office door frame after arriving over three hours late, and couldn't figure out if he was hurt or not, Stella had rushed him straight to the ER, fearing he'd had an aneurysm. Turned out he was only burned out. Really, really burned out. And according Dr. Tiang, about to collapse and have all sorts of permanent system shutdowns if he didn't get some serious rest.

Apparently his body hadn't received the urgent memo that he was Connor MacKenzie and that he needed to remain an indestructible human. Instead, it was going rogue and humiliating him into submission.

He had the weekend before he returned for his follow-up. A weekend to cure himself enough to prove that the man with the medical degree was over exaggerating. Sure, Stella had booked this place for two weeks, based on the doc's initial recommendation, but she had to be nuts if she thought Connor—who could complete a merger from start to finish in less than thirty-six hours—was going to need longer than an extended weekend to get over a little fatigue.

Connor sipped his drink, willing his mind to wind down enough that it would shut off the never-ending list of things to do, so he could relax. He absently patted his shorts pocket for his smartphone. Right. Stella had done something with it so he'd be forced to unplug on this executive retreat—she even got Em in on it, if he'd hazard a guess. Some retreat this place was. It was more like real life detox for the plugged-in businessman. He tapped a finger on the sweaty vodka glass. The worst and scariest part was that he couldn't summon the energy to care that he'd dropped everything to go hang out on a remote island. He just couldn't get there.

And *that* freaked him out.

He had mergers, acquisitions and glad-handing events he needed to take care of, and he'd gone totally off grid.

He raised his sunglasses and rubbed his eyes, being careful around the bruising on his right. He ran a hand over his face, wondering who he'd become. To his right, the old wood screen door that led to the living room banged shut with a *tap*-tap-tap, a loose bit of screen flapping in the breeze. Everything in this place was falling apart. He really needed to talk to Stella about what he expected in a retreat.

"Are you ready for supper?"

Connor turned, half expecting his mother. He flipped his shades down a moment too late. Oh well, he couldn't keep the bruise hidden forever, and she'd obviously seen it when he'd stared at her in the bathroom.

Smooth move.

"Mr. MacKenzie, are you hungry?"

She came closer, her brown curls leaving wet circles on her T-shirt just above her breasts. Those perfect breasts that defied gravity, thumbing their nose at the planet's forces. For a moment he wondered if he wasn't allowed the vodka. Was it her own personal stash that helped her get over the quiet desperation that had to be her life if she lived in shoddy suits and this run-down place? He could sense her need for something more. It was all there in her eyes, waiting to be let out, along with a hungry fire and intelligence. It was the kind of hunger that would lead to her overworking herself to death for his benefit.

Just what he needed. An opportunity to get a ton of work done when he was supposed to be kicking back.

"All right, I'll check again later."

Impatient lady.

Although, maybe it was him. Everyone seemed to expect answers from him before they had even stopped talking these days. Which was perplexing. He was Mr. Snap Decision and had instincts that killed in the business world. He owned Toronto.

He…was feeling slightly queasy.

She'd said something about eating…

That might be a good plan. He wasn't sure he'd eaten today.

"Yeah, food."

"*Yeah, food?*"

He sighed at the contempt she was trying to hide in her voice. Oh, right. Manners.

"Sorry. Food. *Please.*"

"Much better."

"And could you hustle it up?" He loved the way her expression turned from satisfaction over his apology to mild outrage, her high cheekbones flushing. "I'm hungry and beat."

"You really aren't the king any longer, are you?" Her sad tone held a touch of pity.

He snorted to himself. As if he was someone pitiful. Didn't she know who he was? Anger flashed through him, and before he could tamp it down, fatigue was causing him to say things he was already wishing he could pull back. "And you think you can top my position with your shoddy suit, and acting as my babysitter in a falling-down cottage? What do you think *you* have that will get you to the top, sweetheart?"

Man, maybe he *was* burned out. Usually he could hold on to his anger and not be such an ass, especially to an assistant. They put up with more than enough crap without him giving them attitude.

"Good grades haven't done it yet," she said, pulling her shoulders back in defiance. "So yeah, why not babysit some washed up has-been?" She sat in the chair beside him, grabbed his drink and knocked it back.

He blinked at her, trying to prod his brain into processing this new side to his assistant. Was she being insolent? Insulting? Or simply delivering his own secret fears in a blatantly direct way that felt similar to a hard-hitting turn-on?

He liked her. A lot.

"Has-been, huh?" He forced his hand to unclench.

She leaned on the arm of her chair. "Where did you go?"

He stared at the dancing trees, buying time in order to delve meaning from her words. He hadn't gone anywhere but here, and he had a feeling her question had to do with the pitiful look she'd given him earlier. He blinked long and hard, and took a sip of vodka, but his glass was missing. Brain definitely not engaging. All cogs plugged with something gooey.

Connor blinked again and the glass was back in his grasp, the woman at the screen door. He blinked again and she was gone. He peered into his empty glass. Damn. Was it the vodka clogging his mind? He didn't think so, seeing as his assistant with the perky breasts seemed to have downed over half of it, and he was a man who could hold a drink. He'd had plenty of training in business meetings and was known for being able to knock them back for hours on end and still retain his sharp business edge.

Which meant he was fried, if a few fingers of vodka had him gummed up.

Or...

Nope, probably just fried.

Sleep. He needed two full days of sleep, then he'd be better again and could go back to Toronto to finish the merger for some dumbass company that had grown too big too soon, and was ripe for this T. rex to devour. Oh, life. So beautifully predictable.

His assistant reappeared, coming at him in fragmented chunks of information. First at the door, then closer. Then in the seat next to him. A fresh drink appeared in his hand. One in hers. She was tipping her glass to clink against his, and hers cracked from the impact.

His world was tipping.

He shoved his sunglasses back up his nose and tried harder to focus, to control his movements.

The woman let out a bitter, jaded laugh, rubbed her eyes, then chucked her glass over the veranda railing, leaving an arc of clear liquid streaming through the air.

She lifted the bottle to her painted lips instead of getting a fresh glass.

Ah yes, he preferred this version of his assistant so much better. They could get into such fun.

She was staring at him.

"What?" he asked.

"Where did you go?"

He closed his eyes. She was confusing.

"You. Where did you go?" She was drawing out her words as if he was new to the language.

"To business school?"

"Are you on drugs?"

He laughed. She was funny, too.

"Are you?" she asked.

"No. Maybe I should try some."

She let out a sigh so heavy it could rival any teenaged girl having a conversation with her parents. "What's your deal?"

He shrugged.

"No, really. I came to see you last October at the Metro Toronto Conference Center, where you were the keynote speaker and were talking about the confluence of—"

"Yeah, yeah, yeah." He couldn't concentrate when she used long sentences. He was still trying to figure out "October" and "Metro Toronto Conference Center" and what that should mean to him. He pointed to himself. "Five-words-or-less lane."

"See?" She turned to him, her knee pressing into his leg. Her skin was smooth. She shaved a long way up her thigh, and he wondered where she stopped. A smooth leg, compounded with the fact that he knew she left her bush natural, was unbelievably hot. She hadn't done that weird trim-up thing to make it look like an afro with a Mohawk.

He studied his own leg. He was wearing shorts that seemed familiar. He fingered the material. They were nice, but he didn't recall owning shorts that fit. Did his assistant buy them?

Wait. He'd already had this conversation with himself, and the hem was slightly frayed and they were loose in the waist. Part of his brain wanted to recall these shorts.

His assistant sat back, slouched in the wicker chair, the bottle back at her lips. "Where'd he go?" she asked. "Who's the douche who showed up today?"

Connor let out a laugh. This woman played hardball. "I really like you, too."

"My name is Maya. Since you have obviously forgotten it already."

"Says who?"

"I can tell." Her voice became slightly breathless, her face alight. "Can I call you Connor?"

He had been right earlier. She was some new grad who thought he'd spout a million-dollar tip if she hung around him long enough. There had been a time when he'd got off on feeling as though he was someone magical, but now it was just another thing dragging on him. He was too busy to mollycoddle newbies and explain every little thing. Besides, most of what he did was instinct based on knowledge and experience, as well as being able to read people. And oh, tarnation, why did his head hurt so bad?

"Can I?" she repeated.

"I don't care what you call me."

"Thank you." She sat up, her chin set in a chippy way that sent off warning systems in his brain. "Connor, I think you should know that I recently graduated with distinction from the University of Toronto…"

Oh boy, here it came. The sales pitch. I'll work for you for free if you just give me a leg up. Let me stalk you. Be your shadow. You'll never know I'm there.

He closed his eyes, and when he opened them again she'd moved on to talking about something else.

"...and so if you need anything at all while you are here on vacation, let me know."

He'd fallen asleep. Thank goodness he was wearing his shades, so she likely hadn't noticed.

"...I know I'm not intimately familiar with all of your systems, but I'll do my best to help you enjoy your time here at Trixie Hollow while—"

"Trixie Hollow? What is this? Disneyland?"

"It's the cottage's name."

"Sounds like Disneyland."

She appeared taken aback and he fought off an apology. Old money and their cottage names. How had he forgotten? He was putting his foot in it, left, right, and center, as though he was trying to do the hokey pokey with a bunch of toddlers.

"You should build a real cottage." He knocked back his drink and winced, surprised to see her smile. He had kind of been hoping to ward her off so she'd go find some food. He needed to eat, then sleep. Maybe take turns doing each one until his doctor-mandated penance was up.

She stood and shook his hand. "I was going to offer you a refund and put you on the next boat out of here, but I think we're going to get along just fine, Mr. Mac—Connor. I'll go fetch supper. Stay here and enjoy the view."

With a hop in her step, Maya vanished into the cottage, and Connor shook his head, wondering when he'd get off the island and back into his life, where everything made sense.

MAYA SET OUT PLATES and cutlery on the old painted table on the veranda. While she worked, she played a podcast about developing effective calls to action, stopping every so often to make notes. It was a typical gorgeous Muskoka evening, and they would be able to see the water, the trees and the busy bird feeder as they dined. The bugs wouldn't be too bad if she lit a mosquito coil or two upwind from where they sat.

Smoothing her shirt over her ribs, she closed her eyes, shaking her head in disappointment. So far this day had been a humiliating, gut-punching disaster–everything from Connor handing off his bag as if she were a bellboy, to him busting in on her in the shower. Thankfully, she hadn't been having one of her Connor MacKenzie fantasies. She straightened a fork and stepped back. On the bright side, she supposed the chances were fairly high that she wouldn't be having any more of those fantasies to worry about.

What had he been thinking, walking into the bathroom and throwing back the curtain? Other than him believing everything in the world was for him, and the only reason other people existed was to make his life easier.

She snorted and let the kitchen door slap shut behind her as she went to check on their supper. She still couldn't believe the way Connor had just stared at her as the water poured over her skin. His eyes had been so blank, so assessing, with no hint of lust or longing. She was a hot babe, so what the heck was his problem? Why hadn't he reacted? He'd just stood there and gazed at her as if…as if she was an asset he was considering merging with.

Well, if he was going to be like that, then she would be herself and not hold back, as her sisters had recommended. True, being her tell-it-like-it-is self might not be the best way to get the job she wanted in Toronto, but the temptation to throw his dumbassed, boring, washed-up self in his face was simply too strong. Besides, it almost seemed as though he enjoyed her tough and sassy attitude. Plus, if there were sparks flying they'd get a lot more work done than if they were perpetually pussyfooting around each other.

And when he'd suggested building a real cottage? She'd never fallen in lust faster in her life. Her hormones must be in overdrive, because this version of Connor MacKenzie didn't exactly line up with her checklist of what she sought in a man. Yet suddenly she was cooking him supper. Well, that was part of the package deal, but still... She *wanted* to make supper for him, to show him that she appreciated his point of view. That she, too, valued new and modern. Yeah, this place was great and all, but if given the choice between this old cottage and something that kept the mice and bugs out, as well as cleaned up properly, she was in. Maybe if it also had better solar panels, or a brand-new, energy efficient generator. Having her long, steamy shower earlier had probably cost her five bucks, as running the ancient generator to power the aging water heater wasn't exactly economical.

She paused in the small kitchen, wondering if one day they could renovate this place as the neighbors across the strait had with JoHoBo. They'd taken an aged behemoth similar to Trixie Hollow and totally redone it. Nothing was the same, and it looked great. Fabulous, even.

The egg timer dinged. Time to check on the deli pizza toasting in the oven. Done. She tossed a layer of fresh tomatoes overtop, before slicing it on an old cutting board that would double as a serving platter. She had added more cheese and a layer of olives and bacon bits before putting it in the oven, in hopes that Connor might believe she was a real cook and not just dressing up premade meals.

She wiped her hands and carried the pizza out to the table. Maybe he ate out so often he didn't know what home-cooked tasted like.

"Ready!" she called.

She heard a surprised snort from around the corner of the veranda and smiled. Probably woke him up. Good. She could pick his sleep-addled brain for business tips while dining.

She set the pizza on the table and realized the meal wasn't going to be enough. There weren't even appetizers, and only cookies from the bakery section for dessert. What had she been thinking? This wasn't going to do for a man used to Michelin-star meals.

Connor stumbled around the corner, one hand on the wall as though he was about to fall. "Big eater, huh?" He made his way toward her and crashed into the nearest chair, at the head of the table as though he owned the place. His shades were drawn down over his black eye and he moved as though he'd had an incredibly long day. She half wondered if she should take him to see a doctor. He seemed way too tired.

"Um..." Maya stared at him as he started filling his plate. "You all right?"

"Yeah."

Maya sagged into the chair kitty-corner from Connor. She was half tempted to sit on the other end of the table, but it would seem ridiculous whenever they had to pass anything. Tomorrow she'd take a few leaves out of the table, then she could sit opposite him and create an equal balance of power. At breakfast, the showdown would be on. For now, she'd simply be grateful that he was more talkative than when she'd picked him up at the airstrip. Even though he still wasn't the man she'd idolized for years and dreamed of being mentored by. This man to her right was only a husk.

"So, what are you working on these days?" she asked, taking a piece of pizza.

Connor shrugged, consuming half his thin slice in one massive bite.

Maya eyed the pizza. She'd better not take another portion until he slowed down, for there might not be enough. She hadn't counted on him eating way more than her.

"I heard you closed a merger with Stillwater Financial a few months ago?"

He gave a barely-there nod.

She stared at him, her slice of pizza drooping. Seriously? The poster boy for the business world couldn't even be businessy? And when was he going to start assigning her tasks?

"Bad name," he said finally.

"Bad name?"

"Still water. Stagnant. Not refreshing or revitalizing. Not moving or keeping up. Bad feng shui."

Maya dropped her pizza. Had Connor MacKenzie, business king of Toronto's financial district, just spewed feng shui at her? Over a company name?

Silence took over the table, to the point where it felt as though the birds at the feeder were screaming.

Maya couldn't understand it. Last night she'd had one of her best flying dreams, which were always a sign that something good was about to happen. Being suspended above the ground, propelled forward without having to walk, had been exhilarating. She'd never quite gotten it right until last night, when everything had finally felt easy. She'd been happy knowing she was in the right place at last.

Which only made Connor's lack of enthusiasm that much more confusing and crushing.

"I'm moving to Toronto in the fall," she said, hoping the

subject of a job would come up. Namely, that she could come work for his company, CM Enterprises.

"You prefer smog and traffic jams?" Connor shoved another slice in his mouth and pushed himself away from the table.

Maya wiped her fingers on a paper napkin. "My word." He couldn't possibly eat like that at business meetings, could he? People would run away in horror. "Have you ever tried tasting your food, or do you enjoy resembling a vacuum cleaner?"

Connor blinked. Then his shoulders straightened and a blip of fear pulsed through Maya's system. Uh-oh. This was the Mr. MacKenzie she'd seen in Toronto. The one she'd been expecting. And now he'd arrived, after she'd verbally slapped him across the face.

Good to know what woke him up, but holy hell, why had she? Her sister Melanie was right. Maya needed a filter between her mental gas pedal and her mouth.

"I was hungry," he replied.

"I can tell."

"Did you say you have a degree in business?" His voice was calm. It had been all afternoon, but this was scary calm. A look-out-for-that-incoming-pink-slip kind of calm.

"Yes." She gripped the table, not daring to say more.

He patted his mouth with the cheap napkin she'd set out, and threw it on his plate. "That's nice."

"Graduated with distinction."

"Good at writing resignation letters?"

Oh, ants on a stick. She'd just poked her head into a fire ants' nest, hadn't she?

"Just kidding," he said.

Damn those sunglasses. She couldn't get a gauge on him.

"What are your plans while you're here?" she asked, struggling to keep her voice even. "I can help with keeping on top of any projects you're in the middle of. Stella said to take a load off of you so you can enjoy your retreat."

"I'm fine." Connor stood, shoving his chair across the veranda with a scraping sound. "I'll be heading back to Toronto on Monday."

"What? For a meeting? I can come."

"I'm sleeping for the next two days, then I'll be heading home." He fingered the neck of his shirt as though looking for a necktie to straighten. He suddenly seemed very Mr. MacKenzie, the King of Toronto. "I doubt I'll be coming back so don't plan anything special on my account."

"But you booked two weeks!" Maya stood, panic setting in. She'd told her sisters he was renting the place for half a month, and she'd quit her crappy job for this. It was Maya's turn to cough up a painful amount in order to save the cottage from the tax man, and the only way she could do that was if Connor stayed. If he didn't, she knew she'd feel compelled to offer him a refund even though there wasn't time to find a new renter on such short notice. She needed him. With shaking hands she smoothed her shirt and rolled her shoulders. Then she gave him a big smile. "I know we didn't get off to a brilliant start, but you can't just leave."

Shoot. She sounded desperate.

If Connor left, she'd have to face failure and her always-the-hero big sister, Hailey, who'd been secretly bailing out this place for the past five years, to the point of remortgaging her own home and business. Summer was already a quarter over. They were running out of time.

"I can and will leave," Connor stated. "Keep the balance unless you re-rent the place."

"You signed a...a—"

"It doesn't say I have to physically be here."

"Okay, true." Maya spread her palms on the table. *All right, girl, stay calm. There's an opportunity here. Failure is the best way to learn.* And she was failing, so what could she learn, other than that Connor MacKenzie was a big letdown who made her want to cry so long and hard everyone for miles around would need to build arks?

She inhaled slowly. Opportunity. Opportunity. "Before you go, let me ask you something. What would you do to change this retreat?"

"Other than bring in a phone, air conditioner, exterminator, carpenter, maid, interior decorator and—no offense—a cook? Other than that?"

Maya leaned forward. "Yeah, all that." *Tell me something I don't know, sweet cheeks.*

"I'd sell it. The land—premium. And a private island? Gold."

"I've received an offer from a developer."

Connor leaned forward, intrigued.

"Want to check it out? It's in the boat. I haven't had a chance to read it yet."

"Do I have to walk down that path?"

MAYA RAN UP THE PATH, clutching the offer from Rubicore Developments as she shoved her curls off her forehead. Should she scan the papers before presenting them to Connor, so she'd have her own view on them? She didn't want to be in the dark if he read it first and then began referring to clauses she knew nothing about. Maya slowed, fingering the sealed envelope. What if the conditions were so awful that Connor would think she was a dolt for sharing them with him?

But if it was a good offer, she and her sisters could sell the island before it was taken from them. They would be able to live happily ever after with a nice, big, fat check and no more worries about repairs, renovations, and killer taxes.

Only she was pretty sure her sisters didn't see it that way. In fact, Maya wasn't completely sure she saw it that way, either. Even though, like Connor, she'd love to have something a little less rundown.

She started back down the path to the dock, noticing how dusk was falling and darkening her way. She slipped into a Muskoka chair and peeled open the envelope. Darting a glance across the strait to where men from Rubicore were working feverishly under the protection of the trees, she wondered what they were up to and why they wanted Nymph Island, as well. If they were planning to destroy Baby Horseshoe Island by demolishing things such as the rocky point, then it might be a good idea to sell while the getting was good. Who knew what Trixie Hollow would be worth if it was only a few hundred yards away from whatever they were doing over there?

Holding her breath, she scanned the papers for the numbers. Where were the numbers? She flipped through the pages.

Finally... She leaned back in the chair and refrained from giving Baby Horseshoe the finger, in case Aaron Bloomwood, the representative who had dropped off the offer, was watching.

The offer was disappointing—even if it was better than what any of the sisters had in the bank. It would cover the tax bill, setting them free of the financial burdens the cottage had caused them. But dividing the number by four—five, if their mother wanted a share—wouldn't do anything other than make the big problem go away and give them all a bit of breathing room. It wasn't enough to warrant giving up something that meant a lot to the family. Especially when Maya's cut wouldn't even pay off her student loans.

Leaning forward, she rubbed her forehead. She needed an amazing job, or at least a few editors to start saying yes to the business article series she'd been sending out. But without a really great job she'd stay stuck. She had to go to Toronto, but needed money to set herself up there. Otherwise, where was she going to live until she got a few good paychecks?

The offer wasn't enough to make a difference in her life. Plus, living in Toronto and saying you had a cottage in Muskoka held a certain prestige that made Maya glow inside. She might not be rich. She might not be old money, but she had what most Torontonians coveted.

And she had three sisters to share it with.

Standing, she gazed out at Baby Horseshoe Island. As much as she loved progress, something felt off with what Rubicore was doing over there.

She rubbed her arms, hugging herself. Somehow this offer had changed things for her. She couldn't explain how or why, but she felt more connected, more protective over the cottage, now that someone else wanted it. Maybe it was the idea of giving it up to a developer like Rubicore.

Shaking her head, she started up the path again. She was turning into a softy like her sisters. If Connor still wanted to discuss the offer, maybe she'd ask him about counteroffer tips—just in case her family decided to explore the deal. Maya tapped the envelope against her free hand. It was always good to have a backup plan, especially when Hailey was at risk of losing her home and business.

Maya stepped onto the veranda and checked around the corner to see if her guest was still at the dining table. No Connor. Opening the screen door, she entered the dim living room and spotted him in an armchair in front of the cold fireplace. His shoulders were so broad she longed to trail her fingers over them, and if he'd been anything like the man she'd envisioned, lean down to lay a kiss on his lips.

Not professional in the least, and somewhat unexpected, but somehow so very tempting all the same.

Briskly, she joined him, trying to quell her nerves. It was business time. The way she handled herself with this offer would show him who she was and what she was made of.

She took the chair next to him and pulled the papers out of the envelope, hoping he'd stop gazing at the fireplace. Well, she assumed that was what he was zoning out over. He was wearing those damn shades again. Which was silly, seeing as she'd already noticed his black eye, plus it wasn't the least bit bright in here. Obviously, there was a juicy story behind that bruise, and the fact that he wanted to hide it made her want to discover that story all the more.

She cleared her throat and waved a hand in front of Connor's face. A light snore made his lips vibrate, and she leaned back in her chair. Funny how the King of Toronto just kept disappointing her.

Chapter Three

Connor's body ached as though he'd been tortured. The room smelled like warm, old wood. The bedding was soft with age. He propped himself on an elbow and squinted at the morning light streaming in through the bedroom window. He was wearing what he'd worn yesterday and he was on that island with the over-eager assistant who confused him. What the heck was her name? She had amazing breasts.

He went to adjust his morning wood before realizing that it, too, was broken. No erection, not even a hint of one.

He sighed.

Things were worse than he'd been letting on.

Groaning, he sat up. Why was he so sore? It was as if every muscle had been strung tight in the night. He stretched tentatively, the aches slowly subsiding.

If this was an effect of the fatigue, he might need longer than two days to get his feet under him again.

He shook his head and blinked away the uncomfortable sensation in his head. No, he had a plan. A deadline. He always met his deadlines. Being tired wasn't going to affect that. He'd just buckle down and relax while he was here. Get it done. Then on Monday he'd get back at it.

Simple.

He stepped into the quiet living room, wondering if his

assistant had set up coffee. He stood for a moment, getting his bearings. Coffee to the right. No, left. Yes, right.

Where was she? Wasn't she staying here, too?

He moved into the kitchen, which had been added on at some point and didn't quite match the rest of the cottage, other than for its slightly neglected feel.

He lifted the coffeepot and gave it a shake. Empty. He found coffee in the cupboard, water, hit the brew button and waited. This was a really quiet coffeemaker, considering how old it looked.

He turned to a small radio on the counter and tuned it to FM 96.3. Smiling as the kitchen filled with the sounds of his favorite opera. Humming to the music, he allowed the counter to support him as he watched the coffeepot. What was wrong with the thing? There was no coffee dripping into it.

The screen door banged, followed by the light padding of feet across the living room before another door shut. He hurried toward the sound. He needed coffee. What the hell kind of game was his assistant playing? And where was his breakfast?

He pushed open the closed door and was met with a squeal.

Maya, her hair streaming water, tugged the top of her bathing suit over her exposed flesh. "Didn't we go over this already?" she snapped.

"This isn't the bathroom."

"Do I really have to explain what closed doors mean?"

"What are you doing?"

She grabbed the edge of the door and slammed it shut, Connor barely getting out of the way in time. The lock clicked into place.

"Your coffeemaker doesn't work."

"We're on an island, Connor." There was a bitterness in her voice as well as a "duh."

"And? Hawaii is an island and they have working coffeemakers. Same with Tahiti, Jamaica…"

"We don't have power out here."

He nearly tried opening the door again. No power? But he'd just been listening to the radio. Batteries. Right. Then why have appliances if there wasn't power? That was really screwed up. Wait, hadn't she mentioned something about a generator?

This place required so much work.

He dropped his hand from the doorknob. She was probably fully nude by now, covering those perfect breasts in a fine lace bra. He pushed a fist against his forehead. What was his problem? He was fantasizing about seeing his assistant naked and he couldn't even get a decent erection.

Sighing, he tipped his head forward until his fist was pinned between his skull and the door.

His eyelids drifted shut. He should go back to bed.

The door opened and he fell into the room, crashing past Maya to the floor. His face mashed into an area rug and his shoulders screamed from the effort of trying to slow the impact with his arms.

"Were you peeking through the keyhole?"

He groaned and pushed himself onto his back. "No, I was falling asleep."

"Are you narcoleptic?"

He cracked a smile. "No, but my caffeine levels are dangerously depleted." He licked his lips. His top one was already starting to swell.

"Do you want me to start the generator for coffee?" She leaned closer, taking on a sympathetic caring vibe that made him cover his face before struggling to sit up.

Everything was such an effort.

"I'm going back to bed."

"Do you want coffee?"

He shook his head. The idea of getting to his feet and struggling back to his room was too much to contemplate. Maybe he could just sleep here. It felt good not having to hold up his body.

He stared at her bare ankles. Her long legs disappearing into cute shorts. That fine waist of hers. T-shirt; no crappy business attire. What did that mean? Wasn't she supposed to be an executive assistant?

"You look good from this angle," he said.

She whacked him with her wet bathing suit.

He let out a chuckle. He liked her spark.

"I swim around the island every morning when I'm here. So don't come barging into my room, because I never miss my morning swim."

"Never?"

"Never."

Determined little thing. "I used to swim."

"Used to? What, did you forget how to ride a bike, too?"

"You're snarky."

She shifted her weight as though determining whether to apologize.

He reached for her. "Help me up."

"How'd you get so old?" she asked, struggling to help him. He kind of wished she'd do all the work, but apparently they'd need a crane for that.

"I'm one of those working stiffs they warn you about," he grunted. Oh, the irony of that statement. He definitely did not have something stiff that worked at the moment.

"I hardly think running your own company makes you a working stiff. And you know you can swim while you're here. I'm sure you haven't forgotten how."

Connor, finally on his feet, felt out of breath. He gave a fake perky hop to dispel the worry in Maya's eyes. His entire body was way too heavy to be able to function properly and there was no way he could fake a spring in his step for longer than his little hop. Not like Maya. She was all spring and bounce and perkiness. A spitfire. A sexy, sexy spitfire.

"Maybe later I'll swim around the island."

Maya shook her head briskly. "No, you need to start by going across the strait to the left of the boathouse. It's shallowest there and you might be able to stand if you need to."

"Are you calling me an out-of-shape wimp?"

"Well, you don't exactly look as though you are doing great, now do you?" She crossed her arms over her perfect chest and raised an eyebrow.

"You're such a bitch."

She leaned closer, giving him a proud smirk that made him want to kiss her. "I heard businessmen enjoy that in a woman."

This girl was going to be trouble. The fun kind of trouble.

CONNOR SAT ON THE veranda and sipped his coffee, loving the way the midday sun was scorching everything but him. He still couldn't quite figure out why he wasn't wigging out and stressed about all the things he had to do at work. Normally, sleeping away a Saturday morning as he just had would have anxiety building within him like pressure in a shaken bottle of champagne. Instead, his anxiety merely hovered in the background, a low hum, until he decided to fret about it. Then his heart rate would skyrocket, his chest would grow tight and his hands clench until they ached.

Just thinking about being anxious made his muscles start to contract. No wonder he'd woken up sore. He'd probably slept this way, his subconscious fretting that he was forgetting something important, something lurking behind a corner that would alter his entire business world.

He closed his eyes, trying to focus on the quiet island sounds rather than an engine that was puttering and shuddering as though it was running rich. He cracked his eyelids as Maya thumped by, likely on a mission to do something involving the wrench she was carrying.

He shut his eyes again, promising himself that if he just chilled out and did nothing, thought about nothing, he'd knock the doctor's socks off with a new and improved version of himself. A version that could go back to work and figure out why his latest merger felt as if he was pushing a boulder uphill through slick mud. And maybe figure out why the acquisitions his advisor James Culver had been adding to Connor's portfolio seemed so out of character for the man. Normally, his two advisors were that in name only. They basically sat around, waiting for Connor to hint whether something looked good or not, and even what they should pursue. Then they would help make it happen. Bill Hatfield was great at moving things along, and James had been a solid third in the trio, sorting out details. But suddenly James had started adding projects on his own—with Connor's approval, of course. It was a refreshing change, but somehow it still left Connor more tired than it should.

The engine sound in the background stabilized, running smoothly for a moment before cutting off.

Maya reappeared, her fingertips coated with grease.

"What the hell are you doing? Rebuilding a plane from the war?"

"Generator."

He silently reassessed her. She was sassy and unpredictable, and didn't mind getting her hands dirty—quite literally—if need be. She was also, apparently, smart enough to go to the U of T as well as graduate high in her class.

"What are you doing here?" he asked, shifting his weight, and making the old wicker chair creak.

She gave him a dirty look and continued walking past.

"I meant on this island. Making crappy waffles."

"Hey, those are the best you can buy in a box."

"I was promised meals."

"You've been given meals."

He let out a derisive snort, wanting to see how far he could push her. It was probably her mouth—that mouth with those perfect teeth and lush lips. Her wit. A combo that had probably kept her out of the jobs she wanted or gotten her fired. Or the fact that if her bosses had been like him—only not as broken—they hadn't been able to keep their hands to themselves around her. Or keep up to her. And in the business world there was nothing more threatening to most men than not being able to keep up with a gorgeous young woman such as Maya.

"Nobody said the meals would be fancy," she replied.

"I'm trying to get my health back and you're feeding me processed food."

"What's wrong with your health?"

"Nothing. Just trying to eat healthy." He took a slug of his coffee and went to adjust his shades. *His shades.* He'd forgotten to put them on this morning. Oh well. It wasn't as if she hadn't noticed.

"How'd you get the black eye?"

"Who fired you?" he retorted.

She stepped back as though recovering her balance after a kick to the gut. "When are you going to give me some jobs as your executive assistant?"

"Interesting reaction."

"Listen, Connor…"

"Make sure your sentences are short. My attention span isn't at its greatest."

"Yeah, none of you is."

"Excuse me?" He stood, only to find the world spinning.

"I'm sorry, but you are *not* the man I've idolized for all these years, and the disappointment is a little bit tough to bear when…" Her eyes squeezed shut for a moment and it seemed as though she was fighting something supersized.

"Well, I'm sorry my life isn't living up to your dreams, Maya. But I think it's important to keep in mind that, at the moment, I'm your boss as well as your paying guest."

She stepped closer, looking tired. "Connor, I *am* here to help as your assistant, and I apologize for my attitude. Is there something you need from me? Because I need to make a run into port."

He contemplated kissing her, wondering what she'd do if he did. He gave his head a small shake and sat. They were odd together. She put him off guard, made him act like an ass, but the thing was, he deserved it. All of it. He was a disappointment. Even to himself.

"So? Are you really going back to Toronto?" She jutted a hip, making her legs looking even longer. She was impossible in so many ways, from the length of her legs to her attitude. And the fact that instead of getting miffed at her and her bitchy digs, he wanted to push her into the love seat a few chairs down and make her his. He'd start with her perfect breasts, working his way down to her sweet and spicy ass, then wrap those legs around him to test how strong they really were.

"Hello?" She waved a hand in front of his face, her red nails flashing.

"Monday."

"Will you be back?"

"I hope not."

"Then I won't bother buying you the nice waffles." The screen door banged shut behind her, making a new sound as the screws came loose in the lower hinge.

He switched to the chair with a better view of the hummingbird feeder, spilling his coffee in the process. He needed to go home. If he stayed here all week he'd undoubtedly push the two of them into a situation where his dick couldn't back him up.

MAYA SPOTTED HER SISTER Melanie waiting for her in the marina on her motorcycle. Maya plunked herself on the seat behind her, accepting the offered helmet.

"Seriously? The death trap?"

"It's cheap on gas."

"Next time can we take the car?"

"Sold it."

Maya sighed and secured the strap under her chin. They were all making sacrifices for a rotting old building. What was wrong with them? Was this normal behavior? In one of her sociology classes they'd read a case study where the wealthy, in hard times, would drive their BMWs to a food bank far from home, park a few blocks away, then walk in. They'd keep up the pretense that everything was fine as they held on to their symbols of prestige and money, even when they were losing it all.

Was the Summer family—who had never been well-off—doing the same thing? Were they sacrificing everything to keep their symbol of prestige? The one thing that set them apart from the rest of the locals—as if having a rickety old cottage out here somehow made them "more"?

Or was it something else, such as sentimental value?

Melanie gunned the motorcycle's engine, causing Maya to

clutch her so she didn't get left hanging in the air behind the crotch rocket like an unsuspecting cartoon character.

"Warn me!"

Melanie let out a wild laugh.

"Wow. Who are you and what did you do with Smelly Mellie?"

She laughed again. If she hadn't been wearing one of her ever-present XXL T-shirts, which served to cover her figure, Maya would think something was seriously wrong with her younger sister.

Melanie did an extra lap around the nursing home where their mother resided. Maya figured her sister was either enjoying the cool air as much as Maya was or else was also dreading going inside the most depressing of all places.

As they got off the motorcycle, tucking their helmets under arm, Maya studied Melanie. "You know what would look fabulous on you?"

"If you say black leather…"

"I'm actually thinking of a 1950s dress with the big skirt and tight bodice. You'd be totally hot. Simone's started making them for her boutique."

Melanie scowled at the idea of a dress and headed to the automatic doors. "Well, she'll will have better luck continuing to sell Hailey's photos than me a dress. Is Simone coming today?"

"The honorary Summer sister will be here as always. And don't you wear skirts for work?"

"That's different. They're less dressy."

"Trade in the XXL shirts for me. Please?" Maya clasped her hands under her chin and batted her eyelashes.

Melanie shoved her through the doorway. "So…is he as wonderful as you hoped?"

Maya shivered as the building's air conditioning hit her like a sudden cold front. "It smells like instant potatoes and desperation in here."

"Are you avoiding the subject of Connor MacKenzie?"

"He's an arrogant bum cake." The man was not the career savior Maya had envisioned, and she was confused by her reaction to him. She wanted to mother him and heal whatever was going on with him, but also to fight with him until he yelled and threw things. Then she wanted to take him to her bed and make love to him all night long. The man she'd admired in the TED talks, conferences and newspaper articles had to be in there somewhere.

"Bum cake?" Her sister laughed. "So, you like him, then?"

"Of course. He's infuriating as all hell. I can't decide if I want to hump his brains out or shove him off a boat with a rock tied to his ankles." She let out a frustrated breath. How could she still be attracted to the jerk when he was so disappointing and so…so sexy?

"Is he smart?"

"Freaking brilliant. And handsome." She groaned and rolled her head.

"And rich." Melanie was giving her a grin that meant her sister was totally onto her.

"It's more than that." Such as the power he wielded. Serious panty-wetter. "Anyway, I'll be rich soon enough, too."

"Starting when, exactly?"

"When he lets me do some work as his assistant and I get some experience to take to Toronto." Maya clapped her hands together and let out a breath. "Then my life will start."

"Why are you so focused on Toronto? I just got a job in a law office in Bracebridge, with way less of a commute, a lower cost of living, and a decent wage. Honestly, I'm not sure why people move to the city."

"Because there are *options* in the city. More room for growth. That's where my kind of jobs are, and the men that go with them. Plus one has the added bonus of not having eighty million neighbors coming in expecting special favors, and they don't spend forty minutes of your appointment chatting you up about your family, health, relationships or lack thereof. And there's operas and stuff."

"And you go to operas?"

Maya laughed. "No. But I *could*."

"For your information, meetings with neighbors only last five minutes."

"Forty-five."

"After the warm-up, five."

The warm-up was forty. Forty wasted minutes. Every single time you met with someone.

"Think about it," Melanie continued. "In the city, when you wanted student loans, the loan officer spent twenty minutes verifying your identity and asking about your program. Around here, they already know all that stuff, so they spent the meeting time chatting. You are a person, Maya. It's an easy appointment and they get the information right. Way better service—and it makes you want to go back again."

Maya stuck out her tongue.

"You know I'm right."

"I'm sorry, I thought you were Melanie, not Hailey."

"Maya…" She gave a little sigh.

"Yeah, yeah. Rivalry-shmivalry. We're working together to save the cottage, aren't we? Isn't she letting me have it for the next two weeks, to make a miracle happen by calling the hellhole an executive retreat?"

"What's going on with you?"

Maya ran her hands down her thighs. "Nothing. I'm just

frustrated. I thought going to university was supposed to open my world." They paused to let an elderly man wheel by in his chair. "How's your new job?"

"Fine."

"Fine? Really? A brilliant job in a lovely town with lovely people who speak of lovely things? You're not maximizing your degree, either, are you?"

"Nobody does when they first start out. Especially in law."

"Reality is a wonderful place to be, isn't it?"

Melanie gave a small laugh. "You know what?"

"What?"

"Sometimes you're not bad for a sister. Unfortunately, today's not your day."

"Shut up," Maya said with a grin.

Melanie began walking faster, biting back a smile. Maya matched her stride until they were running down the hall in an attempt to be the first to enter their mother's room.

They rounded the last corner, giggling that none of the nurses had caught them, and ran into Hailey, who frowned and placed a finger over her lips, balancing a homemade triple layer cake on her other hand.

Rivalry? Yeah, it wasn't dead. Look at Hailey. She was already here, had the cake and was therefore going to enter the room first and get the majority of the credit. Of course there was rivalry. It would never die. Rivalry was what sisters did. It meant they loved each other. To death. However that happened to occur.

Mrs. Kowski, one of the residents, edged by with her walker. "That looks wonderful, Hailey." Her eyebrows rose hopefully as she stared at the cake, then at Maya's big sister.

"Come by in ten minutes and you can have a slice, Mrs. Kowski."

"Will do!" The woman increased her pace, heading to the

nearby common room. "Supper around here sucks," she called over her shoulder. "I always have room for homemade cake!"

Hailey pointed to Daphne, who was struggling out of the common room down the hall with a mittful of helium balloons. Her five-year-old daughter, Tigger, was leaping alongside, trying to make the balloons bounce off her mother's head, and causing a great deal of static electricity.

Maya laughed. "Who gave Tigger sugar?"

"Maya, light the candles." Hailey was tense, her mouth drawn into a line.

"Where's movie boy?" Maya twisted to check the hall. No sign of Finian Alexander. Had he already taken off on her sister? Because if he hurt Hailey, Maya was going to kick his ass all the way from California to Canada. Hailey wasn't one to take risks, and she'd taken a big one with the bad boy of Hollywood.

"Just light them," her big sister grumbled. "Matches are in my back pocket."

"Chill. I've got it." Maya snatched them from Hailey's pocket and lit the candles. "Tigger's going to think it's for her. Five candles."

Hailey frowned, the line between her eyebrows deepening.

"Relax," Maya said. "She'll know."

Simone, her long black hair waving in time with her brisk stride, hurried up, a small wrapped gift in hand. "Sorry I'm late. Does Catherine know we're here?" She peeked at the closed door they were gathered around before giving everyone a hug. The others talked over each other as they assured her that she was right on time, and that everything was still a surprise, all while getting themselves organized.

"Who has the gift?" Maya asked.

"I had it delivered," Melanie said.

"I brought her a handmade silk scarf from my boutique," Simone added. "Orange, red, and yellow."

"She'll love it," Hailey said.

Maya looked around. Hailey with lit cake. Daphne with balloons. Melanie in charge of the already-delivered gift. Simone with a one-of-a-kind scarf. Maya was the odd one out. "You guys should have told me to do something."

"You were busy." Melanie pushed open their mother's door, nudging Maya so she entered after Hailey, Daphne bringing up the rear with Tigger. "Now sing."

They all burst into the room, singing loudly as though trying to outdo each other. Catherine's eyes shone as she grinned from ear to ear.

"Look at all my girls!" Mrs. Summer pulled her granddaughter to her wheelchair and hugged her close, stroking the child's wild hair. "And look at your pretty party dress."

"Mr. Finian bought it for me." Tigger beamed at Hailey.

"Mom," Maya said, "we all chipped in and bought you a gift. Mellie arranged to have it delivered. Did it arrive?"

"There's a big box in the corner. What's in it?"

"A television stand," Melanie said as Maya leaned over their mother's chair for a hug. She was waved away as Hailey brought the flaming candles and cake closer.

"Make a wish!" Daphne called.

"For sea monkeys!" Tigger added, gripping the wheelchair's armrest as she bounced up and down.

Maya drew the girl away, afraid her staticky hair would catch fire. "Why sea monkeys?" she asked, as all but one candle was blown out.

"They're cool!" Tigger replied. "Look! Grandma has a boyfriend!"

The women laughed, and Catherine blew out the last flame.

"Either that or my lungs don't work like they used to." She smiled at the girl. "Did you know I used to never miss a candle? Even the year I turned thirty-seven and your grandfather put thirty-seven candles on my poor little red velvet cake. Not a single one left burning."

"But there are only five on this cake," Tigger said. "Five, like me."

"I know, dear."

Hailey began passing out slices of cake and Maya tried to make herself useful, but her sister kept elbowing her out of the way. "How's your hero. What is he? The king of Toronto or something like that?" she asked, finally handing Maya a corner piece—her favorite.

Maya shoved a forkful in her mouth and mumbled something.

"What?" Hailey asked.

"Where's your movie star boyfriend?" Maya asked through a mouthful of cake.

"Screen test. So? How *is* the fabled Connor MacKenzie? Is he as great as they say?"

"Yeah. Great." Maya fixed a smile on her face. If Connor went back early there was no way she was telling Hailey. She'd hide out at Nymph Island alone if she had to. As he had said, he didn't have to be present for the full two weeks. And unless he fired her or she re-rented the place, there was no reason for him to ask for a refund.

"Good. Do you think we could line up more of these retreats?"

"That's such a great idea," Simone exclaimed as Hailey passed her a slice of cake.

Maya gave a half shrug. "Maybe. We'll see. Hailey, can I borrow Mom's old recipe book from you?"

Hailey just about dropped the cake-cutting knife in surprise. "Are you planning to cook?"

"Just a couple of things, such as waffles."

"But you like food that comes in a box. No fuss, no muss."

"Yeah, but it's not exactly executive fare."

"Good point. I could help if you want?"

"It's okay. You're busy, too." Maya scooted in next to her mother as her sisters, Simone and Tigger began trying to put together the gift. Finding they needed an Allen key, the bickering sisters headed off to see if they could convince the maintenance man to come help. Having decided it would increase their chances of success if they all went, they filed out, leaving Maya behind to keep the birthday girl company.

Catherine placed a cool hand over hers. "How are you, Maya?"

Maya angled her head so it was resting on her mom's shoulder. "Okay."

"Just okay?"

"I don't think Connor MacKenzie is going to be my ticket into the business world."

"Of course he isn't." Catherine gazed down at her, and if Maya closed her right eye, she blocked out the side that had been affected by the stroke and could see only the side that still looked like her mom, not a frail old woman who was close to completing her circle of life. Maya's heart constricted, and her mother squeezed her hand.

"Only you can be your own ticket."

"What do you mean?"

"I mean do this on your own. Go and make connections."

"But I am. I have the grades, and the guts and the instinct and the drive."

"But are you connecting with people?"

"Mom, it's the twenty-first century. The internet is popular for a reason—so we don't have to connect. We can just go out and get the job done."

"And are they getting the job done with strangers? Or are connections and networks still vital, my dear?"

Maya pushed away from her mother. Catherine was usually uncannily perceptive, but to tell her to go network and connect? That seemed a tad old-fashioned for what she had in mind.

"Go take someone out for a round of golf?" she kidded.

"I'm serious, Maya." Catherine smiled, the damaged side of her mouth going along for the ride. She tipped her chin. "Try it. And report back."

While there weren't many people Maya listened to, she listened to her mother. "Do I have to?" she whined.

Her mom reached over and gave her ear a playful tug. "Yes."

"I suppose golf would be more fun than sitting around in a boring old cottage with sketchy internet." And it sure beat trying to write business articles for money.

"My Maya." Her mother shook her head and looked to the ceiling.

"Fine. Fine. I'll try it." Maybe.

MAYA PACED OUTSIDE the bedroom where Connor was sleeping. He'd been asleep when she'd got back from her mom's party, his door closed. And it was still shut.

She'd read an entire business book last night while waiting for him to wake up from what she thought was an early evening nap. She wanted to pick his brain about counteroffers, as well as the ideas she'd read been reading about. Enough down time, it was work time.

Was he still here? Maybe he'd figured out how to get a water taxi, and had left.

Or, oh no, what if he'd tried swimming around the island? He was obviously in no condition to do so. She should have followed her instinct to take him to see a doctor. Now his death by drowning would be all her fault. There weren't any riptides or scary currents, but in places the rocky shore dipped straight down into deep water, leaving no easy exit from the unrelenting waves unless you somehow made it around to the quieter side, where there was a sandy, shallow area near the boathouse.

Maya hadn't gone for her own swim yet and debated doing so now, to see if she could find Connor. But then a shuffling sound on the other side of the door made her step back. Connor opened it and stood in the doorway staring blankly at her, his hair an adorable mess, his eyes bleary.

He was hot when he was sleepy.

"What?" he asked.

She gave a shrug, her movements too quick to pass off innocence.

Remembering herself, she pushed a cup of lukewarm coffee into his hand. "Glad to see you didn't drown."

"What?"

"Nothing. Good morning. Would you like to play golf?"

Connor closed his bedroom door.

"Jerk much?" she muttered.

"I heard that."

"Yeah, the soundproofing is bar none."

"You snore."

"It's the mice. I'm going for a swim."

The door opened again, and he was without a shirt. His skin was soft, pale. He needed to get outside for some vitamin D. He had broad shoulders like someone who used to work out or be active, but time behind a desk had done something.... He needed her to feed him and build him up again.

"You're too skinny," she said. "You need a big breakfast."

"How's the water?"

"Cold." She wanted to bond with the guy, not swim with him. Swimming was for her. Alone. She didn't need to worry about him drowning.

"Cold just like you."

"Yes, but the water warms up in the sun." She spun on her heel, then, unable to resist, turned and stuck out her tongue.

"You plan to use that tongue?" he asked, stepping forward with a swagger.

Her jaw dropped. But pushing her shock aside, she strutted back to him, exaggerating her hip sway in a way she knew he noticed.

That's right. Eat up what you can't have, honey.

She leaned close and he licked his lips, his chest expanding. She whispered, "I do, but I promise you won't be so lucky to find it used on you."

He laughed, a rich, deep sound that reverberated through her, making her want to hear it again and again.

"Don't make promises you might not be able to keep," he said, lightly touching her shoulder.

She ignored the shivers and the way her body tightened at his touch. "Then I'll assume you are going to find a way to up your charm." She flicked a look over her shoulder as she waltzed away. "Considerably."

Again, that laugh.

"I'll do my best, Maya." He leaned against the doorjamb, sipping his coffee.

She paused, half turning. "Do you like your coffee black?" She hadn't ever asked him, just brought it out the way she took hers.

He gave a shrug. "I'm easy."

"I'll remember that." She shot him a wink and went to her room to rifle through her bathing suits. Discarding the bikinis as trying too hard, she went for the less obvious, a knock-out red suit cut high on her hips and low over her breasts. She might have to stop swimming a few times to slip the straps up her shoulders again, but that would be worth it, seeing as today was her last shot at convincing Connor to stay, before he went back to Toronto and quite possibly didn't return.

Towel draped over her shoulder, she grabbed the coffeepot from the kitchen, topping up Connor's cup as she walked past him on her way out of the cottage. She paused as she poured, ensuring she inhaled mightily, letting her chest expand and rise, her suit dipping down as she matched the inhalation with a slight back-arching stretch.

Connor's attention strayed to her cleavage.

"There's sun on the end of the dock. It's a quiet place to chill out if you get bored up here."

If she could get him to chill out, stay awake and relax, she could pump him for business advice while sunbathing after her swim. Maybe even find a way to use him as a job reference—even though he'd yet to give her any work to do.

Not waiting for him to reply, she added a wiggle to her hips and made her way down to the water, knowing that if he decided to navigate the path, she was going to get what she'd come for.

THAT WOMAN WAS TROUBLE.

Connor loved a challenge more than anything, but he was too tired. Too old. That hot little red bathing suit had stirred something inside, but still…he was too broken, and way too tired.

He sat on the edge of his bed and sipped the coffee. Black coffee wasn't bad. It was something he'd moved to about six months ago, when the fatigue had started sneaking in. Cut out sugar. Get that caffeine straight into the system.

It hadn't helped. And he missed the warm, sweet creaminess of a double-double.

He set the cup aside. He needed to do something. He couldn't go on this way—barely living. Even if Dr. Tiang said he could go back to work tomorrow, how long would he last before he was running into door frames again?

The push of gravity was strong, and Connor lay back on the bed, staring at the ceiling, his mind blank. He rolled over, reaching for his bag beside the bed. He rummaged through his things, wondering what he should do. No laptop. No BlackBerry.

He was free. But free to do what, exactly?

Finding an envelope addressed to him, he tugged it out and hauled himself into the living room, where he collapsed on a chair near a crammed bookcase. He ripped open the envelope and felt a heavy sadness as he fingered the thick vellum. Rubbing his nose, Connor sighed and read the invitation. He'd already told his kid brother, Curtis, that he'd come to his wedding in Tahiti, but how had he not opened the invitation, when the wedding was only two weeks away? No wonder his brother had called and emailed a few times, to make sure he was still coming to act as his best man.

But how was Connor going to find time to go—assuming Stella or Em had organized tickets for him? Two extended weekends so close together was an insane idea, and familiar anxiety took root and flourished within him. He placed the invitation on the side table and reminded himself that at least it wasn't another ex-girlfriend inviting him to a christening. He sagged further into the armchair.

Real life was moving along without him. He had no wife. No kids. No pets. Nothing to go home to. No one to miss him. Nothing to give him balance, as the doctor had suggested.

Balance. Connor was the CEO of his own company. You didn't get there by balancing your world like a Zen master.

He didn't even know what balance looked like. Was it a week off once a year? Someone to cuddle with? Skipping the high-fat salad dressing?

He snatched up his brother's wedding invitation and stared at the empty box waiting for a checkmark beside the words *with guest*. His eyes burned. It felt like a dig.

Connor knew how his evening would go. He'd sit alone, feeling tired and wishing he was at work. He'd probably resent the time away from solving problems that kept popping up and that only he could solve.

His heart rate increased and he pushed out of the chair, grabbing the first book that came to hand. *The Fall: Tales from the Apocalypse*. Perfect. Something dark and brooding that wouldn't remind him about his failure to get a real life. A life with meaning, people, love and commitment. A life where someone would have his back even through the tough times. Someone who didn't want anything other than his love and company.

Yeah, that's probably what a real life and balance looked like. Pretty much everything he didn't have.

He stood on the veranda for a moment, clutching the book. If he went down to the dock, he'd have to come back up. He berated his old-fogey thinking and made his way down to the water. No sign of his spitfire Maya, just the old boathouse that was trying to yoga-move its way back down into nature. He tugged one of the Muskoka chairs farther into the sun and sat back, letting the rays dig into his skin. It felt good. Warm. Bright. How long had it been since he'd let the sun bake him, make him feel whole and real again? Happy.

Wait... Happy?

When had he stopped being happy?

Too much thinking. He was supposed to be filling his head with healthy thoughts so he could merge back into the rat race as though this pit stop had never happened.

He inhaled slowly, and thought back to the staff retreat they'd had a few years ago. What had that guru dude chanted? Empty thoughts? Clear mind? Something like that.

Think nothing. Think nothing. Think nothing.

But he was thinking something. He was thinking about not thinking.

This was dumb.

He drew in a deep breath and held it for thirty seconds, then let it explode out his mouth. Maybe he should swim. That walk down the path hadn't been so bad; this retreat was already making him feel better. But he'd have to walk back up the hill to get his trunks, then down again, then back up after his swim. Too much work, and the sun felt too good.

Two ducks eyed him as they swam around the corner of the dock, vanishing under the boathouse door. Within a few moments they leisurely paddled out again, tilting their heads at him before heading across to the seemingly vacant cottages across the strait.

Tomorrow he'd have to bring down bread. Tomorrow? What was he thinking? Tomorrow he was getting back on that boat and heading to Toronto, his R&R complete, not feeding ducks.

A bulldozer started up across the water, the sound carrying to him as though it was right next door. Great. He came all the way down here to chill out—okay, and to see Maya wet and dripping in her *Baywatch* suit—and they had to ruin the ambience with a 'dozer?

He turned away, hoping to have a catnap, not wanting to allow himself to get intrigued by whatever project was happening across the water. He was on vacation. Relaxing.

Breathing.
Not thinking about what new project was under way.
Breathing.
Listening to purposeful splashing come closer with each stroke.

Maya.

He pried an eye open and watched her come nearer, until her hand tapped the dock like an Olympic racer. He half expected her to do a flip and push off, to go around the island again in the opposite direction. Instead, she hauled herself up out of the lake, ignoring the ladder.

He should have worn his shades, so he could drink her in. She was hot. Maybe even hotter because he knew what she looked like under that red Lycra. Knew exactly where the streaming rivulets of water were heading as they glided down her chin, raced over her collarbone and vanished into the valley between her breasts.

Thank goodness he was so exhausted, or he'd have an erection so big she'd slap him hard across the face for being a testosterone-crazed member of the male species. Even so, he found he had to drape a hand casually across his crotch to hide his partial.

"Wow, look at you, all awake." Maya scrubbed at her hair with the towel, pausing to tip her head to let water drain out of her ears.

"Restorative powers of Muskoka." He glanced to his crotch. Only not quite restorative enough.

"I haven't heard anyone talk about them since the 1800s," she said with a laugh.

"You've aged well, then."

She smiled, with a welcoming friendliness that made him want to hold her, feel her heartbeat against his chest, her head nuzzled under his chin. That, and peel the suit off her wet skin.

He was lonely. That's what that feeling was. Huh. He'd never thought that would happen, but somehow it had pounced, lingering like a sorry state of neglected affairs.

Maya wrapped the towel around herself and pulled up a chair beside his. "Plans for the day?" she asked. "A little work? Maybe some golf?"

"Not golf."

"Tennis?"

"Too much effort. It's going to be hot. The tree frogs are already singing."

She let out a small, defeated-sounding sigh. "Reading then?"

"Maybe." He flipped over the book, staring at the blurb on the back. Earlier in the week he hadn't been able to follow new project layouts. What were the chances he'd be able to focus on a collection of short stories? He set the book aside. What was he going to do when he went back to work, if his brain refused to engage?

"You okay?" Her cool fingers landed on his arm, and he flinched.

"You're cold."

"Cold bitch, I believe, if I string all your compliments together."

"My apologies. Put like that, I sound like a regular ass."

"Well, it's probably true. My mom told me to make connections with people. Network the old-fashioned way, because I'm…you know…a cold and determined bitch. You understand how it is. Fine for a man, but not for a woman."

Her mouth turned down, and he felt for her, but her mother was right. Most new grads thought good grades made it a given that they would start at a six-figure salary, with three weeks paid holidays. And most of all, that they would be worth it. But they had no connections, were often a liability in their eagerness, and yes, women such as Maya were often dubbed a bitch. Yet she had the guts and strength to really go far if she didn't let the double standard get under her skin and make her resentful.

"Your mother is right," he said. "Make connections and network, get as much experience as possible and work your ass off. Literally. You'll make it."

Maya chewed on her bottom lip for a moment, looking uncomfortable.

"What's your favorite color?" she asked.

"Green."

"Mine, too."

How did he get stuck on an island with a woman like Maya? She probably had a more detailed five-year plan than he did, but was still lacking the basics that five minutes in the business world would teach her. "Are you trying to…connect with me?" he asked. She had to be kidding.

"Am I that bad?"

"Try being less obvious. You know, authentic. Genuine."

"Right. Arlene Dickinson, the entrepreneur millionaire from *Dragons' Den,* said that in her book *Persuasion*."

Connor refrained from rolling his eyes. Maya was so green it almost hurt to even sit here and listen to her.

She nodded as though coming to a conclusion. "Why didn't you finish your business degree?"

"Cutting to the chase now, are you?"

"Why not? Time is money."

"Not at the moment, it isn't."

Her feet had begun twitching and he chuckled. Chitchat was killing her. "Do you know how to sit still?"

"No. Do you know how to talk about things that aren't business?"

"Of course."

"Then start a topic."

"I dropped out of business school because I made more during my third-year project than most graduates did in a year. Wouldn't you quit and follow the trail of money?"

"You fail."

"Excuse me?"

"That was a topic about business."

"I was answering your question."

"New topic."

"Like what?"

"I don't know. Show me how to connect."

"You are persistent. Unrelenting." He'd enjoy it if he was in Toronto and not trying to chill out. In fact, he'd likely have asked her out for a drink by now. But this was Muskoka and his vacation. "So, Maya, tell me why you think I can help you get ahead in the business world."

"Fail again. Business related."

"Maya. For real."

"If not you, then who?"

"You tire me, woman."

She sat back, looking sad and rejected. He couldn't do this. He couldn't lead someone with such passion and eagerness into a world that might give her so much it would consume her. It wasn't the same world he'd stepped into seven-and-a-half years ago, making millions as easily as sweeping up sawdust in a sawmill.

"I'm heading into Toronto at 9:00 a.m. tomorrow. Nothing personal, but I don't know that I'll be back."

Chapter Four

Connor sat in the exam room, twisting his hands. The lab had drawn blood that morning and Dr. Tiang had checked his vitals, and was ready to chat about his conclusions. And despite the fact that it might mean more time off, Connor appreciated how thorough he was being. He'd been livid when the doctor had first pulled him off work, but his perspective had slowly begun to change while he'd been sitting on the dock with Maya yesterday. Seeing her so alive, healthy and vibrant, just lapping up life as though it was a big ol' bowl of milk, he'd realized how far he'd crumbled over the past six months.

And maybe Dr. Tiang could help him find a way to get a life. Get Maya.

Connor didn't want to be sent back to Muskoka, because it would mean he'd failed at being a real man and handling all that the city was throwing at him. But he wanted to go back if it meant he might begin to feel human again.

He tried not to remind himself of Stella's ultimatum—comply with the doctor's orders or she was quitting. He almost laughed at how over-the-top she'd sounded, claiming she didn't want to be the one to find him keeled over at his desk.

But his office couldn't run without him. Who would finesse the latest merger if he wasn't there? Surely not Bill and James.

Clenching his hands, Connor forced himself to breathe. Either the merger would happen or it wouldn't. Two weeks wouldn't settle his fate if he really was the king. And if the merger didn't go through, well, then it wasn't as though his stock was going to suffer due to one deal. Heck, he might even decide to pull out if they didn't get their ducks in a row and meet his requirements.

Dr. Tiang rolled over on a stool, stopping in front of him. Connor was in a suit, ready to go back to work, but he felt like a kid begging the coach to put him into the game again, yet afraid that if he did, he'd let the man down.

The doctor let out a large sigh, his focus not leaving whatever was scrawled on his clipboard.

"Mr. MacKenzie, do you have staff who can take over your business's essential duties for the next…say…two weeks?"

"I'm not running into doors. I'm fine to go back in."

"According to today's blood work, your elevated heart rate and memory test, you are not. You need rest. Two weeks is a bare minimum—just to see what you can accomplish."

"I can accomplish plenty."

"I'm guessing due to your present state that you need something more like months."

"Months?" Connor shoved his hands through his hair and swore under his breath. He needed a haircut. He'd ask Stella to book one when he got back into the office. Damn. Stella. She was going to quit if he went against the doctor's orders. Was this an order? Although she wasn't here, which meant she didn't have to know what the doctor did or did not say.

"I'd like to do a stress test."

"Why?"

"To give you a better time frame for when everything is going to hit the fan if you go back to your previous lifestyle."

"Everything as in…?"

"Heart attack. Stroke."

Connor crossed his arms. He could convince this guy otherwise. That was his job. Sales pitch time. "I have good cholesterol and find my job rewarding. Positive stress is present in my position."

"Not enough of it, according to what your body is telling me. I'd like to say it is whispering, but it's more of an outright scream. I don't think it can yell any louder without having a major collapse. Shall we test your hearing as well?"

Connor glared at the man. "There's more to health than blood work, and my hearing is *fine*."

"Personal problems?"

"I have no personal problems." That was a nice side effect of not having a personal life. "I'm fine. This is how I work."

"Tell me something, Connor." The doctor paused. "Do you have trouble concentrating? Remembering things?"

"I'm a busy guy. I have an assistant and a secretary for a reason. Both good women."

"Have you been experiencing irregular heart rhythms? Increased heart rate? Loss of motor control?" He raised an eyebrow. The doctor knew the answer; that was part of why Stella had brought him in here last week.

"I'm fine now. You were right. A few days of rest did wonders." Connor stood, straightening his lapels.

"Have you lost interest in things that used to matter to you? Possibly your job or your social life? Hobbies?"

Who had time for that kind of stuff? Didn't Dr. Tiang read the financial news? You didn't get in there by hosting poker night for the guys.

"Grown away from family or friends? Mood swings?"

"Go to hell," he said lightly.

"This isn't a joke, Mr. MacKenzie."

"My apologies. Really. I do appreciate your concern and know you're trying to do your job. Warning heard. Now, I need to get back to work, but I promise I'll cut down on my hours."

"Impatience?"

"Ha. Ha." Connor reached for the doorknob.

"Inability to get an erection?"

His jaw tightened. "I don't see how that is any of your business."

Dr. Tiang stood, placing a light hand on his arm. "Connor, if you don't take a break and find balance, you will have a heart attack. That will mean more time off of work, either because it is fatal or because you will lose essential heart function—meaning for the rest of your life you will feel tired all the time. Or worse, you'll have a stroke. We're looking at the possibility of losing the use of one side of your body. Rehab. Do you have time for *that*?"

"I don't have time for *this*."

"You're only human, Mr. MacKenzie. You need to create a personal life that is separate from your business life. You, believe it or not, can afford to save your own life, Connor."

MAYA SHIFTED FROM foot to foot in front of the grimy glass doors to one of Toronto's small tax firms. It didn't seem as though Connor was coming back to Muskoka—not just because last night's flying dream had been a panicky one where she'd lost control and begun to spin backward, but because of the way he'd left with barely a goodbye, his mind obviously already back in his skyscraper, making fistfuls of money. So she figured she may as well go to the job interview, even though the work wasn't exactly what she wanted. Plus Hailey had needed a ride to the airport.

Maya drew herself up, vowing to show Connor MacKenzie that she didn't need to wait around for him to notice her skills or kick-start her career. She could do it herself. She *needed* to do it herself. Adjusting her dress, she took one last breath and pushed through the doors, announcing herself at the large reception desk.

As the woman directed her to the elevators that would take her to the third floor, she added, "You might want to hold your breath."

Maya gripped the tall desk. "Why?"

"You'll see."

Maya slowly made her way to the elevators. *Hold her breath?*

Did that mean tons of other grads had already had an interview with this piddly little company, and she needed luck on her side?

The elevator doors opened and Maya was struck by a scent that was suspiciously similar to feral tomcat. She held her breath and dived into the tight space, repeatedly punching the button for the third floor, hoping the smell wouldn't stick to her clothes. Although chances were the interviewer would be immune to the smell. She shuddered at the thought of getting used to the rank odor, and inhaled without thinking. The doors opened and she fell out, coughing. She leaned against the wall, her interview nerves catching up to her.

She blinked back tears of desperation and drummed up the enthusiasm she'd been practicing in the car. She could do this. She needed this job only to help her get established in the city, then she could move on to something better.

Save the cottage. Save herself. Move on.

A woman in a disheveled suit hurried past her, asking, "Are you the three o'clock?"

"Interview? Yes." Maya stepped forward, hand outstretched. "Maya Summer."

The woman gave it a brief clench, directing her into a nearby, vacant room. "Okay, let's get to this. Why do you want to work for HL Financial and Tax Services?"

"I like numbers." Maya smoothed her dress, mentally chiding herself. She liked numbers? Could her reply be any more lame? "I am well organized and pay great attention to detail. I also have a good memory, and filling out forms, doing math and organizing taxes appeals to me."

"What's your experience with taxes?"

"I've filed my own for several years."

"Any courses? Job experience?" The woman flicked Maya's one-page résumé as she scanned it.

"I am a fast learner and—"

"I don't need a fast learner. I need someone with the necessary skills so they can jump in at a dead run. No coop placements? Internships? Summer jobs that have to do with financial management?"

A scruffy looking cat meandered through the room.

"I was in charge of cashing out each night at the—"

"Snowy Cone? I'm sorry, Maya, but that's just not what we're looking for. From your cover letter it sounded as though you had experience. Why didn't you do a coop while at the U of T?"

The cat began scratching a leather chair at the end of the table. Maya made a *psst* sound and tried to wave the cat away from the rapidly disintegrating chair. It turned to her, fangs and hissing noises.

"Don't pester Freud or he'll spray."

Maya took a moment. Was she seriously considering a job she wasn't that interested in? A job that came with a mean, spraying tomcat who destroyed office furniture and who knew what else? Yes. Yes, she was.

"Why didn't you do a coop?" the interviewer repeated.

"My mother isn't well." Maya pinched her hands between her

knees and resisted the urge to plead with the woman. This was her seventeenth interview this summer, after almost a hundred applications. The only job she'd got was back home as a fill-in receptionist at the dealership, plus her old job at the Bar 'n' Grill—and even that was only one night a week, with the next two weeks off. "I've been going home each summer to help my sisters care for her. That's why I haven't been able to do practicums and gain experience during the summers."

"You haven't done any during the school year?"

"I didn't, no." No need to admit that she didn't know the right people to get those placements. It would only make her sound bitter and full of excuses, albeit legitimate ones.

"Well, I'm sorry to hear of your troubles, but sadly, there is nothing we can do for each other at this point." The woman stood. "Please call us when you have more experience."

Maya stood and tried to remain upbeat. "Thank you for your time."

The woman paused at the door. "If you can afford it, Maya, get some relevant experience, even if it's volunteer work. Offer to help out accountants in your hometown, anything related. It's better than nothing."

Accountant work? She wanted to buy and sell companies and get her hands dirty, not spend all day balancing numbers in a spreadsheet.

"Thank you."

Maya let herself out of the building, then sat in her car, sniffing her outfit for hints of lingering elevator smell. She seemed to be in the clear, luckily. Both in terms of smell and avoiding working in an environment rife with hissing cats. Well, at least one.

Maybe she could drive over to Connor's massive building and offer to work for him in Toronto. Anything. Even the mailroom was sounding good.

She rubbed her forehead and checked the clock on the dash. It would be after four by the time she found his office and got through traffic. Maybe even five. But he'd still be there. Men such as Connor didn't leave early. And after a weekend away, he'd be working extra hard, she knew.

She could beg, plead, whine. She'd do even the most menial jobs, and do them for free. Evenings and weekends she could work in a bar to pay her rent—or stay at Backpackers, the hostel on Dundas, and ride her bicycle. She'd have to do it for only a few months before the lack of sleep caught up with her, but by then she'd have proved herself, and Connor would start paying her what she was worth. Then she'd be right where she'd always dreamed of being.

She pulled out onto the main road, her car stalling in the backed up traffic. She restarted her engine, leaving a cloud of exhaust that made her cough. Damn old thing. Leaning across the seat, she rolled down the passenger window. Warm, muggy city air. Nothing ever felt better.

A man carrying a briefcase leaned in and said, "How much per mile?"

"Oh, um, about twelve kilometers per liter when I'm in traffic like this." She waited for the light to change, wishing she'd locked the doors. In the city you never knew what people were going to do—even if they were wearing a suit. She keyed up a business podcast, ignoring the man.

"I meant what's your rate? Your fare?" Maya frowned. "You're a taxi, aren't you?"

"Oh!" Maya put down her phone, contemplating the man. Picking him up would help cover her interview expenses. Sure, Hailey had given her a twenty for taking her to the airport earlier, but still, Muskoka to Toronto wasn't a cheap drive in this beater. "Yeah, of course. Where do you want to go?"

"Eaton Center."

"That's a long drive." And just about exactly where she was heading.

"How much would it cost?"

"You know what? I'm already heading that way. How about forty bucks? Flat rate."

The man opened the back door, chucking in his briefcase. "Let's go!"

Maya laughed. She liked this guy. He could live by her nickname—Snap—that her sisters had given her, too. Snap decisions and all that—they might tease her about it but the fact was she got stuff done.

"I've never heard of your company—Alvin's Taxi—before," he said.

"We usually work in Muskoka." Maybe she shouldn't get a new car when she moved to the city. She could run her so-called taxi instead of biking and pick up a few fares as needed to help cover the cost of running a car. Well, until the police asked to see her taxi license or whatever it was she needed to operate in the city.

"Must be a lot cooler than in the city right now."

"It's a bit cooler," she admitted. She offered him her bag of trail mix. "Hungry?"

"No, thanks. Mind if I smoke?"

Maya shrugged.

He rolled down the back windows and lit up as her car crawled forward.

"The expressway might be faster this time of day."

"Construction."

The man sighed. "Always construction."

"Do you need to be there by a certain time?"

"Forty minutes."

"Hmm." Maya eased her car forward and onto the curb as she

squeezed past a truck and into an alley. "Hang on. This might be rough." She cruised the alleys, zigzagging her way across side streets until they opened up on a bigger thoroughfare where she could get her overheating car moving at a good speed, cooling it down.

"Did I ever mention how much I like your cab company?" he said, a smile in his voice.

Maya laughed. "We aim to please." She glanced in the rearview mirror. "Where do you work?"

"Roundhouse Exports."

"Yeah? What's that like?"

"Pretty good. Two weeks off, paid. Health spending account."

"What's the work like? What do you do there?"

"I travel a lot. I used to be quality control. Now I'm distributor assessment. We could use a creative problem solver such as yourself. We're always on the lookout for people who can figure out how to maneuver around roadblocks."

"I'm for hire."

He laughed.

"Business degree from U of T. Graduated top of my class."

"And you're driving cab? The economy really is in the crapper."

"Nobody will hire me, because I have very limited experience," she said with a sigh.

"That's always a problem, isn't it?"

The way the silence stretched out between them like a rubber band, Maya knew he was regretting his "come work for us" comment. He was probably wondering if she was unstable or something, seeing as she hadn't been snapped up by some big corporation upon graduation.

The man in the back remained quiet, watching the city pass by outside the window. Maya finally pointed to a billboard. "Seen the Blue Jays this season? I heard they're doing well."

"I don't really follow sports. I probably should, though, as I'd be more popular around the water cooler."

"Yeah." More silence. "So, uh, *is* your company hiring right now?"

"Just menial jobs. Nothing for someone with your skill set."

How did he know what her skill set was? Oh, right, she'd bragged about her marks. Maybe she should shut up about that and just take whatever job came her way. It seemed as though she was either underexperienced or overqualified.

"I'm not too good to start in a small job and work my way up."

"Anyone is lucky to get a job these days. Tell you what…" He shifted, grabbing his wallet out of his back pocket. He flipped it open and passed his business card over her shoulder. "Watch our website—all jobs are posted on it—and if something comes up, apply, and use me as a personal reference. What's your name?"

"Maya Summer." Maya blinked, glad her sunglasses were covering her damp eyes. Finally, a lead. Finally a reference. She held up the card, willing her voice to be light. "Thank you."

He patted the seat and smiled. "Anytime, cab-driving Maya from Muskoka who graduated top of her class at the U of T. See? Remembering you and our connection. Rock solid." He tapped his sandy hair with a knuckled fist.

Maya laughed and read the name off his card. "Okay, Jonah who works at Roundhouse Exports and doesn't follow sports and has a health spending account. Thank you."

Maybe her mom was right. Connections might be the answer she was looking for, after all.

THE DOCTOR DIDN'T KNOW what he was talking about. Connor was not going to have a heart attack or stroke. He wasn't a senior citizen. He was young and alive. He just needed to figure out how to stop being such a pansy and get his work done.

"I'll be working late," he told his driver as they pulled up in front of his office building. "Don't wait around."

He stepped onto the sidewalk, the thick summer air pressing down on him. No cool breezes or chirping birds. Just traffic, exhaust, and heat. He tugged at his collar and hurried to the doors, eager for the relief of air-conditioning. A man stepped out, the door's glass reflecting the hot summer sun into Connor's eyes. It was so bright he was momentarily blinded, his balance failing as he stepped back. A bus honked and a truck ground its gears. Someone bumped his shoulder as he fought to see. A douche in a suit glared at him, barely lifting his head from his phone as he jostled past.

Connor entered the building and glanced toward the Starbucks nestled in its heart. He could really use a massive Americano right now, but the line was out the door. He patted his pockets, searching for his phone. Where had he left it? Was Stella in today? Or had she decided to take the two weeks off as she'd threatened to?

Maybe his secretary, Em, would want to get out of the office for a bit and fetch him a coffee.

He took the elevator to the top floor of the tallest skyscraper in Toronto, First Canadian Place. Landing that primo office space on the corner of Bay and King had shown him exactly who he'd become in Toronto. The king. A man who got what he wanted even if it wasn't on the table.

Eager to soothe his worries and doubts with a good opera, as well as a mindless task such as cleaning out his in-box, he stepped off the elevator. A woman behind his secretary's desk popped up as he approached, her hands doing a strange jittery dance at her sides.

"Mr. MacKenzie?" Her face was a mask of confusion. "I thought you were on vacation."

He paused for a split second, not fully recognizing her. She seemed familiar, but at the same time foreign. "Just an extended weekend, didn't Stella tell you?"

"She said you'd be gone for two weeks." The woman placed a hand on her chest, her posture sagging. "It's unlike you to take time off, and so suddenly. I was worried."

"Did you change your hair?" He still couldn't quite place what was so different about his secretary.

Em patted her dark bob with the pink streak. "Three months ago," she said tentatively.

"It's nice. It makes you look younger."

She beamed. Yep, same woman. Man, he needed to start opening his eyes and seeing things. He stepped into his office, calling over his shoulder, "Can you get Stella on the phone, please?"

Em promptly sat, punching in numbers he should know by heart. He closed his office door and waited for her to buzz him.

What to tackle first? The in-box? Real or virtual? Check in with his merger project manager? His advisors and whatever they were working on?

He ran his palms over his large desk, surprised that they were trembling. He clenched them, willing them to still. He was excited to be back, that was all. That was why his heart was racing, too. It wasn't fatigue, or anxiety, or anything that would lead to him in a hospital bed.

"Mr. MacKenzie? Stella is on the line."

"Thank you, Em." He pushed the worn button. "Stella! We're back in business."

"The doctor let you go back to work?"

He tried not to be miffed at the way her voice rose in disbelief. "Why wouldn't he?"

"Because only a few days ago you couldn't remember my name, and ran into the doorjamb hard enough to blacken your eye, and stopped being able to form full sentences. Not to add you've been looking like death warmed over for about a week. And I mean that in the literal sense."

"Good to hear your voice, too," he said drily. "When can you be in here and bring me up to speed?"

He waited through a long pause, staring at the art on his office walls. He spun and studied the panel to his right. "When did I get new office art?" he asked.

"You've had that since you moved in."

"Have not."

"Have too."

Connor focused on the prints once again. The colors were so subtle, so bland. So…boring. "Did I pick them out?"

"The interior decorator did. You said you didn't have time. You requested something powerful, intriguing and preferably not offensive."

Placing Stella on speaker, he walked to the wall and lifted the first print off. "Well, it's none of the above."

"I agree."

"Why didn't you tell me?" He could picture her shrugging on the other end of the phone.

"You know, paycheck, agree with the boss, et cetera. But I did bring you that new painting I found a few weekends ago."

"Where's that?" He scanned his room, and there it was, a gorgeous, bright sunflower that lacked the gloss of talent. Oddly enough, it made him feel good. It made him feel…love. And not in a hokey way, either. "It's nice."

"I know. You should hang it on your wall."

He crouched to read at the name, and fireworks of recognition flared inside him.

"Connor? You still there?"

He pulled himself out of his spell. "Where did you say you got this?"

"Farmers' market a few hours north."

"Yes. Right. I remember now." He stood and returned to his desk. "Stella?"

"Yes?"

"Have you found that getting projects under way and making a decent profit seems more difficult lately?"

There was a thoughtful pause. "Yeah, maybe?" The way her voice lifted—a voice more familiar to him than his own—he knew she was considering the idea, hefting it in her mind while assessing its worth. "For the past few months things haven't flowed as quickly or smoothly as they once did."

Connor nodded. Thank goodness it wasn't just him imagining it, or creating a story in his head so he'd feel like less of a failure for the ways things had been moving lately. "It is harder."

"Well, the economy isn't what it was when we started."

He leaned back in his chair, assessing the print still hanging to his right. It had to go, too. Maybe after he caught his breath again.

"It is harder to make an easy buck with these stupid economic bounces," he admitted. Was that all it was?

"If it were steady. Even if in decline…"

"Those were the good ol' days, weren't they?" He wanted to hash this out in person. She was his best sounding board and had been with him since he'd started this business. He checked his watch. It was already after five, and it wouldn't be fair to call her back in if she was already gone for the day.

"Why don't you retire?" Her voice was gentle, curious.

"Retire?" He let out a laugh. "Don't you know how young I am? I have a world before me." He spun around in his chair, his power position. There wasn't an office higher in the city and everyone knew it. He was on top in every way possible. "And give all of this up?"

"Yeah," she said softly. She was holding back. What was it?

"I'm missing something."

"A life, for starters."

He laughed. "I'm the king. Who needs a life? This is it! What everyone strives for."

"Everything is business with you and it's killing you."

"Not this again." He fought the temptation to hang up, his anger soaring higher than the CN Tower.

"Don't get snippy with me." There was an edge to her voice he hadn't heard before. "You need time off."

"I don't."

"Take time to reassess, Connor. I'm not saying quit, but you need time away to figure out your next life goal."

He paused, unsure. He had made it to the top, and didn't have any more goals other than to try and knock down any dirty rascals storming his castle.

"You have a stellar grad to help you out over the next two weeks," Stella said. "She and Em can take care of the little things and your advisors can take care of the big things. I hired Maya for two weeks. Everything is under control. Take a vacation, Connor."

"I don't think Maya can be you, Stella."

She laughed. "Of course not. But I gave her an info pack I spent half the night compiling. She's up to speed. She's eager but as quick as a whip. Trust her. She'll get it done and she has Em to lean on. I have good instincts in people. So trust the people you and I have hired and go. Rest. Restore. That merger is an old clunker, and two weeks away from it will enhance your point of view, not kill it. And everyone else has their own projects to keep them busy."

"Two weeks minus the days I've taken off already."

"Don't nitpick, Connor."

"You knew the doctor was going to tell me to take this time, didn't you?"

"I didn't, but I know how to be prepared for anything. You taught me that."

"You're not in Canada, are you?"

"No, Connor, I'm not," she snapped. "Ever think that maybe I need a vacation every once in a while, too? In fact, doctor's orders." Her voice was low, sad almost.

"Why?" His heart was racing again, but he knew that this time it was out of concern for his assistant, Stellar Stella, and not for whatever other reasons usually set it breaking the recommended speed limit.

"I'm pregnant. And I've been working too hard."

"Shit." Talk about left field. Hadn't she married only a few months ago? It was right after the Westing merger, and she'd taken her honeymoon just before they'd jumped on the Everglades deal which closed last fall. Holy cow, it had already been well over a year. How did that happen? "Congratulations."

"Thanks."

"Why do you sound glum?" he asked.

"Because I haven't even told my parents yet and I'm having to tell you. I'm still in the first trimester, so don't even think about telling anyone."

"Mum's the word." He chuckled at his pun.

"Connor, you're a nit."

"So? We're back at work in two weeks?"

"You taking the time off?"

"It's not the same without you here keeping me together, Stellar Stella."

"You're really taking it?"

"No, of course not. I'm going to die at my desk and you know it." Laughing, he ended the call, his humor dying as he broke the connection. He tugged forward a newspaper Em had left open on his desk, and glanced at the photo under a headline that had his name. Who was this old dude who looked as though he was a member of the walking dead?

Connor dropped the paper in realization. It was him. The knowledge hit him in the chest and he turned back to his view of the city, his breathing ragged with alarm. It wasn't a joke. He really was going to die here. He might already be…no, don't think that way.

He moved to the wall, supporting himself for a moment before lifting the second print. A print? Why hadn't he bought real art? He could support someone doing something fresh and new, instead of buying a cookie-cutter image. He dropped the print and a corner of the frame splintered.

The print was him, his life. He was similar to the artist in that he'd made something cool the first time. Something original, new, and alive, not knowing how it would end up. He'd followed his gut and created. Then, boom, before he knew it, he was selling framed reproductions and hoping to ride the gravy train to something big, when in fact he'd sold out and stopped creating long ago. This artist was rubber-stamping his own creativity, Connor his whole existence.

It was time for more risk, and to put something worthy in his obituary. He needed meaning.

He returned to the phone on his desk.

"Is James still here?" he said into the speaker.

"Yes," Em replied.

"Tell him to pop by, would you?"

"Sure thing."

A moment later James came breezing into Connor's office. "How's my favorite boss, Connor MacKenzie, the king of Toronto, doing?"

"You crazy son of a bitch, what's up?"

"Not a lot."

"How's the merger?"

"Bill says it's tough going."

"Why?" Connor took a drink of water from the mini fridge to his right. His throat felt dry and his eyes were burning. Must be the air in this place. Recycled. Maybe he should get some sort of renovation done to improve that. Stella, in her condition, would want fresh air, not this dry, already-breathed crap.

"The usual. Slow backers. Lawyers dragging their feet."

"Speed things up."

"Trying."

"And?"

"Things aren't like they used to be." James leaned back in his chair and propped his fingertips together.

"People are still eager to merge with me." Connor's anger was back. He wanted to snap, lash out at something. It had become like this in his office lately. He flashed from chilled out, relaxed and patient to pissed off and ready to punch something.

"I know, I know."

"Don't placate me."

"It's clause 15, subsection 7."

"Which is?" He should have this memorized, not James, who was only an advisor. James was a details man, yes, but he wasn't the boss.

Where were his files? Connor rustled through some papers on his desk and rubbed an eye.

"I'll work on it with him," James assured him. "We'll finesse things. Massage it along. Don't worry about it."

"Any new potential offers on the table I should know about?"

"Nope."

"Nothing?" Damn the bounce in the economy. One little rise and everyone was sunshine and roses, thinking they were through the storm. They weren't. "I thought Bill was our ideas man."

"You weren't gone that long, my man," James said, tapping the corner of Connor's desk with a knuckle.

"How's your primary industry project going?"

"Okay. Moving along on schedule." James allowed a small smile and Connor relaxed. Maybe if this project went well for James things would finally get easier again.

"Look, I gotta go, Connor." James placed his hands on the chair's armrests and leaned forward. "Meeting with the lumberyard's people for dinner. Golf next weekend?"

Connor managed a tight, polite smile as he massaged the tightness in his left shoulder. He had come to hate golf, as it represented getting cornered by golf partners on the twelfth hole and propositioned for a new project, then having to play nice for another six holes before he could let them down nicely and walk away. Or in James's case, rejecting his play for Connor's company. His advisor wanted a large share of the company's bottom line even though Connor had made it clear that it wasn't up for grabs. Connor owned CME, nobody else.

"We'll play it by ear, okay?"

"Sounds good." James tapped the door frame. "Oh, and hey, are you back again?"

"Can't stay away. You know me."

"I'll let the guys know." James licked his lips twice—a tell Connor had come to recognize as the man being nervous. Why didn't his right-hand man sound more enthused about the prospect of him being back in charge? Odd.

His office door opened and Em came in carrying a notepad, ready for an end-of-the-day debriefing. She smiled as James ducked out, and took a seat across from Connor, falling into Stella's usual routine.

Connor rolled his shoulder, trying to ease the shooting pain that was arching up his arm and into his neck. Probably a pinched nerve.

"You all right?" Em asked, her face pale with worry.

He rubbed his chest. "I think I need to leave. How about we debrief in the morning?" Every breath felt as though he was trying to wrestle a noodle through a vise.

Em stood alongside him as though she was expecting him to fall.

Connor didn't dare speak. He needed a hospital. Now.

MAYA WISHED SHE COULD stand in the entry of the skyscraper housing Connor's business forever. The air conditioner was blasting straight at the doors and the chill was a welcome relief from the heat of her car. She surreptitiously flapped the skirt of her dress to encourage more cool air to move against her skin before reluctantly moving through the stream of employees happily leaving the chilly building in order to breathe real air. Feeling like a salmon swimming upstream, she weaved her way to the elevators, barely making it into the next empty one before the doors closed.

Hitting the button for the top floor, she savored the elevator's fresh scent. She ran her fingers through her hair, gazing in the mirrored wall and thinking of various opening lines. "Hey, how are you? Need someone in the mailroom?" Or "Can I work for you here, since you aren't coming back to Muskoka?" It didn't matter. Every line she came up with sounded desperate and stalkerish.

The doors opened and she stepped out of the elevator, needing to buy more time. They closed behind her and she whirled, almost slapping the down button before catching sight of a serious woman sitting at a desk, watching her.

"Can I help you?" she asked.

Of course he'd have staff that wouldn't let you just crawl back under a rock, but would call you out.

Maya waved and shook her head. "I was going to say hi to someone, but just realized the time." She took a step backward and lifted her wrist as though checking her watch. No watch.

Wow. Moron move after moron move. Way to impress everyone in the big city. No wonder nobody would hire her.

"Well, since you're already up here, let me validate you."

"Is my downtrodden self-esteem showing?"

The woman laughed. "Your parking?"

"Oh, thanks." Maya stepped forward, digging into her straw purse.

"Who were you coming to see?" asked the woman.

"Connor MacKenzie."

"Something important?" she asked carefully.

"Well, um. Yes." To her, anyway. Not so much to Connor.

"You'd better go through and talk to Em. I think she's still here."

"Em, his secretary." She remembered her from the info pack Connor's personal assistant, Stella, had sent her. "Thanks."

Maya moved farther into the office, not liking the concern on the receptionist's face. She kept moving past doors and cubicles until she was toward the back, where there was an open area, tall plants and a vacant desk. A large corner office sat empty, its framed prints leaning against the walls.

Two men were chatting off to the side, their heads bent as though they were up to something. Their brows were furrowed, but the longer they talked, the more relaxed they became, until they were chuckling. The one high-fived the other and let out a triumphant laugh.

A female voice broke her out of her people watching. "Can I help you?"

Maya admired the woman's short bob, complete with a pink streak. "Yes, I'm Maya Summer. I'm looking for Connor's secretary, Emily Duncan."

"You must be Mr. MacKenzie's assistant in Muskoka. I'm glad you're here."

"I am, thank you." Maya straightened her back and smiled. This woman knew who she was! Someone in this big impressive building knew who she was and, not only that, was happy to see her. Her life was beginning. Right here. Right now. "Are you Emily?"

"Em."

"Em." Maya turned slightly to point to the men, who had stopped chatting and were walking away in opposite directions. "Who are those guys?"

Em glanced over Maya's shoulder. "Mr. MacKenzie's advisors. Bill Hatfield and James Culver. Did Mr. MacKenzie call you already?"

"Today?"

"Of course he didn't." The woman frowned, dimpling her chin, as she began walking, assuming Maya would follow.

Maya liked her already. No need to stop talking just because you were on the move—there were things to be done.

"Stella is on vacation, so don't pester her unless absolutely necessary, and I will determine when that is. You go through me for everything. Understand?"

Maya nodded, trying to assess the situation. Something had happened, but Em was talking so fast she didn't have time to mull over what it might be.

"I'm glad you came in. I was going to courier files to you, but this is better. Nice to see who they are going to." She gave Maya a small smile. "You're going to be a busy gal. We need to get you situated."

"Why, exactly?"

The woman narrowed her eyes, and Maya felt as though her intelligence was being tested. "Mr. MacKenzie is taking two weeks off."

"Yes..." But...did this mean he was heading back to Muskoka?

Oh, no. What if he was in Muskoka waiting for her to take him to the island, and she was in his office trying to pass herself off as someone important?

The woman shot her a wicked grin. "If you are asking why exactly you will be a busy lady as Connor's assistant, enjoy the quiet, because when we kick into high gear you'd better have your running shoes on, girlie."

"Check. Got them."

Em laughed. "I like you, Maya. I think Stella did good in hiring you. Not many could take on Mr. MacKenzie in the mood he's been in lately, but I think you might. You just might."

"Oh, he's fine." Maya let out a half laugh.

The woman waved her over to her desk.

"Is that his office?" Maya asked, pointing.

"It is. Stay out unless authorized. And you are not authorized."

Yikes. This secretary was scary under her pink streak and smile. But if this was what Connor wanted in his staff, Maya could so fit that bill. "It doesn't seem like him," she said.

"Then you don't know him."

"Yeah, I guess." She couldn't stop staring into the room. It was so barren. Not stark and modern, but barren. As if it was missing some key element—such as Connor. "He needs a plant. Or some life in there."

"Tried that. I had to water it, so gave up. I don't have time to make his office pretty." Em poured a stack of files into Maya's arms. "This'll do you for now. They're all copies, so I don't need them back right away. But when your position is terminated, all of these files and any notes, further files or anything you have created must be returned to me. To me. You understand?" She waited for Maya to nod before letting go of the stack. "You keep nothing."

That was heavy.

"This is all he's currently working on."

No wonder the man seemed so tired. It was an insane amount of work.

"He's familiar with everything in these files?" Maya couldn't help asking.

"Normally."

"He doesn't now, though?" She tried to get a better gauge of what Em was hinting at as the woman turned to grab a thinner stack.

"This is upcoming stuff. He might refer to it, but you probably won't need it. He will expect you to know it though."

Finally. She was going to be working for Connor in a real way.

"Do you have a box?"

Connor's secretary looked at her, eyebrows raised.

"What?" Maya asked.

"You're not taking public transportation with these confidential files, are you?"

"No, but it would make it easier to get to my car without the wind carrying away half the pile."

The woman grabbed a recycle bin from Connor's office and dumped the files into it. "I'll email you an encrypted file with Mr. MacKenzie's email addresses and other vital info, if Stella hasn't already."

"She did, but he hasn't requested I take care of anything yet."

"Oh, he will. Just give him time. In the meantime, you'd better get fully up to speed while you have a chance. Things will be crazy by Wednesday and you can't afford to get behind. If you're behind, we're all behind. Got it?"

Maya swallowed and nodded. Again, the mailroom was looking good. If only to avoid having the sensation that the entire corporation was resting on her shoulders.

"And if Mr. MacKenzie tries to do any work, you call me. He is absolutely and entirely on vacation. Got it?"

"I thought he was on a working retreat." She was sure that was what Stella had called it. He was taking a bit of a break while she took care of things at his side.

"It's a full-on vacation now, so you do your work and keep an eye on him for us."

"Why? What do you mean?"

"Because I'd like to still have a boss and a job next week."

Oh, that did not sound good. That *really* did not sound good.

Chapter Five

Maya stepped out of the water taxi, cursing the spotty cell service on Nymph Island. At least now she knew that the boat, which hadn't been sitting at the marina where she'd left it earlier, hadn't been stolen since it was in the boathouse. The only question was which sister was out here at the island? And where had Connor gone? Em made it sound as though he'd resumed his Muskoka vacation, but Maya hadn't heard a thing from him.

She flicked her phone, the screen lighting up the night as she checked once again for voice mails or text messages. She paid the water taxi with one of the twenties from Jonah's cab ride and, hugging the blue box filed with files, walked up the dark path, wondering why the little solar lights she'd bought weren't working. Did not enough sunshine filter through the trees during the day to charge the batteries? Or had the box of lights she'd bought at the dollar store been broken or defective? She popped one out and inspected it. Finding a small plastic tab that kept the light from connecting to its battery while in its package, she pulled it out, making the light turn on, although dimly. She continued up the path, shaking her head. How could she not even slow down long enough to notice she wasn't installing them correctly?

A few lights were on in the cottage, and she hoped whoever was there wasn't abusing the aging power system by leaving them on for no reason. The solar panels were still okay, but the battery was a real problem—which meant they'd have to run the generator to boost it, so she'd have to haul more gas to the island. And gas was not cheap. By the time she reached the veranda, she was feeling impatient to tell off whoever was using more than one light. She opened the screen door, and Daphne called out, "There she is!"

Tigger came bouncing over. "I got a chipmunk to eat out of my hand!"

"No way!" Maya dumped the box of files and gave her niece a distracted high five, on the lookout for Connor, as well as any extra lights she could turn off.

Daphne stepped close to her, angling them so her words wouldn't filter past their bodies. "I gave Mr. MacKenzie a ride out here. Where were you?"

"How did he find you?"

"I'm listed on the info sheet you gave him."

"When did he get here?"

"About an hour and a half ago. In a limo."

"No plane?"

"He doesn't seem well."

"What do you mean?"

"I suggested a cleanse."

"Tell me you didn't." Maya reached over and turned off an overhead light, relief seeping under her jitters. "I really need Connor to see me as logical and analytical, Daphne. No offense, but a cleanse doesn't exactly say I'm Bay Street material and that I will get things done in a surefire way, or that everything I do is backed by research. That I don't feel, I act."

"Well," Daphne said uncertainly, "he asked me if it would help clear stress. So I set him up."

"You're kidding."

"I told him yoga was more likely to help, and showed him a few moves. I'll bring some of my videos over later. Do we still have the portable DVD player here?"

"I'm not running the generator for TV."

"It has a battery and it's for our guest! And he really needs yoga. He looks as though he's about to keel over."

"I fed the fairies!" Tigger said, slamming the door on her way into the cottage, having finished a loop of the veranda.

"Not now, Tigger," her mother said. "And *shhh*. Mr. MacKenzie is trying to sleep."

"It's not bedtime yet," the girl complained.

"As a matter of fact, it's past *your* bedtime." Daphne began herding her daughter out of the cottage. She paused, turning to Maya. "How did you get out here, anyway? I have the boat."

"Water taxi."

Daphne pulled her bottom lip between her teeth.

"I can give you a ride into town," Maya offered, "especially since they haven't been giving us a local's discount since Simone broke up with the owner's son, what's-his-face."

"That's unfair, she's not even related."

"She's a Summer sister by heart." Maya placed a hand on her sister's back and guided her out to the veranda.

Daphne paused, waiting for Tigger to catch up. "You should leave Mr. MacKenzie a note."

"Right." Maya turned, hurrying back inside. She turned the corner into the kitchen to grab the notepad, and slammed into Connor. "Oops!"

"I was looking for you, actually."

"Sorry, I was in Toronto."

"Doing what?"

"Job inter—getting files from your secretary. Good to see you here."

Connor crossed his arms. "You'll need to take over the details of the merger. Just the everyday stuff to ensure the wheels stay greased. Items that comes across my desk—push them along."

Maya's heart skipped and twirled. *Yes!* "Great. Let me know what to do, and it'll be done."

"All the info is in the files."

"But—"

"I'm on vacation, just get it done. Stella said you were capable."

Maya stared at him for a long moment. He was serious. Somber. His chin drawn tight with a determination she'd seen in him only during his talks.

"Yes, but…"

"I'm on vacation. Talk to my advisors or Em. They'll tell you everything you need to know." He turned away, jaw clenched, as though fighting the temptation to talk.

CONNOR STILL COULDN'T quite believe he was back in Muskoka, but he'd been so relieved when Dr. Tiang had told him that his chest pains weren't a heart attack that he'd blindly nodded and agreed to take the prescribed two weeks off.

He'd never heard of anyone his age keeling over from stress, although he'd met plenty of people who'd bailed out of the rat race and looked healthier for it. The big question in Connor's mind was were they smart for listening to their bodies, or was this another test of his devotion and ambition? Another hurdle to leap? He was beginning to think…well, honestly, he was beginning to think that maybe he wasn't Superman and that the doctor might be right.

He stood on the end of the dock on Nymph Island and gazed into the water. The only place he knew where he could hide away and fix his life was here. Not Italy or some fancy spa, but here.

With Maya. Only hours from the temptation of too much work.

He rubbed his eyes and watched small fish zip and zag below the water's surface, disappearing under the dock, then reappearing. Swimming really wasn't that hard. Look at the fish, it was second nature, just like it was for him as a kid. He could still do it, no problem. All he had to do was get in the water. Just leap off the end of the dock. Nobody was around to see him stand up to take a break if he got tired. He just had to get in there, and build up from whatever he had until he was healthy again. Until he was buff, and ready for Maya.

The blue boathouse across the strait didn't seem that far. He could swim there and back to get his wind and rhythm, and then go around the island just like Maya did every day.

He stretched his right arm across his chest. Then the other arm. He hummed an aria from *La Traviata*. He carefully dipped a toe in the lake and jumped back from the chill.

Great. Now he was never going in.

He let his toes curve over the edge of the dock and closed his eyes, searching for motivation. Why was he doing this? *For work.* He needed to get back to work.

Meh. Work-schmerk. He wanted to go back to bed, even if it meant tossing and turning and barely sleeping.

What else was there? *Not dying.* That could be good motivation, except that it didn't feel like a particularly real threat.

Maya.

Hmm. The doctor had made it sound as though his lack of solid, regular erections was due to stress and fatigue. In other words, if he took care of himself he might be able to pop one and put it to good use with a hottie like Maya. None of this tired, a-bit-too-soft business he was experiencing.

Smiling, he raised his arms to dive into the water. Motivation found.

The sound of bare feet pattered across the dock and he turned, losing his balance, tipping off the dock as a grinning Maya ran past him, diving out in a graceful arc while he landed with a splash. He came up gasping, grabbing at the slick wooden ladder, while Maya surfaced in a front crawl, taking her away. She rolled onto her back, laughing at his expression.

"It's cold!" he called.

"It's not that bad. Try it in May."

"May! I knew you were crazy."

"Earliest is May 5. It'll get warmer in a week or two, then start cooling down again. Enjoy it while it's good." She began backstroking away at a leisurely, strong pace possible only by those in fantastic shape. "There's a PFD in the boathouse that should fit you," she called, not breaking stride.

"I can swim."

"Stay where it's shallow. My first aid isn't up-to-date."

"Up yours, you braggy show-off," he muttered as she surged into a strong front crawl, disappearing from sight within seconds.

Of course she went around the island; it wasn't that big. It just sounded fancy, saying you swam around this big hunk of rock. Connor pushed off from the dock to follow her, but after the first three strokes, he failed to fall into a smooth rhythm, his breathing and movements all wrong.

He reminded himself to take it slow. He was on vacation and didn't have to make a full recovery today. Maya was handling the business stuff, and she could do a fine enough job to get him through. Right now he needed to focus on himself and rebuilding his strength. Focus on this. One stroke at a time.

He swallowed a lungful of water. He grabbed for the dock, which was still only a few feet away, and coughed it out.

Great start. At least Miss *Baywatch* was on the other side of the island and hadn't seen him flounder.

He began dog-paddling until he was no longer fighting the water, then switched to a modified breast stroke, which was less exhausting. But why wasn't that blue boathouse across the way getting closer?

He turned to see how far he'd come, and frowned. Was there a strong current? He'd been swimming for what felt like ten minutes, and still wasn't even halfway. Sighing, he began moving forward again, struggling to go faster. Puffing great bursts of air, he finally grabbed the dock on the other side of the strait. Farther than he'd thought, and now he had to get back.

He was exhausted. He'd forgotten how much work swimming was. He tested the bottom of the lake. Mushy sand that sucked up between his toes. That was disgusting, but his body felt as though he'd used every muscle and needed a break. He clung to the dock, trying to catch his breath. At least Maya wasn't around to laugh at him.

"What are you doing at my dock?" a voice called down to him. "Need help?"

Connor flinched, almost pissing himself. "Just out for a swim, sir."

"You okay?"

"I'm fine."

"You're breathing pretty hard and are kind of purple-faced. Any arm pain spreading to your chest?"

Connor bit his tongue so he wouldn't tell the man to take a hike, and with a smile, pushed off the dock. "Too young for that," he replied.

"Fifty isn't too young, son."

Fifty? He wasn't even forty. Hell, he was barely in his thirties.

"Thanks." He rolled onto his front and began paddling hard, determined to show the man who he was in the water. He owned Toronto; he could definitely swim across a simple strait. He was just out of practice, that was all. He could muscle through this; he was young and strong. No problem.

But, man, he was so exhausted. It felt as though his bones were filled with concrete.

He raised his head out of the water to inhale a great breath, and just about rammed into an old rowboat skimming toward him.

"Connor, you okay?" Maya whispered.

"What the hell?" He was barely even off Mr. Heart Attack's dock, and she'd been around the island already? Sure, the island wasn't big, but neither was the distance across the strait. Although swimming it made it seem so, that was for damn sure.

Maya raised her voice. "There's an important call waiting for you at the cottage, Mr. MacKenzie." She gave a little wave to the man on the dock behind Connor. "Oh, hello, Mr. Frederickson. Lovely morning."

Connor's heart rate increased to a level he was sure Dr. Tiang would call indicative of imminent failure. "What?"

"Shut up and get in," she muttered, hauling him up by the armpits.

He rolled over the gunnel and onto the boat's bottom, chest heaving with the effort. Maya oared them across the lake as though they weighed nothing. How did she have strength left in her arms to row like that? His felt like a puddle of overcooked noodles.

Back at Nymph Island, Connor crawled onto the dock and forced himself to stand, knowing the neighbor across the way was likely still watching.

"Who's on the line?" He blinked. His eyes were raw and stinging. He wasn't going to make it back up the hill to get the call. He fell into a chair, wondering what kind of disaster was waiting for him to solve. Merger cold feet? Laws in the way?

Finances not able to be liquidated in time? Someone quit? And why the hell wasn't someone else dealing with it for him?

Maya hauled the rowboat onto shore and tied it to a tree. "What?" she called to him.

"Who is waiting on the phone?"

She gave him a small frown and shook her head, then hollered up to the cottage, "Okay! We'll call back in an hour!" She made her way over to the dock and took the seat beside him.

"Who was on the line? I thought there was no phone. Who's up at the cottage?"

"Nobody, there isn't, and nobody," she whispered. "And watch what you say—everything carries across the water."

"Nobody?" Connor leaned back in his chair. "Wait a second... did you just *save* me?" How entirely humiliating.

"No, sir." She looked away, cheeks flushed.

Just when he thought his pride couldn't fall any further...

"Sorry," she murmured, her shoulders slumping forward.

"Nah, it's fine. I can swim again later."

He gave her a gentle nudge of thanks, his muscles screaming at the effort. She shot him a relieved smile, and some of the anxiety in his aching bones let go. He was going to be okay. He wasn't sure how, but with Maya looking out for him, good things finally felt possible.

CONNOR SAT ACROSS from Maya at the dining table on the veranda and clasped his hands together, squeezing them tight. He would not work.

He. Would. Not.

He would dump it all on his assistant and focus on those things Dr. Tiang had suggested to expedite his "recovery." Heck, he might even try a cleanse and some yoga, which Daphne had suggested last night.

But as for the doctor's suggestions? Connor was already doing well.

Daily physical activity? Check.

No caffeine? Working on it. But hot damn, the thought of warm coffee with cream and sugar was so tempting. and the more he thought about it, the more he wanted it.

No sugar. Damn coffee dreams.

Plenty of sleep? A struggle as always.

No stimulants. No problem. Other than the coffee issue.

No drugs, including over the counter. Never had been a thing for him.

No alcohol. Sucky, but possible.

No stress. Ha, ha. The doctor had a good sense of humor.

No work. Again, an issue. But that was why Maya sat across the table from him, unpacking a blue box from Em.

Connor tapped his fingers along the table's edge. This was similar to being in a witness relocation program. He knew where his former life was, just wasn't allow to reach out and contact it.

He mentally consulted the list from the doctor. There was more. What was it?

Meditation. Right. That should be interesting—trying to still his mind.

"I'm going to need fruit and fresh vegetables," he said to Maya. "Nothing processed."

"What?" She frowned at him as she finished piling a humongous stack of file folders on the table. Just seeing all those files full of all the things he should be working on, finessing into a finished project, was making his chest ache and his heart act as though it was crossing cobblestones on stilettos.

"No white flour. Or at least in limited quantities. No more coffee or vodka, either."

"Uh, you know this isn't exactly…" She bit her bottom lip, obviously worried about how best to proceed. Her demeanor changed suddenly, and she stretched her neck from side to side as though gearing up to tackle someone. "You know what? I'll do my best." She pulled up the chair across from him, sat and folded her hands on the table, imitating his pose.

"Thank you. I appreciate it."

"Em gave me copies of the things she feels I will need in the coming two weeks. Can I presume you will be staying for that time?"

He nodded. She was his motivation for getting better, so heck yeah. Not going anywhere but her bed—eventually.

"I went through approximately half of these files last night."

Connor felt his eyebrows dance up around his hairline. Wow. That was a lot of reading and digesting.

"I have a few questions, but I'll wait until I read the rest. Although I am curious where you want me to focus the majority of my attention."

"There should be a master timeline in there for all project completions. It includes checkpoints, deadlines, etc." He reached across the table to tug at a file, but pulled back before touching it. "Red folder at the bottom." He clasped his hands behind his neck, struggling with his urge to grab the folder. Maya puttered through the pile and his jaw clenched, perspiration pricking his forehead.

Unable to resist, and knowing it would be so much faster if he did it himself, he lunged forward, yanking the folder from the pile. He flipped it open and stared at the list of dates. Several had been crossed out, their modification dates penciled in above. More should be checked off as complete.

"You got this yesterday?"

"Yes. Em said it was the most up-to-date version."

They were behind.

He scanned the list. Everything was behind, from a week to two months. He used to complete things ahead of time, eager for the other side to volley the project back to him. Now he had the mammoth company delaying projects, with a series of departments that all had to have their say before anything could be given the green light.

His breathing became shallow and his fists clenched.

He shut the file, wishing there was a way to slam it closed, lock it. He shoved the folder across to Maya, its contents sliding out as she caught it.

"Top page."

Connor pushed his chair away from the table. If he went any further he'd get sucked in, hours vanishing as though they'd never existed. Instead of taking a half step forward he would be taking two steps back in his quest to feel like himself again.

His chest started to tingle.

No way.

He stood, putting space between him and the massive pile of work. He needed to be alive. For…for what? To be his brother's best man. Connor wanted to look good, not the pale, walking corpse he'd seen in the papers yesterday. He wanted to be someone who didn't disappoint women such as Maya.

That was his goal. Get this sexy nymph in his bed by the end of two weeks. Make her eyes light up at the sight of him, not show disappointment. Feel those curves, give her the best sex of her life.

Doable. Totally doable.

"Start with this?" Maya waved the red folder.

"You'll figure out the priorities from that, yes."

"Aren't you going to be working?" She hesitated, and he wondered how much she knew.

"I'm on vacation. I'm totally hands off. Go through Em for anything you need. Stella is away. My advisors have been notified to give you any info you require."

"Wow. You guys are super serious about taking time off. I like it. Do you have a health spending account, as well?"

Connor tried to smile, but couldn't.

"So, if you don't want to talk business," she said, palms flat on the table as she leaned forward, her gaze digging deep into his secrets and soul, "why am I here with you?"

"I thought you got good marks in your classes or some such thing?"

"I did. But why wouldn't you have an assistant do this back in your office?"

"Just the way things worked out, I guess."

He stepped off the veranda and into the area where Maya had said the ice shed used to be ages ago, wondering if this was all a bad idea. He should have gone somewhere else for his vacation. Yet, he couldn't imagine being anywhere but here.

There was a narrow trail that led through the rocks and trees to what he guessed was the top of the island. He was curious to see the view was from there, but more than anything, he wanted to get away from Maya and how she was blowing holes in his resolve not to think about work.

Sure, Em may have blurted out why he was in Muskoka, but he doubted it. As far as he knew, Maya was in the dark and would remain there. It may be pride or vanity, but he wanted her to see him become someone strong again. For her to forget the shell he had become. He wanted to no longer be the man losing everything because he'd never really had anything real to begin with.

He turned back to her, an idea striking him. "You're working here, so I can keep an eye on you, Maya. You're new. Eager. Likely to make errors. Think of it as a trial period. Normally it would be Stella handling this, but she's out of the country."

"But you won't look at the work, and want me to go through everyone back in Toronto…"

Shoot.

This woman was clever. And determined, like the man he'd been not that long ago. Where had he gone? Was he still there, or had he been swallowed by another one? A guy hell-bent on keeping his head above water while he treaded in quicksand?

Maya was searching his face for an answer.

"Just get it done."

He took a few steps up the hill and she called after him, "But this isn't the most effective use of—"

Just shut up, already.

"Consider it a job interview," he snapped, and her back straightened as if someone had inserted a rod. She gave a brisk nod, her nose diving into the files.

He looked up into the baby-blue sky. Why? Why him, stuck here with her? He couldn't make love to her and couldn't talk business with her. This was the worst version of hell. Ever.

Chapter Six

Maya frowned and reread the brief on an acquisition Connor's advisor, James Culver, was spearheading. Grabbing her laptop, she did a few quick online searches. This acquisition made no sense. It was totally out of character for Connor's business. Was he suddenly branching out? Changing direction?

She shook her head. It didn't matter. What mattered was that she filled in any holes that had been created by those on vacation —namely, Connor and Stella. Maya sucked on the end of her pen, wondering what it would be like to work so closely with Connor. Had Stella fallen for him the way she had? All that power, control, and confidence. How could a woman not fall for that? And Stella probably knew everything about him, which meant she could quite possibly be competition. His assistant had almost a decade of experience as Connor's right-hand woman, and who was Maya? Nothing but some eager upstart wanting in, and with a massive crush on a man who didn't seem to exist any longer.

She looked up from where she had the files spread on the veranda table. Connor had gone stomping off into the bush almost two hours earlier, and was just returning. He was sweaty, sleepy-eyed as though he'd had a nap, and staring at her with an odd expression.

"What?" she asked.

He tipped his head in a way that made the warm July sunshine wink off the shine of his hair. He moved toward her, his eyes averted from the table, slipping into the kitchen as though he expected her to reach out and tackle him.

Weird.

She returned her attention to the files. She still wasn't sure what she was supposed to be doing.

"Connor?"

"Yeah?" He appeared at the screen door, the room behind him dark in contrast.

"Am I supposed to be checking your email?"

"Yeah."

"Okay." She gave a nod, encouraging him to say more. "Um, anything I should avoid?"

"Emails from my mom."

Maya froze. Were personal emails going to be mixed in with business ones?

"I'm kidding. She sends her jokes to my home account."

"Should I be checking any other accounts, as well?"

He shook his head. He looked weary, but at the same time, there was something new in him. Determination. Hope. Resolve.

Wowzers. That was a sexy look on him.

"If you want to meet with anyone while you're here, I can set things up," she offered.

"What do you mean?"

"Business meetings. Conference calls."

"I'm on vacation." His voice was sharp.

"Sorry. I wasn't sure—"

"I'll tell you if I need anything." Connor spun on his heel and vanished into the shadows.

Maya pressed her fingers to her temples and let out a long, slow breath. Wow. She grabbed her cell phone and checked its signal. Nope. She'd have to go up the hill Connor had just come down if she wanted to talk to Em.

Grabbing a few files, a notebook and pen, she headed up the narrow path.

It had been awhile since she'd been up here and she smiled at the fairy houses her niece, Tigger, had created since then. They were getting more elaborate the farther she went, ending with one made of birch bark, acorns and tiny pine boughs, featuring a sand path to its door. If there really were fairies on Nymph Island, they were living in some pretty nice digs.

Maya sat on a rock, enjoying the sun's warmth. Although the cottage didn't have air conditioning, the shade of the large pines and maples helped it stay cool, sometimes, too cool.

"Hello, Connor MacKenzie's office, Em speaking."

"Hi Em, it's Maya."

"What do you need?"

"I'm wondering about the sawmill acquisition."

"The lumberyard James is working on, yes?"

"What exactly am I supposed to be doing?"

"Have you worked on an acquisition before?"

"Um, no."

Em let out a sigh. "Okay, well, have you at least read the files?"

"Yes."

"And?"

"And it seems odd that he wants this behemoth, don't you think? It isn't at all like Connor's usual acquisitions."

"And you know his usual acquisitions?"

"I've followed his career in the papers, so yes, I believe I have a pretty good feel for what type of things he likes to acquire."

"Well, his advisors wanted him to branch out and diversify his portfolio, so just move things along as they come through."

"Right. Tough market at the moment."

"Yes. So? What is it you need, Maya?"

"What should I be doing?"

"Have you kept up on his email?"

"No, not yet."

"Then call back when you're done." Slight pause. "So I'll talk to you tomorrow."

"But it's only two-thirty."

"I'm guessing that account hadn't been checked in about four days. Have fun."

Maya clicked off her phone, noting a patch of trampled grass to her right where Connor must have hung out while he was up here. What had he done the whole time? Stared at the sun? Slept? She turned to face the lake. Maybe he'd just sucked in the view. It was a nice one.

Using the data on her cell phone, she logged into Connor's email system.

She swallowed hard. Five hundred thirty-three unread emails.

Maya began scrolling through them, reading names of individuals she'd only dreamed of contacting. There were invitations to cocktail events. Interoffice memos. Newsletters. Ongoing conversations. Where should she start?

A memo caught her eye in regards to Connor's vacation time. Obviously, whoever sent it had forgotten to take him off the list. She opened the email and scanned it. It was very to the point. He was taking time off and his contact person would be her, Maya Summer. An email address was listed for her—a company one she hadn't accessed yet because she didn't know it existed. Crap.

She redialed Em.

"Am I supposed to have office email?"

"Yes."

"Could you maybe share the password?"

"Texting it now."

Maya clicked off, shaking her head. She got the password and logged into her new CME email account, figuring nobody would have emailed her.

Fifty-four messages, and none of them looked like "welcome to the team!" Blinking, Maya trudged down the path. Time to hook up to the cottage's WiFi and do some serious email culling.

As she walked, she skimmed the subject lines. One doofus wanted her to photocopy things for him. Was he for real? Didn't he realize she was Connor's personal assistant, and that she wasn't even in the Toronto office?

This was going to be a long two weeks.

Exciting. But long.

"I DON'T GET IT," she said into the phone to Em the next morning. "I was up half the night and I still can't see how CM Enterprises is going to profit from this acquisition."

The lumberyard CME was working on could do some real damage to Connor's bottom line. It wasn't like his other acquisitions or mergers, and while she didn't have access to every single file of his, she had enough common sense and financial knowledge to know that not only did this not fit a trend, but its purchase price seemed overinflated.

She had tried to broach the topic over breakfast, but Connor had pushed away from his half-eaten egg on toast with something that looked like fear hiding in his gaze. He hadn't come out of his room since.

And now she was getting brick walls from Em.

"Can I talk to one of his advisors?" Maya asked.

"I'll patch you through to James," the secretary said with a reluctant sigh. "But know that this isn't really your business."

"As Connor's assistant in charge of this stuff, I think it is. If there is a problem with the acquisition that nobody else has seen, then as an employee I have a duty to not only tell him, but to look into it more thoroughly." Especially with Connor being so out of it.

"Just don't go getting everyone riled up over nothing. These guys have a lot of experience and sway with Connor."

"Can you put me through, Em?"

She sighed and there was a click on the line.

"James speaking." The man's voice was tough, with an edge to it, and Maya had to remind herself that she wasn't some lowly backwoods gal, she was Connor's assistant. It was her job to get to the bottom of this, and to understand it so she could do right by her boss.

"This is Maya Summer. I'm Connor's assistant while Stella is on vacation."

"Who?"

"Maya Summer."

There was a long pause. Was he playing the I'm-too-important-to-remember-some-lowly-assistant game or was he waiting for her to proceed?

"I was talking to Em, and she said you could answer some of my questions."

No reply. Was he still there?

"I'm sorry, *who* are you?"

"I'm filling in for Stella. I have the necessary clearance, if that is your concern."

"Have you worked with Connor before?"

"I have not."

"What are your qualifications?"

"Connor hired me." She kept her voice low, dry, and unimpressed. She was not going to prove herself to this man. She needed information and he had to give it to her. "I'm his representative—"

"No, you are not, but carry on." His tone told her she was going to have to do some serious convincing to get him on side. "What do you need from me that Connor doesn't already know?"

Wow. His mother must have trouble distinguishing him from a donkey.

"I have a few questions about the lumberyard acquisition."

"Do you now?"

"Yeah. Namely, how is Connor going to profit from this? I must be missing some pieces in my files."

"I'm sorry, I don't have time to explain this to someone who doesn't understand. This is my project and *my* assistants are taking care of the details. Connor can continue being oblivious as to how hard we're all working to keep him afloat."

Damn. Was this one of the situations where she should have tried connecting with him, such as her mother had suggested? He was totally shutting her out, which only served to make Maya more curious about what she was missing.

"What is the overall purpose of this acquisition?" she asked.

"I think this is above your pay level."

"And I think you are being difficult. Seventy percent of corporate mergers fail, you know."

"This isn't a merger, it's an acquisition, so what exactly is your point?"

"Why would a financial company take over a sawmill?"

"Lumberyard."

"Same difference. But this is like adding a chair to a cloud."

"Look, there are a lot of nuances in this business that secretaries aren't aware of."

"I am not a secretary. I have a degree in business and I understand that this one says fail all over it unless we do something."

"*We?* How long are you here for?"

"Two weeks."

"Right. So, not a royal we."

La-di-da-da.

"I still don't understand how this overvalued *lumberyard* fits in, and will make Connor money."

"Maya, is it?"

"Yes."

"Worry about your job. I'll worry about mine."

"All right, then shall I send this overvaluation to accounting and see what they think?"

"It's already been sent." What little patience had been in his voice was gone.

"It's not marked in the system."

"I'll let my assistant know."

"And what should I do when the shareholders ask why Connor's financial company is acquiring a sawmill?"

"Well, since you will not be invited to that meeting, I'll express that we are interested in growth and positive value. Merging and acquisitions is about expanding our reach. This helps build a new direction for the company."

What a load of bullpucky.

"We know what we're doing, Maya, so you worry about getting his highness coffee, doing photocopying, and staying out of the way. My assistants will continue to deal with this project." He hung up the phone and Maya smiled.

Oh yeah, there was something worth investigating there. She could feel it.

CONNOR TRIED TO MAKE his hands stop trembling. Could someone be addicted to work? Because his hands were shaking as though he was suffering from withdrawal as Maya passed her phone to him, an app open to the interoffice message she insisted he read.

He sucked in a deep breath, loving the dry, old-wood smell of the cottage. He'd been fine all morning and all afternoon by distracting himself with the new business of taking care of his body. Of avoiding Maya when she got that intense, hungry look. Which was pretty much all the time since she'd opened the box of files from Em.

But this. He should push the phone away. Right now.

"It's your advisors," Maya said. "Tag teaming me."

"Tag teaming?" Connor took the phone.

"They—well, just James really—doesn't trust me and is going to sandbox me."

"Why doesn't he trust you?" His heart clenched as he thought of the information she had access to. Stella had vetted her, but Stella had been pretty eager to get out of Dodge. What if Maya wasn't who Stella thought she was? What if…?

He skimmed the message and let out a relieved sigh. James was only freaking out over her eager questions. Typical spitfire Maya stuff. He could get over that.

"How'd you get access to my account?"

Maya's shifting back and forth ceased, and she took a sharp breath. "Stella gave it to me. She said important things might come through this and to check it a few times a day."

Connor kept a firm grip on one end of Maya's phone, not releasing it when she gave it a tug. She seemed apologetic. Confused. But the thing that struck him the most was that she'd brought the message to him instead of deleting it. That had to count for something.

He released her phone. "How did you rile them up, anyway?"

"The sawmill lumberyard thing. It doesn't fit your profile."

"My profile?" He studied her.

"Yeah, why lumber?"

"What?" His mind refused to chug forward. He wasn't sure if it was the fire in her eyes or the soft, feminine scent wafting his way, but he couldn't seem to think.

"I don't see how it can bring in a profit for you."

"Look, my advisors are a bunch of butt-kissing pricks who usually wait for me to advise them. They aren't dumb, but this is the first time James has made a suggestion—a decent one at that—so I'm going to go with it. Both James and Bill are good businessmen. They made a plan and James made a compelling presentation. I trust them."

Maya nodded slowly, holding his gaze. Man, she was strong. It made him want to hold her in his arms and let her heal him one day at a time.

"I see," she said. "Well, maybe you shouldn't trust them explicitly. Maybe they're still too green."

"Green?"

"If they always come to you? Maybe they still need overseers."

"Are you offering?"

"Is that what you need?"

Connor ran his fingers through his hair and let out a chuckle. She'd go running the other way if he told her what he needed from her right now.

"No, but I'd like to know what you think." He moved closer, not sure what kind of game he was playing. But the way her eyes grew rounder and her chest expanded as she leaned nearer, he knew she felt whatever was surging through him, too.

"I…" She appeared to be puzzling through something. "It's a gut thing."

"Well, unless it is vital, I'd suggest you let it go." He bent nearer as though he was going to kiss her, and her lips parted. "You're smart. Fix whatever needs fixing. I trust you."

He leaned away and she caught herself, straightening up as she shot him a slightly dirty look. He waved his arms as though making his way out of a spider's web, and headed to the screen door, wishing vodka was on the recover-faster list. Hanging out with Maya was confusing him. It made him want things he shouldn't. Such as sleeping with his assistant.

His hands were shaking again, and he rested against the railing, inhaling the island's pine scent. He needed to clear his mind and ignore the three hundred questions he had running through his brain. Maya might be trigger happy, but she wasn't dumb. Her reputation was at stake, and he knew she wanted a good reference. Hopefully, that would keep her in line until he could get back to work, in a week and a half. All he had to do was remember to breathe and take care of himself, and it would all work out.

THE WOMAN SERIOUSLY wouldn't quit. She was all business all the time. Didn't Maya know how torturous it was hanging out in the same cottage as her? Connor rubbed his face and blinked twice, trying to summon patience, and enough of an attention span that he could focus on what she was saying. He'd been sitting so still a chipmunk, tail raised above its striped back, had scuttled within a few feet of him. Then Maya had come barging out of the cottage as though her hair was on fire, her eyes lit up with passion.

Damn it all. He used to seek out that sort of passion to spur his own. Now he dreaded it. He rubbed his chest and steadied his breathing.

"I was reading your emails and you got this." She passed him a piece of paper, her body practically vibrating with excitement.

"You're printing off my emails?" He willed himself not to care that she was printing what was probably confidential. It was her paper, her ink. But dammit, what else was she copying? And was she shredding stuff when she was done? "Did you clear the background check and sign the company's confidentiality and noncompete agreements?"

"Of course I did!" She tapped the paper. "This is a business proposition that I think has some serious potential. And no, I'm not printing out all your documents like I'm a federal agent collecting a case against you. I can see what you're thinking, Connor."

He passed the sheet back to her, but she refused to take it. "I thought I told you I was on vacation."

She held her breath for a few seconds, then sat in the chair across from him, elbows propped on her knees. "I know, but..."

"I don't want to be bothered. If it isn't vital, let it go."

"Then why didn't you hire someone in the city?" She stood again, her body arched toward him in a way that was definitely intriguing.

If he were twenty years younger...

He rubbed his eyelids with a thumb and index finger. They were almost the same age. He needed this vacation so he could get his life back. His *self* back. And while he was at it, find a much-needed boner—if only to manually release his pent-up sexual frustration.

"Delete those emails, Maya. They're junk. And then leave me alone to chill out. *Capisce?* I'm trying to take a vacation."

"But they're looking for a financial backer, and you would be perfect for this."

"Because I have money? I don't have time to babysit a project with a bunch of newbie entrepreneurs who have sunk their life savings, plus some, into some lame project and want me to magically make them millions."

Her lips curved in a smile. "You watch *Dragons' Den*?"

"I used to, but that has—"

"Kevin O'Leary has a cottage not far from here."

"Are you having him over for coffee to tell him about these people? I believe both shows hold auditions, Maya."

"You're such an ass." Maya flashed an impish grin that made Connor want to up their banter to see what it took to get to her.

"You ever heard one of those stories of people who've won the lottery, Maya?"

She nodded, her lips in a perfect pouty frown of disapproval. He wanted to kiss her until those lips were a bruised cherry red.

"People appear out of the woodwork, all with ideas on how they can spend your money," he continued. "They get it, spend it, and forget about you once you're broke again." He waited for her to see his point. "I'm that lottery winner, but I'm not some dumbass. I protect my investments."

"This would *be* an investment, though. They have a product that—"

"Maya, it doesn't matter. They all have a great pitch. Well, okay, not everybody."

"They want forty thousand and are offering you fifty percent of their company."

"Maya…" The more she talked, the more he wanted to know. It was that damn curiosity that had always served him well. But he was too tired. Too tired to start learning about a pile of new businesses. Especially when he could barely run his own company and seemed to be playing shadow tag with the grim reaper.

"Won't you consider them?"

He crumpled the paper and chucked it back to her. She caught it, looking determined, as though she was figuring out which angle would work with him to get what she wanted.

"Are they personal friends or something?"

She jerked her chin up, obviously insulted.

"Then what?" he asked.

"It sounds solid. I'd like to meet with them."

"You have forty K?"

She shook her head.

"I like you, Maya."

"But?"

"I'm on vacation! I said I don't want to be involved in anything unless it's an emergency. This is *not* an emergency. I need rest. I haven't had a vacation in years, and right now I am trying to keep a promise to myself. One where I kick back and don't think about work for two weeks. If you can't help me with that, I'm going to have to go elsewhere."

She swallowed quickly, her posture straightening. "You won't even know I'm here. I mean, that I'm working. That you have emails—"

"Get the vodka, Maya. You're strung way too tight."

She paused on the edge of her chair.

He closed his eyes. "Just get it. We both need it."

She banged her way through the loose screen door, and he let out a quiet curse. Wasn't anyone going to fix that rotten thing?

Chapter Seven

Maya passed the half-empty liquor bottle back to Connor. They'd started off mixing vodka and Coke and using glasses, but that had been hours ago. Since then, she'd roasted veggies on the barbecue, as well as chicken breasts that, despite their blackened edges, had been pretty darn good, if she did say so herself. Or maybe it was just the vodka that made everything taste as though it was the best food she'd ever cooked.

They were almost to the bottom of the bottle now and had succumbed to passing it back and forth, swigging as they went. She was beyond drunk. And she was hot. They were breaking heat records in Toronto and, despite it always being cooler out on the island, she was feeling the heat. The hot air pressed in on her, inescapable, and the way her shirt was sticking to her skin was driving her wild. If the lake wasn't so far away, she'd go for a dip.

"So what do you like most about being out here?" Connor asked, passing back the bottle.

She ignored it and peeled off her T-shirt, tossing it across the veranda, not caring if he could see her nipples through her lace bra. He'd seen more in the shower and hadn't done anything to be worried about.

"Freedom."

"To whip off your shirt?"

"Yeah." She leaned her head against the back of the wicker chair. "And you?"

He smiled. "Yeah, I like that you enjoy the freedom here, too."

She laughed. "Are you flirting with me, Connor MacKenzie?"

He leaned closer as he offered the bottle again, his lips near hers. "Maybe. You said I had to up my charm. However, you seem to enjoy it when I'm an ass. It makes your eyes twinkle with mischief." He raised his chin. "You like the challenge, don't you? Trying to one-up me."

"Is this you trying to be charming?" He was so close, her own breath was being reflected back at her. All she had to do was ease a tad forward and she'd be kissing her boss.

He stood, offering his hand. "Would you care to go for a swim with me, Maya Summer?"

"I would." She rested her fingers against his palm, wondering what he would do if she pulled him down and pressed his head between her breasts. What would he do if she removed her bra?

"Maya Summer, you are drunk."

"That's why my sisters always make me drink margaritas. Otherwise I get drunk too fast." She allowed her chest to brush his as she stood, her nipples hardening with the light contact. She shivered despite the heat and tipped her head back. Connor's eyes were dark pools of lust, and she wanted it unbridled. Here. Now.

Sex with me?

Did she say that out loud? She didn't think so. She hooked a finger through a belt loop in Connor's shorts, and pulled him to the steps that led down to the path.

"Don't we need towels?" he asked.

"There are some down there."

"Bathing suits?"

"My oh my, you need an introduction to the freedom that is Nymph Island."

"Fitting name."

Connor kept up as she headed for the water. Once her feet hit the dock, she shimmied out of her shorts, turning to watch Connor. The big question was whether to swim in her underwear or to skinny-dip. The sun was still shining and anyone who was over on Baby Horseshoe and had half decent vision would see her. But Connor already had, and that was all that mattered right now, because she wanted him to see her again and to react.

He tossed off his shirt and tightened his abs, his attention focused on her own bare stomach.

"You're too skinny," she said with a laugh. "Quit sucking in." She waved at his shorts, daring him to drop them.

His cheeks flushed as he slowly unbuttoned his shorts, allowing them to fall to the ground.

She reached behind to unclasp her bra, noting that Connor seemed to have stopped breathing. She flicked it to the side and shimmied out of her lace panties, giving him a wicked wink.

"Coming swimming?" she asked, just before taking a shallow dive off the end of the dock. The water felt amazing as it rushed past her naked skin, and she came up grinning. "Feels great."

Connor stood at the edge, studying the water's depth.

"Come on, Connor."

"It's broad daylight."

"And?"

His shorts came off, and he was in the water before she could take him in.

"Hot damn, that's cold!" He let out a gasp, treading water quickly.

"You're going to tire yourself out. Put your feet down."

He relaxed and straightened, his broad shoulders sticking out of the water. Maya came closer, keeping eye contact. He wasn't giving off signals. Not a one. None saying for her to back off. None saying to come closer.

She paddled near him, rolling onto her back so her breasts bobbed to the surface, drawing his gaze. He was interested. Good. She could handle polite and shy.

Turning in the water, she glanced up at the cottage peeking through the leaning trees that hugged the shore. Almost laughing, she thought of her mother and sisters' beliefs that this place was a matchmaker, and that destiny had a hand in them falling in love if they spent time here with the right man.

Destiny better know Maya wasn't looking for love. She was after a good time and a hot job. And right now, judging by the desire coiling Connor's muscles tight, he might be able to fulfill one of the things she was after.

She splashed him playfully, and he seemed shocked for a second, before responding with a splash of his own. She rolled and dived, coming around to his bare ankles, giving them a tickle as she surfaced behind him, resisting the urge to nip at his lovely round tush. He laughed, looking younger than he had since his arrival. He reached for her ankle as she swam away, and she let him catch it, reel her in, curious to see what he'd do with her once he had her. Hopefully, touch her in all the places she touched herself while thinking of his power, intrigue, control, and sexuality.

He pulled her in, one hand over the next as he worked his way up her leg. She laughed and squirmed, playing along. He wrapped her legs around his hips, gripping her waist, his naked body scorching where their skin met. Without warning, his lips were on hers, taking her, turning her on beyond belief. Everything about him that she admired in the business world was at home in his kisses, too.

He deepened the kiss, consuming her breath and any willpower she might try to summon.

Oh, yeah. This was what her body wanted.

She wrapped her legs tighter around his waist, the water buoying her up. She didn't feel his erection, and slipped lower, seeking it, wanting to feel it rub against her opening. His hands distracted her as he cupped her tush, lifting her as his mouth slid off her lips, down her neck. She floated back as his lips pulled at her wet skin.

He lifted her higher, his warm mouth clamping on her erect nipple. Her skin was sensitive in the water and cool breeze. The idea that anyone could see them kicked her longing into a higher gear. She needed him.

She let out a low moan. "Yes, please."

He gave her a nip, his palm moving to her other breast.

"Ohmigod." He was good. Really good with his hands and mouth. She was going to do something wild in the water if he didn't back off.

She really hoped he didn't.

She caressed the nape of his neck, keeping her body tight to his, wishing he would move his fingers south.

Connor walked them to the shallows, keeping them low so they'd stay partly covered by the water, his hands moving over her back as they fought in a lip-lock that would leave her mouth red for days.

"Take me Connor," she groaned.

He sat in the sand, Maya in his lap, and she brought his hand down between her thighs, wanting him to feel how turned on she was. He let out a stuttered breath and slipped out from under her. "Not here," he whispered.

She stood slowly, letting him see her fully nude before him. "Come to the boathouse." She led him into the small building, dumping the stack of towels they kept in a cupboard onto the floor. Connor's body pressed tight to hers, not allowing her more than a butterfly's breath away, and they fell onto the towels together, their lips meeting again. She tried to straddle him, but he snatched up her hands in his, pushing her down so he could lean his torso over her, pinning her in place.

"Touch me, Connor."

He ignored her, taking in every detail of her wet skin. Slowly, he lowered his mouth to her chest, licking streams of water off her trembling form. He relaxed his grip and she swept her hands free, pulling his chest tight to hers.

"Don't be so impatient," he grumbled as she tugged his palms to her breasts.

"I want you everywhere."

She ground her hips against his thigh, where his body had her pinned. He trailed his fingers along the tender skin of her exposed side. She shivered, and tried to reach between their bodies so she could stroke him.

He was being so difficult. So...so in control. She loved it even though it frustrated her like hell. There was something sexy about a man who could and would stand up to her anywhere, anytime. He would never let her bulldoze him, and the knowledge that his power extended to the bedroom pushed her desire deeper.

Connor licked her nipple, blowing warm air on it as his damp hair ticked her bare shoulder.

"You're killing me." She pulled on his shoulders, wishing that he'd quit worrying about turning her on, and make love to her.

He moved slowly, building the tension within her. She was going to come before she even got to touch him, feel him inside her.

"I want you," she said, her body heat soaring. "Now."

"You're sexy, Maya. You deserve time."

"I want to come so bad. Touch me."

His hand slipped between her legs, and she ground against him as he rubbed her into a frenzy.

She needed something to hold on to. She was so close.

He tweaked her nipple as he thrust two fingers inside her, curling them as he stroked her. She let the wave hit her, ride over her, shuddering down her spine.

"Say my name," he said, his voice low.

"Connor the King of Toronto and Bay Street and All Things Amazing."

She ground against him one last time, loving the way his laugh vibrated against her chest. "I need more," she pleaded. The man had opened a floodgate of lust and need.

He laughed as she went limp under him, her arms falling loose by her side. "I'm serious. Do me again—for real this time. That was exquisite."

He lightly grazed her shoulder with a finger. "Imagine how it'll feel if you let me take my time."

"I will explode," she murmured, listening to his heart tap out a steady beat. She was still pinned by him, and all she could think was how much she wanted him to roll his weight all the way onto her and make use of everything the Y chromosome had gifted him with.

She shifted slightly and propped herself on an elbow, her breasts pushed into his chest, their legs still tangled. He closed his eyes, the bags under them grooved and dark, his bruise still an ill shade of green. How could he be so worn-out? He was Connor MacKenzie, unstoppable. Maya's dream was to become the female version of him—someone who owned the business world with ease and grace—but this wasn't part of the dream.

She trailed a finger down his body, edging closer to his still-hidden crotch. She wanted to stroke him, make him light up and keep this party going. He drew her hand away, kissing her wrist, then sucking her ring finger in a way that made the muscles at her core contract. She lowered herself onto her back once more, inviting him to join her.

He shifted, blocking her moves to reach his penis, his expression mischievous. "You are every man's dream, Maya. Responsive, sexy, beautiful, smart as hell."

He began caressing her torso in a dance that lit her nerves on fire. His lips joined his fingers, making sensitive paths on her skin. Finally, he lifted his chest over hers, but lower to rest between her legs. She parted for him in encouragement, but he was positioned frustratingly low, his mouth moving south in slow circles on her stomach, his breath steady on her skin.

He was going lower. She tensed, waiting for him to touch her with his tongue. She threaded her fingers into his hair. She couldn't believe he wouldn't let her satisfy him first. He was even better in bed than she'd imagined.

His movements stopped and a gentle breath tickled the skin just above her triangle of hair.

"Connor?" She propped herself up on her elbows. Another puff of breath followed what sounded like a gentle snore. "Are you *asleep*?"

If this was destiny playing a joke on her, destiny was a fat-assed bitch.

CONNOR BLINKED AWAKE. It was dark. Cold. And he was sleeping on something uncomfortable. Water was lapping under him, but he was dry. A dock. The boathouse.

Maya?

He patted the area around him. He was alone on the towels Maya had thrown out of the cupboard in their haste to touch each other. She wasn't a nymph, after all, but a siren who had dashed him upon the rocks as he'd predicted. He stifled a groan, his mind filling in details he wished were attached to the brain cells the vodka had surely washed away. How stupid could he be? He'd come incredibly close to revealing his secrets to Maya. She was a lot like him in that she valued strength and virility, and he had neither. She'd almost seen how weak and broken he was, and that would have been a game changer. A killer. What was wrong with him? She was the sexiest, most stimulating woman he'd ever met, and all he'd managed was a partial erection. Sure, way better than he'd managed over the past month, but still, nothing near the display of manhood he expected of himself, or would be truly representative of how he felt about her, sexually.

She'd moved so boldly. Shed her clothes, called him to her like the siren she was. Of course he'd followed her and her song. She'd been hot. Naked. Wet and willing, but he hadn't been able to satisfy her in the way a man should. Sure, he'd given her an orgasm, but it was humiliating how he'd had to fend her off to protect his secret. Connor draped an arm over his eyes, his head aching, his pride broken.

His mind drifted to her expression as he'd taken command of her teasing body. There was nothing he wanted more than to feel himself surrounded by her, up to the hilt. The longing created an ache inside him so severe it was as though something had been torn from him.

As soon as she noticed he was broken, she'd be gone. And for some reason that mattered to him. He'd been stupid to allow things to go so far—and not because he was her boss.

Connor sat up, his head swimming, his brain an overinflated balloon in a vise. The digging sensation behind his eyes intensified. The doctor had been right about abstaining from alcohol. Holy hell.

Sighing, he curled up on the towels under him, using one as a blanket over his shivering, naked form. Maybe later he'd go searching for his clothes, then make the awful trek back up to the cottage.

He'd actually been feeling better earlier, so what did he do? Get drunk and finger-bang his more-than-willing assistant. He was his own worst enemy, and yet all he could think about was finding some way to get an erection so he could show Maya just how much of a man he really was. How much he wanted to finish what they'd started.

He rolled over, trying to get comfortable, and his body thanked him with a stab, stab, stab in the temples. Pain in tandem with his heartbeat seared through him and he let out a groan.

Quiet footfalls sounded on the dock, then came into the boathouse. He glanced up as Maya crouched beside him, clothed again, flashlight shining on him. She didn't seem angry, only concerned. He was becoming an invalid.

He sat up, his head screaming at him to put a gun to it and end his misery.

"Hey," she said. "How are you feeling?"

Wow. Lots to dive into there. *Let's start with tattered human, followed up with crappy morals and no sense of honor.* Who took things that far with an assistant while both parties were drunk?

"Sorry about that." He wanted to stand, but couldn't figure out a way to do so without informing his head that a change in altitude had occurred.

"Sorry about what?" she asked, her voice edged with caution.

"Taking advantage."

She laughed, sitting on the boards with her knees drawn under her chin. "You gave me a better O than I can give myself. Nothing to apologize for there."

He glanced at her, checking to see if she was jerking his chain, but was unable to read her expression with the light pointed away from her face.

"Really." She handed him his clothes, then set the flashlight down beside her. She scratched her forehead as though feeling shy.

He reached up and drew her down for a kiss, freezing at a sudden memory. Had he...? Oh, no. He'd fallen asleep while preparing to go down on her. He swallowed a bitter lump of humiliation and released her, slipping into his shirt, unsure how to go about pulling on his boxers without dangling his flaccid penis in her face.

"Uh, did I fall asleep?" he asked, his voice thick.

She laughed shortly, the sound held back by something similar to disappointment, he suspected. Or worse.

She stood, turning away to adjust the cupboard's contents, which had to be still in disarray from her yanking out the stack of towels like a madwoman. Connor quickly tugged on his clothes, almost falling over as his head was showered in shards of pain. His shirt felt odd like it might be backwards, but Maya passed him several bottles of water. She grabbed an air mattress from against the wall. "Can you bring the towels?" she asked.

He gathered them, careful how he moved his head, and followed her out to the dock, where she dropped the air mattress. She took the towels and began busily arranging them while he downed one of the drinks.

Connor hesitated beside her, not sure what she had in mind. He didn't want to fall asleep with his tongue on her clit, and he didn't exactly think his screaming head would let him do anything as active as penetration, assuming he could even rise to the occasion.

"Have you seen the stars since you've been out here?" She turned to him, swinging the thin flashlight beam his way. He winced and held up a hand to shield his eyes.

"I haven't."

"Come." Using the flashlight's beam, she directed him onto the bed she'd made, complete with sleeping bags. Two.

Thank goodness. He could be smooth without taking things into no-man's land.

He sat carefully and slowly, then looked up as she turned off the beam of light. "Holy cow." Stars were crowding the sky as though there wasn't enough room for all of them. The more he stared, the more he could see, filling in the inky background.

"I know. Amazing, right?" She sat on the opposite side of the mattress, and in the dim light filtering across from the opposite island, he watched her sit with her knees folded against her chest. All he could think of was how he wanted to make love to her. Not screw her brains out, but to love her slowly and luxuriously. To feel every curve, luscious and deep. To learn her body as if it was an ancient, endangered language. To honor her temple, and let her know how precious and rare she was. Strong, feminine. He wanted a completely different kind of satiation than he had when he was younger. He wanted to take his time. Memorize her scent. Her taste. Her responses.

Without questioning himself, Connor reached over and stroked her cheek with the back of a finger. She leaned into his caress.

He lay down on his back, hands tucked under his head to form a pillow, struggling to keep his eyes from drifting closed. "Do you know the constellations?" he asked. He wished she'd curve herself into the hollow of his shoulder and warm his side with her heavenly body.

"A few," she admitted from her side of the mattress. "It looks like we could reach up and touch them tonight."

"Yeah." His eyelids succumbed to the pull of gravity, but he promised himself he wouldn't fall asleep on her again. Not until she did.

"Another reason you love it here?" he asked, allowing a playful note into his voice.

"That and being able to, um, well, do private things outside." She laughed.

He laced his fingers with hers. The silence between them stretched with unspoken words. "That's a definite turn-on, you know."

He wanted her to know he loved how bold and brave she was. To let her know that he supported her strength. He admired her, and found her nothing less than amazing in every way he'd discovered thus far.

"I'm really sorry I fell asleep."

"Connor, it's okay. Really. I know you're here for a break, and as I said, having a nice big screaming orgasm brought on by a handsome guy isn't exactly a heartbreak for me."

She joined him on her back, her pose echoing his, her chest rising with every breath. It was hard to enjoy the stars with her by his side. He opened his eyes, the world spinning slightly.

If he knew Maya, which he really didn't, she'd show her bared chest to him again. The odds were great that if he didn't blow it tonight, she'd be rocking those hips over his by the end of his vacation, her breasts bobbing deliciously with the motion. He only hoped he could explode whatever low expectations she had of him, as well as somehow, in the next nine days, find a way to retrieve his manhood from the dark hollows of his fatigue.

CONNOR AWOKE WITH Maya in his arms. He blinked and looked at her again, checking to make sure she was really there: a beautiful woman in his arms. A caring and smart woman who had his back and was… Damn, he had to stop thinking or he was going to turn into a bowl of mush.

He barely dared breathe as he watched the mist rise off the water over Maya's shoulder. It had been years since he'd slept this well. And on an air mattress on a dock, with mosquitoes buzzing around him all night, no less. It had to be the magic of Maya.

A few hundred yards away a boat motored past slowly, voices drifting across the water, breaking the quiet spell of the sunrise.

The craft turned between the two islands, and Connor hoped the sound wouldn't wake Maya, so he could savor having her in his arms a little longer. Tipping his head to watch the boat, he inhaled Maya's scent, a subtle blend of pine, lake water and something else distinctively hers.

The boat puttered to a stop at the dock across the strait. Maya had said whoever owned the place had given her an offer for the cottage and that she'd show it to him, but she hadn't done so yet. What had happened?

Maya stirred as voices carried across the water once again.

"Good morning," Connor whispered as she propped herself on her arms, blinking at him, then at her surroundings.

"I drank a lot, didn't I?" she asked.

Regrets.

He hated mornings after. He was about to see self-loathing and disgust in those blue eyes of hers, or else a thrill that she'd bagged something good and was expecting a ring to come sliding onto that finger he'd sucked last night. And they still had to work together.

"We did, yes."

"Hmm." Her face became a scrunched up version of barely awake. Her eyes cut to his and he knew exactly what had just struck her mind. A flood of pink crossed her cheeks and he traced the color with the pad of his finger.

"You're blushing."

She dipped her head and giggled. "Did I really say all that

horny stuff to you?" Her giggles turned to guffaws and he turned her over, needing to see her face in order to judge her reaction.

She was honestly amused. How about that?

He pinched her ass and laughed, letting her know she was safe with him. Always.

Connor wanted to kiss her. He didn't want to revert back to their professional shells. At the same time, he hadn't hired someone to be his girlfriend, and things could get awkward if she felt uncomfortable about their romp. And she *was* embarrassed.

Time for a distraction.

"So?" He tipped his chin toward the island across the water. "They gave you an offer?"

Maya's expression changed to one of interest and hope. And that fiery passion he'd come to look forward to seeing. "They did. Not a great one, though."

"Market value?"

"The island hasn't been appraised, but I'm guessing it's quite a bit below."

"Hmm."

"We may take it, though."

"Why's that?"

"We owe taxes." She stood, shaking out her sleeping bag before briskly rolling it into a tight wad, her jaw clenched. "Hungry?"

"Yeah." He rolled off the air mattress and onto his hands and knees. Damn. The bed had felt good. Connor gazed up the path. Would he make it? His head wasn't sending out piercing signals as it had been last night, but he felt as though he'd slept in a desert with his mouth wide open despite downing a few bottles of water before sleep.

He licked his lips and tried to get some moisture to return. Good thing he hadn't given Maya a good-morning kiss, or she'd think she'd been kissed by the dying.

He watched her long, trim legs as she moved. He wanted to feel them wrapped around him again. Wanted to have her soft breasts in his hands, under his lips.

Maybe, with Maya as his goal, he really could pull his health together. In the meantime, he had the monumental task of holding her off. He again glanced up the dirt path to the cottage. As with anything worthwhile, the first few steps were always the hardest—as would be the hundred crunches and push-ups he planned on doing that day in order to bulk up again.

Chapter Eight

Every time Maya looked at Connor, her body reacted. To say her crush had returned would be similar to calling McDonald's a small, family-owned burger stand. Now that she knew what his body could do to hers—with only his hands and mouth when he was dead tired—she was raring to go. All the time. She needed to find out what he was capable of when he wasn't hammered and about to pass out. But most of all, she needed to find out how he felt to make love to.

Moving across the kitchen as though he owned it, Connor laid a hand just below her waist and leaned across her, grabbing the saltshaker off the back of the stove. He looked at her, a hint of something in his expression, and her body moistened, tightened and yelled, "Charge!"

She willed the reaction to fade so she could return to the business of making breakfast and being his not-quite-so-personal assistant—she needed a reference from him, not love.

Love? This stupid cottage was getting to her. Anything between them was a temporary sexual affair and nothing more. It definitely wasn't the whole "fall in love on Nymph Island" thing that had been happening in her family for generations, starting with their great-grandmother who had been gifted the cottage by a secret admirer. Neither she nor Connor had the time or desire to do anything as stupid as fall in love. They had goals. Walking down the aisle was not on the horizon. Getting him to rub the tingling tension out of her nipples? That definitely was.

No, a reference. That's what she wanted, not for things to get complicated, and sexual encounters always wound up that way.

Oh, my. He kept coming closer to get items. If he reached across her chest one more time she was liable to push him down on the floor, pour pancake syrup over him and then lick every inch of him clean.

"How are you feeling this morning?" she asked, after clearing her throat.

"Thirsty as a camel in the desert."

"Is that a lot?"

"I imagine so."

She passed him the jug of orange juice from the fridge as they continued to work to the sound of the generator chugging away, making scrambled eggs and her mother's waffle recipe from scratch. Maya stirred the eggs and bit her bottom lip. Maybe if Connor was in a good mood she could convince him to dig deeper into the entrepreneur's proposal with her, because her gut was telling her it was something that could make Connor more money than a lumberyard, as well as change lives. And if she made him money, she might just get a tad of it, too—or at least a steady job.

"All ready?" He reached across her, taking the stack of waffles. She inhaled when his arm brushed her breasts.

"All set," she squeaked, joining him outside, trying to ignore the way she had nipple hard-ons that would rival last night. It was going to kill her going back to "just colleagues."

"Ever miss eating outside when you go home?" he asked, taking his seat.

"Maybe I eat outside at home." She winked at him and dished herself two waffles.

"Nah. You don't."

"How'd you know?"

"Too time-consuming. You're all about reaching your goals. Eating outside is a luxury that doesn't pay out dividends."

Maya laughed. "Am I that obvious?"

He nodded, scooping eggs into his mouth. "Only because I think a lot like you do."

"Yeah?" She leaned forward, eager to hear what he had to say.

"Yeah. But you need to learn to chill."

"Hey, wasn't I watching the stars last night?"

"Yes, and you were drunk." He shot her a grin, taking her in with his gaze, consuming her in a way that made her want to rip her shirt off and straddle his lap.

"Your point being?"

"Want to hike around the island with me today?"

"I have work to do."

"Oh, work." He shook his head mockingly, as though she was making a big deal about trivial things, not keeping his butt out of hot water.

"It's *your* work."

"And I say cut out for a bit and take a hike."

"There's a lot to do, Connor. And I really don't think I should slack off or things will pile up."

"It'll still be there. It'll always be there. You never get to the end of the pile. Trust me. I'm on vacation, and as the island's guest, I demand you guide me so I don't get lost."

"It's a small island."

"Chicken?"

"Why would I be chicken?" She pushed back from the table, her chair legs scraping the veranda floor.

"I think I see a yellow belly."

Maya stood. "Connor, it's not funny. I have a dream and it's not to be someone's paid slave for the rest of my life. You said this is a job interview, and I'm taking it seriously. I want to be able to do things such as pay Nymph Island's taxes, own a penthouse in Toronto and get a real job that invigorates me."

"This work doesn't invigorate you?" He leaned back, crossing his arms, daring her.

"Heck, no." She braced her palms on the table. "Would checking emails all day invigorate you?"

"A penthouse isn't everything," he said quietly.

His tone suggested he'd lost something. Maya gave herself a shake. The man had everything and he was acting as though he was missing some stupid little thing such as picnics in the park.

"Invite some friends over if you're lonely in your big fancy penthouse."

"Who said I was lonely?" They stared at each other for a moment. "And friends I've met where, exactly?"

"Functions, work, the gym."

"Maya, to be the king means making sacrifices. Have you considered the fact that your life—this dream of yours—might land you in the same pile of poo I'm living in?"

"I know, balance and all that." She crossed her own arms and jerked her chin. "And can I just say, some pile of poo."

"Do you know balance, Maya? Do you really?" He placed his hands flat on the table. "Because I think you don't."

"More than you do."

"Then as your boss, I ask that you prove that by teaching it to me."

"What? Don't go pulling the boss card on me! We're—we're…" She wanted to say "equals," but that wasn't entirely true. He hadn't even allowed her to touch him last night. He'd given her pleasure, but wouldn't let her reciprocate.

Why was she even thinking about last night? This was about work. And he was her boss.

It was all so infuriating.

Connor stood up in turn, so close she had to step back so she wouldn't kiss him and forget her anger. He said in a low voice, his breath tickling her neck, "Then come for a hike. One walk won't determine your whole destiny."

She had a feeling that he was very wrong, and that a hike could indeed determine her destiny. She just wasn't sure how.

MAYA PUT HER HANDS on her hips and watched Connor finish slathering sunscreen across the bridge of his nose. Grinning, he reached out and dabbed a drop on hers.

"Don't get a burn," he chirped.

"It's not even 9:00 a.m."

"Smile, Maya. This is fun."

"What's with the sunny disposition?"

"What? A guy can't be cheerful?"

"You're up to something."

His grin grew even wider. "Nope."

She rubbed in the sunscreen and hoped this stupid hike around the island would be worth the time away from work. Connor had an incredible amount of email come in every hour, and it was up to her to cull that pile, not go stomping around in the bush. She hadn't slept well on the dock, and wanted to do things with Connor that, in the light of the day, weren't exactly appropriate, seeing how much power he held. And not just as her boss.

"Ready?" she asked.

Connor did a quick bend to touch his toes, then straightened. "Ready."

"Sure you can handle a hike? There are some steep slopes and loose rocks. The path is barely visible." She eyed him closely. A few days in Muskoka were making a difference, but she could tell the man was still not quite himself.

"Trust me. I grew up outdoors."

"Um-hmm." Sure he had. If the outdoors was shown on a television screen.

"I was in Boy Scouts." He leaned closer. "And Beavers, too, you know."

"Big deal. Wasn't everyone?" She mimicked his pose, loving the way his eyes twinkled in challenge. "I was a Brownie *and* a Girl Guide."

His lips twitched in amusement. "When does a Beaver become a Boy Scout?" Using a low, sensual voice that sent cool tremors up her spine, he said, "When he eats his first Brownie."

Maya snorted, trying not to laugh at the lame joke. "So, you never actually became a Boy Scout, then?"

"I'm sure there's still time." His gaze roamed over her figure in a way that made her want to tug him down on top of the sun-warmed rocks and let him earn a badge or two.

HE WAS DYING. There was no other way to express what this hike was doing to Connor and his body. His lungs burned as though he'd inhaled acid. His legs had lost feeling and he was stumbling along, staring at Maya's perfect posterior, to keep him placing one foot in front of the other so he wouldn't lose the view.

How could one island be so big? Why hadn't he brought water? Or a hat? They had to have been hiking for at least an hour.

"Almost there!" Maya called back in a singsong voice.

Connor fumbled on the rocks, reaching out to catch himself on a nearby branch. The sapling bent under his weight and he went down in a sweaty heap behind Maya, who was skipping up the rocks like a mountain goat.

"View's great!" she said, shielding her eyes. "Over there behind that island is the inlet to the Indian River."

Yeah, his view from the blueberry bush that had broken his fall was great, too. He could eat berries and stare up at Maya's figure until he passed out.

Maya turned, a silhouette against the glaring sun. She scrambled down to him. "Are you okay?"

"Of course." He popped a berry toward his mouth and missed. "Just getting some antioxidants."

She tugged him out of the bush. "Wait until you see this view across the lake. You'll love it. Totally different from the top of the hill over there." She pointed behind them, and he studied the terrain. What in blue blazes? That had been *downhill*? This hike was starting to feel similar to his life: even downhill felt uphill.

He groaned, his quads leaden. He trudged the last few feet to where Maya stood waiting. The breeze brushed against his hot skin, and he thought about walking down to the water for a dip, clothes and all.

He fell onto his butt and loosely hugged his legs, trying not to wheeze as he stared out at the dark blue water.

"Another ten minutes that way, and there's a nice view of Windermere if you've got 20/20 vision."

"How long did we hike?"

Maya shrugged. "About ten to fifteen minutes."

"That all?"

"I know, it goes fast, doesn't it? Suddenly it's like—boom!—middle of nowhere."

He glanced at the broad expanses of rocks, trees, and water surrounding him. Middle of nowhere. Panic seeped into his soul and he fought the hit of adrenaline that urged him to run back to the cottage so he could check his email. Check his voice mail. Anything to prove he was still part of Toronto. That he existed and was still alive and needed. That he hadn't been completely forgotten. It was already Thursday. He hadn't been unplugged this long since before he started the company.

"You've been checking my email, right?"

Maya laughed. "Feels disconnected up here, eh?"

He gave a brief nod. He was tempted to take his sticking shirt off, but wanted to be more buff for Maya. Even if he felt dead after the hike, he decided he was going do some exercises to help build his muscles again. He had all day to fit them in, and would do them one at a time. On the island there was nothing but time, and a body that wasn't doing his life justice. He should be a hot bachelor, not a defective, useless old man.

"And yes." She leaned closer and laid a hand on his forearm. "I have been checking your email."

"Good."

"Nothing pressing so far. Just a great opportunity to become a venture capitalist."

Some of the tension within him shook loose, knowing Maya was on top of things. He tried for a smile, which felt awkward. Add smiling to the self-improvement list. Connor tipped his head back, allowing more of his skin access to the sun's vitamin D.

Wait, did she say venture capitalist? That sounded *sexy*. Powerful.

No, don't bite the bait. She was fishing. He wasn't a dumb fish.

Right.

He peeked at Maya. Her fitted red shirt showcased her narrow waist, and she was gazing down at him with...dammit. That look again.

"Don't stare at me like that."

"Like what?"

"All passionate and full of fire."

She laughed, thinking he was joking.

"Anyway, I already told you. I don't do that kind of stuff."

"I was doing some research on funding entrepreneurs—"

"*Dragons' Den*?"

"Well, no…but yes, kind of." She sat next to him, hugging her legs. "Their product could change the world, Connor. They could help children." She pivoted to him, her knee pushing into the side of his leg, and an ember flickered to life within him. He wanted to fan that ember into something that roared and consumed his soul.

He watched her expression, willing himself to hear her out, but not get involved. She needed this and he could handle it. It wasn't work, it was listening to someone else's dreams. He was being a mentor. That's all she wanted from him, and he could be that person. Hell, he'd mentor her any way he could just to keep her close.

"They have a product in a niche that has very little competition, and their device could become the standard in cleft palate surgery for children. Less pain. Faster healing times."

"If it is such a narrow niche, how do you assess the market? How do you know this invention will do all they promised? Has it been through clinical trials?"

"Investing in niches is always a risk." She pushed the tips of her fingers into his bare knee as she said "risk" and he felt the ember flare into something larger. Was it her, or was it work-related? And were the two inseparable? "But the payoff could be huge—and not just financially."

"And?" he asked, hating the way he was being sucked in, and yet he couldn't push the topic away to save himself.

"For forty thousand you could either win huge and change lives, or go home."

"Broke."

"Um, sort of. But only if we got scooped."

"Scooped?"

"There's no patent filed."

"No patent? What kind of hooligans are you dealing with?"

"This is why they need you."

"I'm not a babysitter. But seriously? No patent?" Something in his chest fizzed, and he closed his eyes to regain control of his reactions. You didn't sit on a great invention and start shopping it around without a patent. How amateur were they?

"They're working on it. They're doctors. This device is less clunky than what everyone's currently working with. They know what they need, but they require assistance getting there. And fast. You could help them. I know it."

"I don't have that kind of time."

"I do."

"For a cut?"

"Naturally."

"What if we lose? Do you lose, too?"

Maya's chin jerked upward in a move that he'd come to equate with defiance and determination.

"Yes. Then I lose, too."

"Even the investment money?"

"Well, no."

"But you still think it is worth the risk?"

"I'd like to meet with them."

Connor sighed. He was going to have to let her run with this or he'd never hear the end of it.

"Have you ever met Arlene Dickinson?" she asked.

He shook his head. He knew who the woman was, though. She'd taken over a communications and marketing firm out in Calgary, and had gone on to expand it into a major business with an office he'd recently worked with in Toronto. Plus, she'd written a few books and was the star of several business-type reality shows such as *Dragons' Den*. She did all that and wasn't an exhausted washout like he was. What the heck was his problem, anyway?

"Well, what she says is capitalism isn't wrong. Capitalism without a heart and social conscience is. And this project has both. It's perfect."

"Why are you pursuing this?"

"Because I think it will make you more money than the lumberyard, which I still don't understand your involvement in."

"You don't have to understand it, you realize?" The familiar squeezing sensation returned to Connor's chest.

"As your advisor, I think you should take a look at the proposal and give it serious consideration."

"First of all, you are not my advisor. You are an assistant. A temporary one at that." Maya's face fell and he tried to soften the blow. He had to live with this woman, and she could go bad news on him if he wasn't careful how he treated her.

"Second, I really need a vacation, Maya. I love your passion. I understand it. Admire it. You'll go far." He held up a hand to stop her from butting in. "Here's the deal. You need to stop hounding me on this."

She inhaled to speak, then bit her lips and nodded. "But…" He waited for her hope to return. "If you do your research, go meet with these people and still decide that you want to back them, then I will fund it. You and I will be equal partners, but I will be a silent backer. It'll be no secret that I'm involved, but I don't want to get tied up in things or advise anyone. I can't right now. Understood? It's all you."

He waited as Maya sat silently, her face lit up like a little girl at Christmas.

Before he realized it, he was flat out on the rocks, being peppered with kisses. Then Maya leaped off him, her mouth moving a mile a minute about all the things she was going to do, and how he was going to be so proud of her, and that he'd never regret his decision, as well as something about how she loved him and everything in the world.

Connor exhaled, feeling strangely remorseful. What untamable beast had he just unleashed? And why did her offhand remark about love leave him feeling empty inside?

Chapter Nine

Maya glanced at Connor, who was as still as could be in the veranda's hammock. He'd lain down after their hike, hours ago, and hadn't moved since. He had muttered something about crunches, and promptly passed out.

She wanted to wake him with the news that the entrepreneurs had agreed to meet with her. First by phone and then, if that went well, in person. She didn't really need to talk to Connor, of course, but she wanted to. She wanted to hear his thoughts, get advice, but most of all, get him pumped up about the idea—and preferably decide to come along with her as team lead, because she knew she was going to want to meet the entrepreneurs after tonight's phone call.

In the distance, a garbage barge motored between the islands, and Maya squinted to see where it was heading. She leaned over the railing for a better look when she recognized Daphne and Tigger on the barge, coming her way.

Great. She did not need company distracting her right now.

Maya hurried down to the water, grabbing her niece, who by then was bouncing around on the end of the dock, trying to get the attention of anyone aboard the passing replica steamship *Wenonah II*.

"They can't see you, hon. Too far away."

"They might if I bounce higher."

Maya shuffled her niece out of the way and helped Daphne tie up the barge.

"Is this a good time?" her sister asked.

"For what, exactly?" Maya eyed Shawn, one of Daphne's protest buddies, the man running the boat. "We don't have any garbage. Well, not enough to warrant the barge, anyway."

"Oh, I'm not collecting trash today." Shawn grinned, standing tall beside Maya's kid sister.

"Shawn is taking his arborist's training and said he'd check some of our trees." Daphne smiled up at him, her soft sundress flowing around her in the breeze.

"Oh." Maya ran a hand down her thigh and calculated how much this was going to cost. The island's treetops were swaying even in this light wind. If one of the massive white pines fell on the cottage she'd be wishing she'd found a way to cough up the money to have it and any other dangerous trees taken down. Especially since Hailey had had to cut off the insurance a few years back, leaving the place unprotected.

"For free," Daphne said behind her hand so only Maya would hear. She flashed Shawn another beaming smile and skipped to help him unload some tools from the barge.

"Will it be noisy?" Maya asked.

"Depends on what I need to do," he replied.

"Any chance you could take down some of the trees leaning out over the water?"

The man shook his head. "Doubtful. I think there are a few government agencies that would get sticky about the shoreline—fish need places to lay eggs, and those trees, as well as fallen ones, create protection for them. Unless you have a permit to do work along the shore?"

"We don't." Her attention drifted to where their land was eroding in places, with waves undercutting tree roots and eating away the land near the boathouse. A few years ago they'd asked for an estimate on having it built up, but both the red tape and the cost were so overwhelming that the sisters had decided to allow nature to take its course. For now, anyway.

"I'll take Tigger up to the cottage." Maya turned to collect her niece, and found her already halfway up the path. "Tigger!"

"Oh. You still have your guy here," Daphne said, her hand flying to her mouth.

"He's asleep. Or was. Just do your tree thing, and I'll keep the kiddo out of everyone's hair. Oh, and Shawn?"

"Yup?"

"There's a big tree above the cottage that leans pretty badly that we're worried about. Can you check it out?"

"Sure thing."

Maya heard the screen door slam as she hurried up the hill. She hoped Connor wouldn't be bothered by having his space invaded.

Puffing slightly, she landed on the veranda moments after the screen door slammed a second time. Her niece was standing in front of Connor's hammock, twisting her hips back and forth to make her fluffy dress move.

"What happened to your eye?" Tigger asked. Her hands were cupped together, sunflower seeds for her chipmunks dropping onto the veranda.

Connor, slightly bleary-eyed, his face shadowed by stubble, blinked at her. "I ran into a door frame," he answered, his voice husky.

Maya let out a huff of amusement. Really? He couldn't have gotten a little more creative?

Connor smiled comfortably, not edgy as he had been when he first arrived. He seemed to decompress after every nap, and a little more of the old Connor MacKenzie came out to play. "I know. I sound like an abused woman. At least it wasn't a doorknob."

"Tigger." Maya reached for her niece. "Come on. Let Mr. MacKenzie sleep. I need to put on lunch—"

"I already ate lunch," she replied.

"It's for me and Mr. MacKenzie."

"I thought you said he was going to sleep?"

"And I think you have some chipmunks to tame."

Tigger held her fingers a fraction apart, dropping seeds as she turned to Connor. "I came this close to petting one."

"Tigger has the classic Summer sister issue of impatience."

"I screamed," the five-year-old said wisely. "Not because I was scared, but because I was excited. I wanted my mom to see. I scared the chipmunk away."

Connor's gaze drifted up to Maya.

"I'm her aunt," she said quickly. "Daphne, my youngest sister, is her mother." Maya gave Tigger a little push. "Go find your chippies. I think they're hungry."

"I saw one up on the veranda earlier," Connor said, his voice having lost its huskiness. "I thought it was going to steal my sock."

The girl turned back to him, her mouth dropping open. "Really?"

"Really."

"Tigger, go play and let our guest rest."

The girl reluctantly went down the steps to find chipmunks.

"Sorry," Maya said to Connor.

"Why? She's cute. And she's got that persistent, quick-as-a-whip Maya thing going on. I've never seen someone wrap around you like that and beat you at your own game."

Maya wasn't sure if he was complimenting her or poking at her. "My sister and an arborist are looking at a few trees. I hope they don't disturb you."

"Why so formal?"

"Formal?"

"You're acting as if I'm a guest."

"You are."

"Suddenly you're not calling me names, and you're acting as if you're a butler or something." He tapped her hand with the back of his. "Treat me like a friend taking a vacation."

"Um. Yeah." A friend with some serious benefits. "All right. Want a drink?"

Connor stretched, slipping his hands behind his head, lost in the view of the boathouse and calm water below. "I shouldn't."

"I meant water or juice or something."

"Sure."

"I'm going to start a late lunch. Let me know if you need anything."

"What time is it?"

"Two."

"Seriously?"

"You napped for three hours."

"Nice."

"Yeah. Oh! And I talked to the entrepreneurs."

"Great. Take it away, Maya."

"I'm going to chat on the phone tonight."

"Great. When's lunch?" He stood, his focus elsewhere.

"Twenty minutes."

"Great. I'll be in my room. Let me know when it's ready."

Maya watched him leave, her heart going with him.

MAYA SET CONNOR'S LUNCH on the shortened dining table and sliced a fresh peach for herself. She'd eaten earlier, but still wanted to sit with him. Pick his mind, flirt a little. And whatever else happened to come up. Preferably in his lap.

Connor pulled out her chair, and waited for her to sit before pushing it in. Then he took his spot across from her, frowning at her plate of sliced peaches.

"I ate earlier," she said.

"I could have made my own sandwich."

"Nah, it's part of the deal. I'll eat a snack with you, though—if you don't mind."

Connor shrugged and dug into his sandwich. Halfway through, he cocked his head, listening to a tapping sound coming from behind the cottage. "Is that a woodpecker?"

"I think it's Shawn checking trees." Maya listened, not hearing the normal sounds of her niece playing.

"For what?"

"Rot, I think. There are some big pines uphill of us and one big one that needs to be taken down."

Connor lowered his sandwich. "Should I be worried?"

"I don't think so..." Maya wiped peach juice off her elbows with a paper napkin, thoughts of picking Connor's brain or flirting with him forgotten. "Have you seen Tigger lately?"

He shook his head.

"I'm going to go investigate." Maya stepped off the veranda onto the flat area where the ice shed used to be, her senses on high alert. Big trees freaked her out. It wasn't windy, so they weren't swaying and creaking as they did in a storm, but nevertheless, she couldn't seem to chill out.

Stepping through wildflowers and ferns, Maya climbed up to where Daphne and Shawn were standing on a moss-covered rock, checking on a hemlock growing out of a crack.

"Did you see this?" Shawn called. "This tree is growing in barely anything."

"Yeah, cool. Have you see Tigger?"

Daphne pointed to a spot a hundred yards to their right, just above the boathouse path. "She's collecting stuff for a new fairy house. Totally involved."

Maya sagged in relief as the girl flounced through the underbrush, a long blue cord trailing behind her as she squatted to pick up another treasure to add to her bunched up skirt, which was acting as a basket.

"How are the trees looking?" Maya asked Shawn.

"Overall, pretty good," he replied, stepping a few paces uphill to tap at another trunk.

"Any that need to be taken down?"

"I've got that leaning one you mentioned set up for taking down. The guide ropes are ready so it falls in the right place. There's another massive white pine up near the crest of the hill which gets the full brunt of the wind and could use a topping so it doesn't come down in a big storm. I don't think it would reach the cottage, but if it did…" He waved dismissively and continued uphill, checking more trees, pushing against a few and performing other tree mumbo jumbo.

"He's cute," Daphne whispered.

"Don't fall under the spell of Nymph Island," Maya teased.

"He's literally a tree-hugger. What could be more perfect?"

Maya assessed Shawn, noting his lean build, Greenpeace T-shirt and scruffy, handsome looks. He probably would make a good fit with her hippie sister. "Hey, Shawn?"

"Yup!" he called.

"You seeing anyone?"

"In the trees?"

She rolled her eyes. "Romantically?"

"Why? You interested?"

"No, but my sister needs a date for a…" She waved a hand at Daphne, gesturing for her to hurry up and find an excuse.

"I don't know!" Daphne whispered, her cheeks pink.

"For a movie. She wants to see Finian's new movie." Maya shrugged and Daphne nodded. "You heard Hailey's dating him?"

"I did."

"Yeah, well, he has a new movie coming out and we'll be going to the opening night in Bracebridge. Daphne needs a date. It's an action flick. Want to come? We can't promise anything special, because Finian and Hailey will be in Hollywood, but it would be cool if you came."

"Who are you taking?"

Maya stole a glance at her sister. "Um, me?"

"Yeah, if it's like a couple thing. I have a friend who might want to go, too."

Maya froze, glancing again at Daphne, whose attention was fixed on something behind her. This wasn't the time to be a good mother and watch her daughter; Maya needed help or she'd be sitting beside a tree-hugging guy with dreadlocks for two hours. Not that there was anything wrong with that—it was just so far off track compared to what she usually sought out that it would be like a penguin searching for a mate at the north pole.

"She's going with me," a male voice called out.

She turned, relieved to see Connor coming up the hill, ducking under Shawn's colorful tree guide ropes. The way Connor was moving, she could tell his quads ached, but he didn't let on. His face was a mask—the same business look she'd come to admire.

Daphne held out her hand as Connor met up with them, and he took it in a gentle shake. "Daphne Summer," she said. "You must be Connor MacKenzie?"

"I have one of your paintings," he replied, head tipped to the side.

"You do?" Her voice squeaked slightly.

"Yeah, my assistant picked it up on a whim. A big sunflower."

Daphne turned to Maya, a question in her eyes, and she held up her hands in surrender. "I didn't buy it, Daph. Totally unrelated."

Her sister whispered, "Destiny..."

"So? Can I come to the movie with you?" Connor asked. "It's been a while since I've seen a flick in a theater."

"It's this weekend," Daphne said. "Simone and our mother are going to join us, too." She turned to call up the hill to Shawn, "So? You coming to the movie with me or what?"

"Just tell me where and when," he yelled back. "And heads up! I'm taking down the leaning pine. It'll fall east of you so don't move that way. You should be fine where you are."

"Got it," Daphne called.

Maya swept her gaze over the group, making sure everyone was out of Shawn's way as he started his chainsaw. Everyone accounted for, including Tigger who was now picking flowers near the cottage.

Daphne glanced at Maya and Connor with a grin. "So? You two going together?"

Connor raised his eyebrows and Maya pretended to be put out, but inside she was doing a happy jig that would rival Riverdance. "Yeah, sure. Why not?" She ran a finger up Connor's chest and flicked his stubble-covered chin affectionately. "I hear this guy cleans up pretty good."

He grinned in a way that made her feel as though he was seconds away from pouncing on her and kissing her until she begged for mercy. Which, for the record, would take a really long time.

"Oh shit!" Shawn yelled. "Oh shit! Timber!"

Maya's attention turned upward as movement caught her attention. A big-assed tree was tipping toward them, gravity pulling it downward. One of the blue guide ropes was missing and it was angling toward them in a blur.

Her eyes flicked to where Tigger was playing, singing a song to herself. Directly in line.

Something blasted her shoulder, and she spun to catch her balance. Connor. He tore past her, heading for Tigger, while Maya grabbed her sister, who was rooted in place, her face a mask of pain and horror. With strength born of desperation, Maya dragged her back, away from the falling tree. Jerking a glance over her shoulder, trying to see if Connor had reached her niece in time, she tripped on an exposed root and sprawled to the ground, hitting hard enough to wind her. Daphne landed beside her, her knee ramming into Maya's side.

"*Tigger!*" Daphne screamed, as the tree landed, shaking the ground, followed by a rain of boughs and broken branches. Other trees shuddered and dropped torn leaves and limbs as the giant thudded to the earth.

"*Tigger!*"

"She's okay!" called Connor, his voice strong.

Daphne scrambled toward the sound.

Maya pushed herself onto her back, her lungs shrieking for oxygen. She stared at the sky, unable to inhale. There was a new hole in the canopy up there, where the tree had come down. Maples reached for each other across the space, like outstretched human hands in a Michelangelo fresco.

Breathe, body, breathe.

Slowly, as her lungs recovered from the shock of impact, she drew in slivers of air, fighting the blackness that coated her vision. She carefully tested her limbs. She was entirely numb. Where

Daphne had landed on her ribs there was an odd, vague sensation that she knew would soon become a shaft of pain, a trail of fire in its wake.

"You okay?" Shawn's face appeared above hers and she jolted, her lungs heaving into action. She nodded, unable to speak, gasping like a stranded fish.

"Take it easy." Connor knelt beside her, holding her shoulders. Tears pricked her eyes, and all she wanted was for him to hold her close so she could sob against his chest. "I think you knocked the wind out of yourself. Tigger is fine."

They stared at each other for a long moment. Then, finding her voice, Maya whispered, "Thank you."

Connor shrugged, struggling to shake off what she could see in his eyes. He sank to the earth, drawing a trembling hand over his mouth. Then he looked at Shawn and abruptly popped to his feet.

"You stupid son of a bitch! You could have killed us! What the hell were you doing up there? Do you know anything about trees? You could have *killed* that little girl!"

Maya pushed herself off the ground, pain finally catching up with her and stealing her breath. She wedged herself between the two men, pressing a hand on the chest of each as she tried to focus.

Shawn's body was shaking under her palm. He apologized in a fluid stream, barely pausing to breathe. "It was an accident. Man, I am so sorry. I'm so sorry. I don't know what happened. I had all the guide ropes in place and checked twice. No wind. I cut it right. I swear. One of the ropes—something happened."

"I guess no charge for taking that one down, huh?" Daphne said feebly, coming around the massive fallen tree, her daughter clinging to her like a baby monkey, one of the guide ropes dangling from her waist like a belt.

Shawn paled and stepped away from Connor, whose fists were clenched, his neck muscles straining.

"Don't you double check your work? Who takes down a tree around kids?" Connor snapped.

Shawn bent over, hands on his knees. "It went over like a tipsy bridesmaid. Oh, God. Have mercy on me. I swear I'll never..."

Tigger giggled at Shawn, the severity of the situation not registering, as she slipped out of her mother's arms. "That whole tree came down!" She snuck her hand into Connor's, her fingers vanishing in his grip. "Thank you for saving me, Mr. MacKenzie."

He gave a tight nod and blinked twice, his expression changing from one of rage to something else. He gave a large exhalation and, gently releasing Tigger's hand, pivoted to move briskly down the hill and into the cottage.

"That was exciting," Daphne said in a low voice. Her body was shaking and she looked as though she was fighting tears.

"I'm not allowed to touch ropes anymore," Tigger said sadly.

"Is the cottage okay?" Maya asked her sister. She squeezed her fingers into a fist, fingers that still pulsed from being pressed against Connor's muscled chest.

"Two broken windows." Daphne tipped her chin up as though she could keep from crying if she just got her head positioned right.

"I'll pay for them," Shawn said quickly.

Maya nodded, her mind already on other things. Namely, Connor, and what was going on in that heart and mind of his.

CONNOR SWIPED AT HIS dry eyes as Tigger solemnly stared up at him. He stopped the hammock from moving so it wouldn't hit her. She looked too precious and fragile in her party dress, the lace along the edge tattered from climbing trees and chasing chipmunks. There were dirt smudges from where he'd tossed her into the underbrush as the tree came crashing down behind them, sending chunks of earth, grass and leaves flying through the air as though a bomb had gone off.

"Do you have any sugar?" the girl asked.

Connor tried to focus on the here and now, and the fact that everyone was safe. Tigger. Him. Even the freaked-out-looking Maya. He'd never witnessed fear so raw and stark in anyone before, and Maya had been the last person he had ever expected to see it in. He'd wanted to hold her, tell her it was okay, but he feared that kind of act would have enraged her—for making it seem as though she was weak and in need of consolation.

"Do you?" Tigger repeated.

"Uh, no."

The girl's lips curved into a frown, her chin dimpling with disappointment. *Oh, no. Don't do that to a man.* His hands were still shaking from his mad dash beneath the falling tree, saving her from what would have been certain death.

Him. Connor MacKenzie. A broken man had just saved a life. Lord have mercy on his soul, but all he wanted to do was burst into tears. There was too much aftermath clawing its way through him and he was failing at battling it back. He was too tired to be the stoic male, and too tired to deal with more female disappointment.

"Am I supposed to have sugar?" he asked.

"Old men always have candy."

Shock set him back. "I'm not an old man!"

"Yes, you are."

"Prove it."

"You move like an old man. You're old, and old men have candies." Tigger's jaw was set in a way that reminded him of Maya.

Laughing, he shook his head, unsure how to make her see his point. "But I just saved you!" he said. "I just ran across and—" he gestured wildly "—and swooped you up! Old men can't do that."

"Tigger," scolded Daphne, coming up the veranda steps.

Birds were chirping in the background, again. It had been eerily silent after the tree had fallen. He peered around her for Shawn's form. She was alone, which was good. He didn't want to see Shawn until he stopped shaking and his heart rate returned to normal. Otherwise, he might find himself behind bars for manslaughter.

Sure, it had been an accident, but Connor couldn't help pouring all his adrenaline-fired blame on that man's shoulders for not seeing that the girl had removed one of his most important safeties. He'd almost killed Tigger. Almost. If Connor hadn't been there… If he'd been a moment slower…

He needed to stop thinking.

Connor tried to give Daphne a reassuring smile, but the truth of Tigger's words hurt. He bowed his head, sneaking a peek at the disappointed little girl in front of him. "Sorry, kiddo."

Tigger thrust out her lip in a pout that instead of making him want to give her a scolding, tore at his heart. Such an obvious tactic, and yet he couldn't believe how well it was working on him. No wonder old men carried candies; it wasn't for low blood sugar, it was to eliminate the chance of having their heart torn from their chests by cute kids. Especially once you had realized just how fleeting life really was.

Daphne angled toward Connor, blocking her daughter's view as she dropped a Werther's Original caramel in his hand. She gave him a smile, pressing warmly as she closed his fingers around the candy. "Thank you."

He gave a small nod, not daring to speak. When Daphne

disappeared into the cottage, he opened his palm, revealing the golden wrapper to the small girl.

Tigger's face lit up and she bounded over, her dress flouncing as she snagged the candy.

"Thank you!" She gave him a quick squeeze around his neck that about guaranteed he'd need to see his chiropractor when he went back to Toronto, and said, "Told you you were old!"

"Yeah, yeah, you got me." He swung his legs up into the hammock and set about rocking it, ready for a nap like the old man he was, as he watched Tigger shuck the wrapper and pop the candy into her cheek in a second flat, making her resemble the chipmunks she was trying to tame.

Maya came onto the veranda, her movements revealing her pain. Whatever had happened on her side of the tree hadn't been pretty. Her forehead wrinkled as she caught sight of the candy tucked in her niece's cheek.

"It's a good thing my competitors don't know her tactics," Connor said. "I'd be done for within a matter of minutes."

Wincing, Maya flopped into the chair near the hammock, setting the old wicker creaking like an arthritic in a storm. "Sugar winds her up." Maya bent her arms, gazing at her elbows, which were a dirty, bloody mess.

"Aw, Maya. Look at you." Connor sat up, taking her in. Her knees were a disaster, and her chin was scraped, as well. "Are you okay?"

Maya's bottom lip quivered slightly before she tucked it into her mouth, pinning it under her teeth. She gave a tight chin lift in acknowledgment.

"Have you checked the windows?" he asked.

"No. I came to see if you were okay."

"I'm fine." He held out his shaking hands and laughed. "Like a rock."

She smiled, her face pale. He reached across the space, just about falling out the hammock as he gave her shoulder a quick squeeze, letting his touch linger when she blinked back tears.

"It's okay, Maya."

"I know." She waved at the wetness in her eyes. "This is stupid."

He let out a low whistle as he caught sight of the torn skin on her palms. "Look at your hands! Come on, let's clean you up." Connor leveraged himself out of the hammock, then paused, noting his muscles were screaming in a new way—from hard use rather than fatigue. The sprint to Tigger must have built up an incredible amount of lactic acid. He paused again, then pushed himself all the way upright, ignoring the myriad of sharp muscle pains. So, he was officially on the road to recovery. How about that.

Maya hobbled to the screen door, trying to hide her pain. But her hips still swayed in that sweet way that made him want to pull them against his, and he smiled, remembering why he'd done all those crunches, the hike, the swim. Heck, maybe he'd even add a few more push-ups before bed.

CONNOR STOOD AT THE doorway to the bathroom, watching Maya dig through a medicine cabinet.

"Come in," she said. "Close the door."

That was an offer he was willing to accept. He shut the door behind him, amazed at how well it closed, given the cottage's age. Connor gently directed Maya to the bench under the window, cringing at the condition of her knees.

"Where shall I start?" He looked up and spotted the wound on the underside of her chin. He bent his head, assessing the extent of the damage. "You did a real number on yourself."

"Better than being hit by a tree."

"Any day of the week." He sorted through the first aid items. "I think we need to clean you up for starters. Do you have a facecloth?"

Maya pointed to a basket on a shelf to his left.

"Apparently, I am blind." He shot her a reassuring smile, not sure his doctoring skills would be up to par. But honestly, a chance to touch her bare legs? Only a fool would turn down the opportunity to play doctor on a woman such as Maya.

Connor filled the sink with warm water and swished the cloth around while glancing at himself in the mirror. He might be handsome again one day if he could ditch those bags under his eyes. And maybe get that greenish bruise to go away completely.

He turned back to Maya, kneeling in front of her. "Want an aspirin or something?"

"I'm fine."

He began dabbing at her knees, finding that the dirt stuck between every tiny crease in her skin. He rinsed out the cloth and tried again, using more water, letting it run down her leg and onto another cloth.

"Sorry," he said when she flinched. There were a few big tears in her skin, but luckily, nothing too deep. He slowly wiped her legs with the dry cloth, cleaning her down to her toes. Such lovely, gorgeous toes. Downright sexy.

Maya presented her palms. "These are going to be fun."

"Is that a rock lodged under your skin?" He removed the tiny pebble, and lowered her hands into fresh water in the sink. "Let them soak." He brushed the hair off her face, his moves slow and gentle. "They must be numb. You didn't even flinch."

He needed to add bicep dips to his repertoire tomorrow. And another swim. Maybe both. Because he swore as he brushed against Maya his body felt stronger, tighter. And he liked it. A lot. With her back against his chest, he reached around her, helping her clean her palms. It was something she could do on her own, but she didn't seem to mind the help. He inhaled her scent, watching as she matched his breaths, leaning back against him.

Mmm. This was good. Innocent, yet entirely erotic.

He slowly scooped water in his palms and ran them up her forearms, letting the warm liquid spill over her bare skin. She shivered and he moved closer, his body stretched over hers like a shadow. "You cold?" he whispered in her ear.

She shook her head and tipped it back against his shoulder. Allowing himself to cross the line, he placed a light kiss on her neck before returning his attention to her hands, hoping she felt as tempted as he did.

When her palms were fixed up, he gently spun her to face him, her back to the sink. He let his gaze linger on hers, then slowly lifted her arms to see her elbows. Her face pinched in pain and he stopped.

"What's wrong?"

"My ribs hurt."

"Ribs?" Keeping eye contact, he tenderly lifted the hem of her shirt, asking for permission.

"Oh, for crying out loud, Connor. You've seen me shirtless twice." She whipped off her top, her breath catching with the sudden movement.

That bra was as sexy as anything he'd ever seen in a Victoria's Secret commercial. Its satin dipped low over her curves, pushing them up in a bounty that stirred his testosterone into a whirlwind. He blinked back the need that tore through him, fighting the temptation to lower his face to her breasts and tug her dark nipples out of their hiding spots….

"My ribs are lower," she said, her voice sensual, teasing.

"Yeah, I know. I'm analyzing your assets." He bent close as if he was going to bite her neck, and she arched her spine, pressing into him. He reached behind her and pulled the plug from the sink, draining the murky water. Then he leaned back, eyebrow raised. Her cheeks flushed as she bowed her head to check her ribs.

"Ouch," he said. "That's some welt."

He touched her skin, sending goose bumps across her midriff as he shifted her to get a better view.

"I'll get some ice," he said, stepping out of the bathroom.

On the other side of the door he took a moment to compose himself. He wanted to screw Maya senseless, and was playing a dangerous game in there. One where he wouldn't win. One that would end in his humiliation, because even as stirred up as he was, he knew he couldn't commit to the level their bodies surely desired.

Not yet.

He returned with ice wrapped in a damp tea towel, unsure whether he should apply it himself or excuse himself before he got in too deep. Maya glanced up at him, and there was something in her expression that made him drop to his knees and gently press the ice pack against her red skin. She inhaled, pushing her chest out as she curved away from the cold. He'd like to watch that move again and again. He reapplied the pack, and she placed her cool hand over his, folding herself against him as he fell back onto his heels, clutching her. Within seconds his fingers were knotted in her hair, tipping her head back to gain access to her mouth, kissing her with full force, pushing every emotion roaring through him into the kiss.

Her fingers slipped under his shirt, lifting it away from his body and over his head. He suppressed the urge to tense his muscles so he'd seem firmer under her touch, and caressed her shoulders. He ran his hands over her breasts, hooking his fingers in the edge of her bra to draw her nipples free. He pushed his palms back up her chest in a fluid move. His hands met at her neck, and he swooped them around behind her head so he could tilt her back and kiss his way across her collarbone. Her fingers trailed down his chest and he shifted her so she could grind against his partial.

Come on, buddy. Now's a good time to come up and say hello.

"I want you bad," he whispered, and she sucked on his tongue, making him think of what she could do to a hard-on. He groaned and unbuttoned her shorts.

"Auntie Maya?" called a sweet voice.

Maya tipped her head up, looking dazed, her curls a riot around her perfect, flushed face. She pressed a finger to her wet lips.

The doorknob began to turn and Connor leaped into action, his abs screaming with the effort as he unceremoniously dumped Maya on the floor, her breasts bouncing. He grabbed the knob, not allowing the door to open fully. Slipping out into the hall, he smiled at Tigger.

"Hey, kiddo. Need the facilities?"

"The what?"

"Bathroom? Your aunt is just finishing up." He pointed to the heels of his hands. "She's going to be sore for a few days."

"Does she need a Band-Aid? I have some princess ones in my mommy's purse."

"You know, she might like that."

Tigger quirked her head. "Where's your shirt?"

"Oh…" He ran his fingers through his hair as Maya joined them.

"Hi, Auntie Maya." The girl danced into the bathroom, shutting the door behind her.

Connor stepped to Maya, pinning her against the wall, his lips on hers. She lifted her legs, pressing her heat against his crotch.

He pushed forward, grinding into her, barely able to breathe through his passion.

They kissed as though it would be their last, until the sound of the toilet flushing broke their embrace. Maya dropped her feet to the floor and straightened her top. Without a word, she stepped into the living room, her ass swaying as though it held the secrets of the world.

He was a doomed man.

Chapter Ten

Where the heck had Connor gone?

Daphne, Shawn, and Tigger had left, and the two of them finally had the island to themselves. Maya's work was done for the day, and she wanted to dive right back into what they'd started in the bathroom. The way he'd caressed her skin when he'd dried her legs made her want to lay herself out so he could dry her all over. All. Over.

Damn him. Where had he gone?

Hearing footsteps on the veranda, she hurried around the corner to catch him, scaring a nuthatch off the railing. Connor looked wiped, his black swim shorts clinging to his wet legs. Not seeing her, he trudged forward, disappearing into the cottage.

Maya had come to know that look. It meant she was facing another evening tweeting distribution system jokes to Steve from Roundhouse Exports, or else watching *Dragons' Den* reruns she'd saved to her hard drive. Not so bad. Except the way Connor had revved her up meant she'd be spending special time with her vibrator, since he and his delicious mouth would be snoring only one bedroom away. She lifted her head to the sky and whispered, "Destiny, you are one mean bitch."

It didn't help that the way Connor had rescued Tigger was a total turn-on. She'd never realized it, but apparently she had a thing for heroes. Every time she thought of him dashing off to save her niece, an unrelenting heat spread through her.

Maya made her way into the cottage and sat down with *All In* by Arlene Dickinson. While she read, she kept Connor's closed bedroom door in her peripheral vision. She could swear he was snoring already.

She sighed and flipped a page, wishing she had the courage to wake him up by slipping under his covers wearing nothing but her lust and longing.

Her cell phone rang and she jumped up, crossing the room in a few strides. What the heck? She never got reception in the cottage.

"What's this?" a male voice replied when she answered.

"Um? Who is this?"

"James Culver. Connor's advisor. And I demand you tell me what the hell this memo is about!"

"Oh! Right. Sorry." The phone got scratchy and she froze, not daring to move in case she lost the connection. "Connor is considering backing these entrepreneurs. It's all explained in the memo. I sent it to you, Bill, Em, and Stella so you'd be in the loop. A contract is in draft with Legal. I'm taking care of it all so you and your assistants don't have to worry about it."

"Worry about it? Are you kidding me? You're gambling away Connor's money on some dental device and you've been here how many days? Some of us work really hard to make sure Connor makes money, not loses it. We get pestered like this all the time by people who would love to suck him dry. You need to drop this idea."

"Connor gave it the okay."

"Connor's on vacation and not making major decisions right now. I'm the one he left in charge of the office, and I say no. This agreement happened under my watch, and you not asking me first sets a precedent that I will be dealing with long after you're gone."

"Um, what kind of precedent?" She glanced at Connor's closed door.

"Word is going to get out that anyone with a half-baked idea can come to us for money and support. We'll never be able to do any real work—work that makes us a profit."

"And buying a lumberyard is going to do that?"

"And turning to venture capitalism is?"

"Uh, yeah. It is." She placed a hand on her hip. "I don't understand why you're getting in such a flap over me advising Connor on something out of character, when you seem to have done the same thing yourself. Except I'm only gambling 40K and you're gambling well over ten times that amount. My project could pay off big. I fail to see how yours could."

"I have a lot of experience and know what I am doing." His voice trembled with anger.

"I sure as hell hope so, because I like Mr. MacKenzie."

"Oh, so that's what this is about? You want to play house with the boss?"

Maya made sputtering sounds. "Wow. Just wow."

"Do your job and stay out of my way."

"Consider it my pleasure," she said, hanging up.

She set her phone down, letting out a slow, long breath.

"You've met James?" Connor said, leaning against the doorjamb to his room, arms crossed.

"I have had the unfortunate pleasure of landing on his bad side, yes."

And this was the moment when she lost her job for not getting along with his team. Crap. She was actually starting to enjoy the work.

"You handled yourself well."

"Thank you." Maya stiffened her spine, not daring to let her relief show.

"I'd even say you got the upper hand." Connor pushed off the doorjamb, wincing.

"You okay?"

"Yeah, just a sore shoulder." He flashed a brief smile, but gave her a wide berth as he hurried past her into the kitchen.

She followed, giving his butt a slap as he dug around in the fridge for a snack. He straightened, banging his head on the freezer above.

"Ow!"

"I am so sorry!" Maya laid a hand on his head where he'd bumped it, but he slipped away, avoiding her touch. She nudged her chest against him, offering herself, but he dodged her again, clutching his skull in a way that told her he was faking most of the pain.

Hurt seared her soul and she backed against the counter, letting him grab a peach before stalking out of the kitchen.

What the hell was his problem? Whenever she got close, he ran away.

Maya bit her bottom lip. He didn't want something with her, fine. But she didn't want "something," either. She wanted one thing. Sex. Okay, two things. Sex and a job reference.

MAYA STOOD ON THE DOCK, the morning sunshine streaming down on her. There was something new and renewed about Connor today. Something she couldn't quite figure out. He would dance near, then close up and move away. But it wasn't just that. There was a purpose and drive flaring in his eyes that made her own heart beat a little faster in anticipation. It was as though he had his own secret project he was working on, and it made her curious. She wanted to help him and be a part of it, but knew she had to be patient. Then maybe, just maybe, he'd let her in.

Connor hauled himself out of the lake, panting, as water streamed off his broad shoulders. Maya held out a towel and stopped herself from staring at the way his muscles bunched when he raised it to scrub at his dripping hair. His haircut was just past neat and tidy, and starting to look slightly shaggy. She adored how it made him appear less serious.

"Good swim?" she asked.

"Yup."

"Go across and back?"

"Yup."

"Still don't want to come with me to meet the entrepreneurs?"

"Nope."

"You are a man of many words this morning."

"Yup."

Sighing, Maya shifted her weight and toyed with the boat's key chain which was made of foam so it would float if accidentally dropped in the water. "I could use your help, you know."

"You said you had it covered."

"I do, but it would be nice to have you along."

"Just keep shaking that sweet ass in that little suit of yours, and remember to listen."

"I'm a good listener."

"I wasn't done," he said, his tone slightly sharp.

"Sorry. You had more sexual harassment masked as a compliment?"

He shook the last of the water out of his hair with a grin, catching himself on a chair as he lost his balance. He toweled off his torso and sat down.

"Well?" she asked.

"Patience, Maya."

"I have to leave soon if I'm going to make it on time."

He peeked out from behind the towel as he patted his brow. "Are you *driving*?"

"Um, yeah. That's what people who aren't *you* do."

He gazed off into middle distance. "Okay. Long story short?"

"Preferably."

"You already act as if you own the place, and I know you won't let them blow sunshine up your ass."

"Sweet ass, I believe you called it?"

"Fine, blow sunshine up your sweet ass." He reached over and gave her a light slap on the closest butt cheek. "You can file the sexual harassment suit later."

"You wish." She gave him a wink and he grinned again.

"Basically, go into any meeting assuming the other person is trying to get the better deal."

Maya sighed. Could he get any more basic?

"Be *patient*, Maya."

She licked her lips and tried to act as though she wasn't insulted by him wasting her time with trivialities.

"People will tell you anything. You have to check their facts. Don't take anything at face value. Ask questions most folks would be too uncomfortable asking. Repeat yourself if you have to."

"Got it."

"Listen. Pause. Reflect."

Maya nodded. "Listen, pause, reflect." She should probably add connect in there, too, seeing as it seemed to be a point of weakness with her usual tactics.

"Circle back if you have to. Take notes. Act like a lawyer ready to catch them lying. They wouldn't come to you if they could do this on their own. What can you offer that they haven't been able to accomplish? But most importantly, what can they bring you? It *has* to be mutually beneficial." He banged a fist on his open palm for emphasis. "What are your odds of success? And above all, they need to be a helluva lot more invested than you ever will be if you're backing them financially."

"Right. Okay." This was the stuff she'd been waiting for. Now why wouldn't he come with her and help sort through it all, making certain she didn't miss any cues or hints about problems that could bite her in the butt later? "Sure you don't want to come and hash it all out afterward? Draw the agreement over the coals?" That would be so much fun.

He leaned closer, his expression full of haunting shadows. "Business isn't just theory, instincts or snap gut decisions, or even research. It's more than that, Maya."

He stared at her for a moment, and shivers ran down her spine. The wrong kind of shivers.

"Can you do this?" he asked.

She nodded and took a gulp of air.

"Good." He sat back, his face softening, the shadows gone.

"What do you love most about this business?" she asked quietly. "The chase? The catch?"

The shadows returned. "Ask them about their lives. Break the ice. See if they have kids."

"Kids?" She didn't want to talk sippy cups, she wanted to talk turkey.

"It'll reveal their core to you. Who they are. As well as how distracted they are from their own work."

"You prefer to deal with people without kids?"

"I didn't say that. Just keep your eyes and ears open, as there are hints as to who they are in everything they do and say. Then wait at least two to three days before giving them a decision."

"That sounds like a dating rule—don't call for three days after getting their number."

"Business is a form of dating, Maya."

She opened her mouth to ask what the two of them were

doing, then closed it again. She had a meeting to attend. Connor would reveal himself in time. All she had to do was figure out how to be patient.

CONNOR ROLLED OVER to check the clock, his abs killing him. Only nine at night. He slung an arm across his eyes and wondered if it was a raccoon or Maya he'd just heard. He was guessing Maya. Either that or a really steamed thief.

He smiled, thinking of a robber coming in here. Other than the ancient furniture, which might actually be worth something on the antiques market if it hadn't been so well used, the place didn't have much of value other than Maya's laptop and printer. And even the printer was probably some thirty-dollar loss leader from the local computer shop.

He considered getting up to find out why she was pissed, but thought better of it. If her appointment with the entrepreneurs hadn't gone well he could deal with waiting until she'd cooled down, since the long drive obviously hadn't worked.

Thinking of Maya, he smiled and curled onto his side, lulled back into near sleep by the bed's warm comfort. The door banged open; the scent of coffee filled his nostrils.

"You work with jackasses," Maya announced, plunking a cup on his bedstand.

"Coffee? It's nine at night."

"Nine in the morning."

"Well, then. Good morning, sweet cheeks." He flipped himself over to flick up the shades, trying to hide his morning wood. He glanced down and sighed. Still nothing to hide. How much sleep did a man need?

"It's almost afternoon," Maya grumbled.

"Great." He squinted as light bleached the room. "I'm supposed to sleep."

"Says who?"

"I'm on vacation. That's what people do when they are on vacation."

"Right. Well, your advisor, James? He tried to fire me yesterday."

Connor winced as the coffee scorched his tongue. "Do I want to know why?"

"I went by to get more files on the sawmill and he told me to butt out."

"I thought you were meeting the entrepreneurs?"

"Oh, yeah." She sat on the bed beside him, the anger dissolving. "They were great. I think I'm going to go with them."

"Wait a few days," he warned. She was so damn impatient. She listened to her gut only long enough to get the first few chords of the song, then floored the engine, ignoring the rest of the tune. Every time. He needed to teach this girl to slow down before she floored it into a brick wall, as he had.

"I'll wait." She sounded reluctant.

"Good. I'm holding you to that."

He stood to leave his room, then turned back to Maya, who had her wavy hair pinned up in a way that made it look messy, elegant and sexy all at the same time. Hot damn. He was finding it difficult to keep fighting the urge to kiss her.

He pinched the bridge of his nose and focused on what had made her angry. "Why exactly does James have a problem with you?"

She shrugged. "I ask too many questions."

"What kind of questions?"

"My usual nosy ones." She gave him a smile. "You're not mad, are you?"

"For asking questions? No, not really." But the effect of those questions was intriguing. James, like anyone, became edgy when stressed, and Connor could see how Maya's inquisitiveness could get under the man's skin. He used to do the same to James eons ago, when they'd first started working together. But he'd thought James had mellowed. Was leaving the company in his hands too much for his advisor?

Connor gave Maya a reassuring tap on the elbow. "James is carrying a heavy load right now. More so with me gone, so don't take it personally. I turn into a supreme prick who wants things done five minutes ago, and for everything to be lined up so I can fire through them like a sergeant major general when I'm busy. It's normal." The familiar tightness associated with work expanded in his chest, which he rubbed with the heel of his hand. He gave a light laugh. "I should ask him if he wants to take over some of my projects."

Connor considered the idea, blocking out Maya's flabbergasted protests. James dealing with all the details he had to shovel through on a daily basis had unusual appeal. Could Connor walk away from the entire company, and not just his projects? He had enough to retire on, and James had enough to buy him out, as well as a deep desire to be king of the hill.

If Connor wanted to keep his foot in the game he could do some consulting here and there. Or just drift off into the sunset. Living in Muskoka, he wouldn't need a lot of money once he had a roof over his head, and the sale of his penthouse in Toronto would surely cover the cost of a nice year-rounder out here. He knew other businessmen who'd done it, such as Tristen Bell, formerly a die-hard real estate mogul. They'd done a few deals together and come out laughing. Then Tristen had suddenly pulled up stakes and vanished. Rumor was he was in the area. If Tristen had enough to pull out, then so did Connor.

He interrupted Maya's continuing argument about his life, his business and how he couldn't ditch it. "Could I get a ride into Port Carling sometime? I want to look up someone."

"You can't retire. You can't give it up. You're at the top of your game."

"And why not? I've delayed my own gratification for too long." He let out a laugh, deepening it as Maya's expression turned from one of agitation to one of fear for his sanity. He placed a gentle kiss on her nose. "You need to lighten up, Maya."

Sipping his coffee, he headed outside to his favorite place on Nymph Island—the hammock. When he'd first started his business, during university, his satisfaction had come from making it into the big leagues. As the years went on, he kept telling himself that when he finished the next deal, made the next million, he'd take a break and join the jet set life he'd always dreamed of having. But he'd never given himself that gratification, and never allowed himself true vacations for fear of losing his position on the totem pole. He hadn't even gone to Italy to enjoy *Barber of Seville* in an old opera house.

So why not now? Why not cut out and enjoy what he'd earned? He was never going to do it if he stayed at CME. There would always been one more thing popping up as an emergency, changing his plans. This, out here in Muskoka, was real life. The life he'd been missing.

Chapter Eleven

Connor shook Tristen Bell's hand and pulled him close enough to slap his back in a friendly man-hug, getting a warning growl from the massive Bernese mountain dog sitting at his friend's feet.

"Don't mind him. Maxwell Richards III is a friendly old coot," said Tristen.

"Quite the name." Connor gave the dog a scratch behind the ears and, seemingly satisfied, the big animal wandered off to collapse in the shade of a large maple.

"He came with it."

Connor sized up the former real estate tycoon. He was trim and fit, his hair a bit longer than the sharp-edged Bay Street image Connor was used to. In fact, Tristen had adopted somewhat of a casual, woodsy style.

"You look ten years younger than when I last saw you in Toronto. Are you doing some hot young thing?" Connor's attention moved to the large, renovated cottage sitting behind him. "They've got to be crawling all over you."

His friend laughed. "Are you kidding? After the way my ex-wife took me to the cleaners there's no way I'm getting on that horse anytime soon. Even for a one-nighter."

"How'd she get the better lawyer?"

Tristen laughed again and tipped his head as though asking

Connor how much he wanted to hear. "I pretty much rolled over and played dead."

"Uh..." Connor shifted, unsure what to say to the toughest negotiator he knew.

"She showed me that nobody liked who I'd become." Tristen's face tightened, but before Connor could puzzle it out, the man's expression turned to one of lightheartedness. "So here I am. Like the place?"

They both looked at the two-story clapboard house, which featured a fair amount of stonework along its bottom.

"Love it."

"Thanks. Did it all myself."

"What?" Connor tried to hide his disbelief.

"Kidding. I tried, though. Turns out I'm not great at plumbing or wiring. But I designed what I wanted, and got in there when I could, and helped. Turns out stonework's my thing. You don't have to be able to measure things quite as precisely."

"Stonework?"

Tristen took a few steps to the side and pointed to the chimney that extended up the other side of the building.

"Wow."

"Did a patio out back, too. Want to see it?"

Connor shrugged, trying not to compare the man's pride with that of a new parent.

Tristen led him from the parking area and across a veranda that was similar to Maya's, but in better shape. Rounding a corner of the cottage-turned-year-round home, they found themselves on a stone patio overlooking the water.

"Laid them all myself. I have them in sections in hopes that the frost won't heave it too badly. So far, so good."

Connor nodded, his focus drifting to the cushy outdoor furniture sitting under an awning a few feet away. Man, that looked comfortable. And the way his quads were still aching from his dash to save Tigger two days ago, nothing had ever seemed more welcoming.

Tristen moved to a small outdoor kitchen and opened a fridge. "Beer?"

"Yeah." Connor peered over the small wet bar to check out the space. He withdrew his hand as his friend offered him a bottle. "Actually, you know what? I'm trying to cut back."

Tristen sized him up, then returned the beer, along with his own. He pulled out two bottles of water instead and passed Connor one. "Going to run a marathon or something?" he asked lightly, taking a seat in the outdoor living room.

"Something like that." Connor eased himself into a chair, hating the way his abs screamed at him. The good news was that it no longer took him all day to get in one hundred crunches. Too bad it still hurt, as though someone was spearing him repeatedly.

"So? How's the city? How's Connor MacKenzie Enterprises? Done any amazing real estate deals since I've been gone?" He downed half his water, then set it on the stone-topped table, which was actually more like a large ledge around a built-in fire pit.

Connor licked his lips. The last thing he wanted to do was talk business. He gave a small shake of his head and pointed to the renovated cottage with his bottle. "I love this place. So quiet." He could almost see Port Carling from their location on the small bay, but not quite. There was a low drone in the background from passing boats heading to town. "Does it get busy?"

"Yeah, weekends in July and August. You can tell when it's a weekend, like today, but it's still not too bad. I don't mind the sound of boats. Smells a hell of a lot better than Toronto's traffic." Tristan let out a laugh and crossed one leg over the other, slinging an arm over the back of his seat.

"Ever miss the city?"

"Never."

"Yeah. I'm not missing it as much as I thought I would."

"How long have you been out here?" Tristen asked.

"Less than a week."

"How long are you taking?"

"Two weeks, I guess. One left to go."

"Good on you."

Connor sat forward, resting his elbows on his knees. "It's weird, though. I'm not as stressed about being disconnected as I think I should be."

Tristen nodded, taking another gulp of his water. "Once you get over the withdrawal, it doesn't seem as vital any longer, does it? As though it loses its meaning."

Connor fidgeted with the label on his bottle of water.

"So?" his friend asked.

Connor looked up to find Tristen watching him in a way that told him the man knew exactly why he was there.

"I'm burned out." He rubbed his forehead, feeling haggard, washed up.

"Well, a vacation is a good start." His friend's brow furrowed and he focused on the water below. "I thought you'd be the type to work until you dropped."

"Apparently I'm at risk for a heart attack, stroke…the works." Connor took another swallow of water, hoping to dispel the desperate lump that had formed in his throat.

"You're pulling my leg!" Tristen sat forward, echoing Connor's pose, with elbows resting on the faded knees of his jeans.

"Wish I was." He took a few more gulps of water, struggling against the undertow of emotions.

"What are you going to do?"

Connor swallowed hard. He took in the quiet getaway Tristen

had created for himself. "How..." He cleared his throat. "How did you..."

"Leave it all?" The large dog had found them, and he plopped his massive head in Tristen's lap, momentarily distracting him. He roughed up the dog's head affectionately, then tipped his own head back and forth a few times so Connor couldn't tell if he was imitating the dog or weighing his reply.

"Well," Tristen said finally, "how much do you know about my final year in Toronto?"

"Not much. I went to call you one day and you'd pulled up stakes."

"Yeah, I wasn't in a good space when I left."

"Understandable."

Tristen let out a long breath. "Basically, I was working too much. You know how it is. I never saw the wife or the kid. She wanted another, but I was never around, and so it never happened. You know how all that goes. You try and make them happy with the big house, the diamonds, and the Escalade in the driveway. Anyway, she got tired of it and left me. Got a fancy lawyer. Same story as half the guys on Bay Street. But I was tired and began to wonder why I'd done it all. Why did I make all those cutthroat deals and rise like cream if she didn't care and it didn't make her happy? Work and deals lost their meaning when she left me. It may sound odd, but I discovered I didn't know her, my kid, my friends or even myself. So I gave her half the business, then sold my half and said good luck."

"You walked?"

"Yep." He leaned back, crossed his legs again. "I came up here, bought this fixer-upper in October three years ago. Been renovating it ever since."

"You're not working?"

"I have savings. She got only half, right? Don't need a lot other than for renovations. Oh, and taxes. The taxes around here are enough to give you a coronary. But I love it. It's quiet. The neighbors are hardly ever around. Deer walk through my yard. Nobody is yelling at you for letting squirrels live in your trees, or if you don't rake your leaves and they blow into someone's yard. It's peaceful in all the ways I need."

"Being retired, don't you miss working?"

"Of course. Anyway, I couldn't pull out entirely. I still sell a little real estate here and there, but nothing major. And I don't try to undercut people anymore. I got tired of being that hard-assed, ruthless son of a bitch everyone admired but dreaded, you know? Everyone deserves a fair deal."

Connor nodded, understanding where Tristen was coming from. People were in awe of Connor and his success, but also jealous and sometimes snarky about it. Especially if he came up well ahead of someone else in a deal.

"So, did it…" Connor leaned back, enjoying the comfort of the cushions, unsure how to frame his next question. "Your identity…"

Tristen gave him a crooked smile that had to be a hit with the ladies, and said, "My pride and vanity? Did it take a hit?"

"Yeah."

"Sure you don't want a beer?"

"Trying hard not to die here, man."

Tristen leaned forward. "It's that bad?"

Connor nodded, and his friend tucked his shaggy hair behind his ear, his broad shoulders stretching his shirt with the mild effort. "Well, you know what they say. Work hard until you retire, then die the next day. You're just such an overachiever that you're trying to have it all now."

"That's why we're friends, man. You always dish your manure fresh and straight up."

Tristen laughed, but suddenly turned serious. "Yeah, it hurt my pride a little. Still does when people from my past act as though I broke down or something. But the thing is the so-called 'hole in the world' that I left back in Toronto got filled in pretty damn fast. Some other guy stepped up and took my place. People probably don't even remember me anymore. I wasn't as vital or as irreplaceable as I had believed. And yeah, my name is on a lot of papers for some major building projects and land deals in the city, but nobody is going to create a statue or name a park for me. My daughter doesn't even know what my favorite color is. How sad and pathetic is that? She still sends me a tie for my birthday. That's how little we know each other."

"She doesn't come out?"

"She's seventeen."

Connor didn't have a wife on the horizon, but he could see how any relationship he might start could very well end the way Tristen's had if he didn't make some major lifestyle changes.

"You gonna quit the rat race?" his friend asked. "I know of a nice little year-rounder not too far from here that you could get at a fair price. Needs a bit of winterizing, but it would allow you to modernize it at the same time."

Connor laughed. "You're still the same guy, angling for a commission, aren't you?"

Tristen's smile didn't reach his eyes. "If you quit the rat race, you can't go cold turkey, Connor. That kills men like us. You need a project even if it's joining the Lions Club or serving coffee at the local coffee shop three days a week. Don't just go pulling the plug, or it will get pulled on you. You know what I mean?"

Connor's heart lurched. Was his cold turkey vacation going to cause him to keel over?

"I can see what you're thinking," Tristen said. "Vacations are okay. You need them. What I'm talking about is for you to ease out—if you're considering pulling out. Or throw yourself into something new. Fill yourself with something fresh and rewarding."

"Like a job." Why did that sound so unappealing to his ears?

"Or a girl."

"Are you looking? I hear they have a thing for old money and you're last name rings a bell in that regard. Pun intended."

"Always looking." Tristen shot him a wink. "But never seeking, my friend."

Connor smiled and finished his bottle of water. The idea of coordinating a transfer out of the rat race was exhilarating but also exhausting.

MAYA STARED AT THE PAGES sent from Accounting. How on earth was this math supposed to add up to the lumberyard being worth that much? Yes, everything balanced, but some of those numbers couldn't be correct. Knowing she'd get an earful, she hiked up the hill to perform due diligence, trying to talk herself out of making the call. There were more pros than cons to contacting the office. In fact, the only con would be that James would get bent out of shape again—but only if Em told him that Maya had called. And she could handle that if it meant she could finally rest assured before Connor signed the deal.

She punched in the number for Em's home phone and paced a path through the underbrush on top of the hill.

"Em? It's Maya. Sorry," she added quickly. "It's the weekend and I know I'm a pain, but I can't get the math to work for the sawmill."

"Maya, we have—"

"Accountants, I know. But I can't figure out how Connor is going to come out ahead on this deal. I know I'm just an assistant, but I can't ignore this, as I simply can't see a sawmill being worth this much. And why would he want a lumberyard in the first place?"

"I have a call coming in," Em said. "I'll phone you back in a few minutes, okay?"

"Fine," Maya grumbled. She hung up the phone and rested its cool plastic against her chin. A boat puttered into the strait and Maya hurried down the hill, wondering if it was Connor returning from his trip ashore to visit his friend. When she got within sight of the dock, she relaxed. It was Connor. Smiling, she made her way to his side as the man in the boat pushed off. He was handsome. And familiar.

"Who was that?" she asked Connor.

"Tristen Bell."

"Oh, a Bell."

"Yeesh. Women and old money."

Maya laughed. "There are a few of them around these parts, you know." She gave him a haughty smile. "Plus, I'll have you know that some of us are looking for love. Not someone with a big fat bank account and a name that makes gold diggers woozy."

"That's what they all say until you buy them a Porsche." He slung an arm around her shoulders and she hoped he wasn't planning on having her support him all the way up the hill. Her ribs were still tender where Daphne had landed on her, and he was pushing against the sore spot. "So, what did you do this afternoon?" he asked. "Enjoy having the cottage all to yourself?"

"Yeah, an afternoon off because your incoming work slows on weekends." She snorted and pushed his arm off her shoulder as they moseyed up the path. "I sunbathed nude on the dock and had an orgy in the woods."

"Damn. I missed all the fun."

"Yep." Her cell started ringing, and she hurried back to the dock for better reception. "I'll see you up there," she said to Connor.

"Boyfriend thanking you for the orgy?" He waggled his eyebrows.

She held up the phone. "It's Em."

She answered the phone, hoping he'd take the hint and leave so she could say whatever came to mind without worrying about him interrupting or getting offended with whatever cockamamie idea popped out.

"Hi, Maya here."

"Hello. Maya? I'm not sure how much I can help you with the lumberyard deal. Maybe I could put you in contact with someone on James's team."

"I'd rather get your vibe on this first." Maya stared out across the water, her attention drifting to where they were building a new cottage. Everything was changing. Everything was uncertain. But nothing was heading where she wanted it to go. Heck, she hadn't even heard the usual chaos emitting from the far side of Baby Horseshoe Island, where the teen camp was.

"Is something amiss in the state of Denmark?" Connor asked, startling her.

Maya held her thumb over the phone's speaker. "I can't vouch for Denmark, but I think Toronto might be a safe bet." She waved him away, ignoring how he was rubbing his chest as he did whenever she got in deep with his business, and moved to the end of the dock.

"So, what do you need?" Em asked.

Maya lowered her voice, flicking her gaze over her shoulder to ensure that Connor was, indeed, heading up to the cottage. "The sawmill doesn't fit Connor's profile. I can't see how he's going to make money from owning it. And its valuation seems inflated."

"Connor has gone over everything already. In this economy it is good to diversify and have some primary industries in your portfolio."

"It feels like a bailout."

"James knows what he's doing."

"Did he bring this deal to Connor?"

"As far as I know."

"Em? Is this a bad time for Connor to take a vacation?"

"It's never a good time for the CEO to leave the office."

Maya pushed a hand through her curls, wanting to get Em to the point where they could discuss office conspiracies, as she had at least one in mind.

"You can trust me, Em. I need your help to figure out why I have a bad feeling about this deal. We need to save Connor." She glanced up the hill to where he was finally disappearing into the dusk and trees. "Is there a relationship between anyone working on the deal and the lumberyard owner, maybe? A connection? Anything?"

"I can look into it. You really think something is up?"

"Do you think it's possible someone other than CME might be benefiting from this deal?"

"It is a possibility," Em said carefully. "When you're dealing with millions of dollars and massive deals, people can get greedy. But they're signing in less than a week, Maya. The timing on all of this is very inconvenient."

"Then we'd better hurry. You search for connections and I'll dig deeper into the valuation. I'll call you tomorrow."

Maya hung up and wondered how someone such as Connor could let something like this slip past him. Was James really that good, or was she that far off the mark?

"MAYA, STUFF LIKE THIS happens all the time." Connor downed the last of his orange juice and pushed away from the table. He needed to escape before she had him several hours deep into her projects. It had been all he could do to walk away from her and her call with Em last night on the dock.

"This is important, Connor. Imagine you had a child with a cleft palate and cleft lip. Wouldn't you want little baby MacKenzie to feel less pain before and after reconstructive surgery? To have the best shot at proper healing? These guys have an invention that will ensure that. Medical devices are a growth industry—five percent per year. It'll be a home run, Connor. They just can't get the licensing in place in time to give this thing a real shot at making it."

Damn her. She was making him feel, making that tug to jump in so friggin' irresistible.

"So?" he said. "You've been to business school. Use your connections to nudge things along."

"My connections?"

He almost laughed at her confused tone. "Yeah, you know. The people you hung out with. Built connections with, added to your network. Hobnobbing?"

She stared at her plate, face blank.

"You did network?" he asked.

"Yeah, of course!"

"So then, get on your phone. See who can help you out."

Maya smiled and pushed away from the table.

"Finish your breakfast first."

She promptly pulled her chair back in place. Laughing, Connor walked to his room to put on his trunks. Today he would try swimming around the island, and spend the afternoon thinking about early retirement and whether it was something he should implement.

He took his time going down the winding path to the water, breathing in the summer morning air. Closing his eyes, he tried a new method of being present in the moment, counting the number of bird species he heard calling to each other. The distinctive chick-a-dee-dee-dee of the chickadee, the knocking of a woodpecker. A nuthatch walking upside down on a tree to his right. Damn. He'd opened his eyes. He sucked at being present.

Ditching his towel and sandals on a chair, he dived into the lake, coming up several feet from the dock. He slowly warmed up with a back crawl, determined to make it around the island by taking it easy.

The water felt good, and he wondered if he'd be able to keep swimming when he returned to the city. It would have to become part of his routine. He laughed and choked on a mouthful of water. There was no way swimming would stay in his routine once he returned. A few late night meetings and he'd sleep through his opportunity to swim. Add an early morning meeting, and soon he'd be completely out of the habit.

He needed to find a way to have it all. Being away from the office for a week without contact hadn't been nearly as bad as he'd feared. He was even beginning to enjoy not having anything pulling at his attention. He could stay with one line of thought without distraction.

On the far side of the island, the current turned against him, and the waves grew as the wind ripped across the open lake. Hugging the shore, Connor took his time, watching for places he could climb out if need be. The way the waves were eroding the bank here and there created small inlets that he could possibly use if he didn't mind getting dirty.

A few minutes later he found himself back between the two islands, sheltered from the waves and wind.

Almost there.

When he reached the dock again, he smiled and swam to shore so he could walk out of the water instead of trying to haul himself up onto the dock with his burning arms.

He heard a light, friendly voice, and spotted Maya on the dock. When she saw him emerging from the water like a sea monster, she turned away, holding her cell to her ear.

She was reminding someone who she was and where they had met.

Good, the girl was contacting her network.

He stood on the dock in a growing pool of lake water. He smiled and toweled himself dry. He felt strong. Alive. Virile.

This morning he'd awoken to a partial. Better than what he'd had in ages. The hope he'd felt—the relief—was overwhelming to the point of tears. He could fix himself. In one week he would be at his brother's wedding as best man, and he was going to look good.

He gazed at Maya's long legs from under his towel as he rubbed it through his hair. She shifted position, her frustrated mood revealing itself even though her voice hid it perfectly. She clicked off the phone and turned to him, the smile on her face tight.

"What?" he asked.

"You made it around the island?" Her voice still had that light, friendly tone she'd been using on the phone, but he could tell her calls hadn't gone well.

"I did. Did you go?" She shook her head. "Why not?"

"Lots of work to do."

"Don't sacrifice your health for my work."

"Don't flatter yourself."

"I'm not. I just know what should be a priority."

"Because you've been good at following them?"

"No, I haven't. That's why I know what they are." He tossed his towel on the chair beside him and squared off with Maya. "You find someone to help?"

"Not yet."

"Why not?"

"Because apparently my network doesn't remember who the hell I am."

"Ah." He crossed his arms and leaned against the boathouse. He couldn't help but smile. He'd met so many ambitious people similar to Maya, who knew everything, except how to hang out and be human, not realizing that human connections were still ninety percent of business. "You handed out cards like they were candy at a parade, but didn't chat up the crowd?"

"There wasn't time. And anyway, people don't need me nattering on about stupid things, or acting like a desperate student or grad."

"Maybe they do." He watched her for a moment. "How many people remembered you?"

Maya turned to stalk up the path, and Connor called out, "Try Nolan McKinley. Tell him I sent you. Get his direct line from Em."

Maya turned slowly. "Thank you. I will."

"And take the time to be friendly and real. It's not all just business, you know. Remember? It's like dating."

"You sound like my sisters and mother."

"Smart women."

"Apparently," Maya said with a heavy sigh.

CONNOR STRAIGHTENED HIS tie and studied himself in the mirror above the bureau. Was he too dressed up for a movie? What was Maya wearing? Man, he hadn't been this nervous getting ready for a date since high school, and going to Finian's new film with Maya and her sister and that dumbass tree guy wasn't even a real date.

He needed to stop thinking. The more he thought about Maya these days, the more he found that his own life wanted to blend with hers. It was as if the old Connor had been an immovable, impenetrable statue made of metal, which had somehow rusted while he'd been busy digging through never-ending paper. Now he felt that, if he reached out to touch it, that statue would crumble before him, becoming nothing more than a pile of oxidized dust.

Who was he? He had no clue.

Connor buttoned his shirt cuffs and studied his reflection again. Whoever he was, he looked pretty good. Almost like the old Connor who used to take on the world.

He dug through his bag for his wallet, and wondered what Toronto would be like without Maya. What if she moved to the city? Would he be able to feel her presence the way he did on the island? Would they meet up for drinks after work? And the bigger question, would he finally get his gearshift working, and be able to treat her as a real man should?

He sighed and adjusted his fly. Not even forty and his johnson was letting him down.

Connor entered the living room and found Maya waiting for him. She took him in, not breathing, then turned away, busying herself with finding the boat key, which he'd noticed was always kept on the mantel.

"Do I look okay?" he asked. He immediately felt like a woman for the way he cared way too much about what her answer would be.

"It's just a small-town movie theater. You're fine." She lifted out the skirt of her dress. It was something soft that clung to her curves in a way that made him want to create a sculpture of her.

She was a Greek goddess, demure and incredible, easily the sexiest thing he'd ever seen. He reached for her, then pulled back his hand. He had to keep his focus. He needed her, but he wasn't ready. Not yet. He had to make sure he was worth the wait, because he knew she would be.

If she was still there.

MAYA COULDN'T LOOK AT Connor. If she did she might be tempted to run a hand down his arm, and he'd been giving off weird vibes. Was being on a fake date with his assistant bothering him? If so, then why had he stepped in and offered to go with her?

Because he was a nice guy. He'd saved her from going on a blind date with one of Shawn's friends, then turned around and saved her niece. And right now, he was also helping Daphne by going out tonight. He probably didn't even want to be on a date with Maya.

Wait, did he like Daphne? Was that why he'd offered? He wanted to be closer to Daph?

Maya glanced at him as she parked down the street from the movie house. No, he couldn't. He didn't. Not the way he looked at her. Maya was the only one. Or at least the only one this week.

Maybe Connor didn't find her sexy.

Maybe he knew their night of getting it on had been too much, gone too far. She'd been too forward. Too bold. But he was an alpha, a powerful businessman. Why the hell would he want demure? She'd seen the way he responded when she came on to him. He wanted her, and he loved it when she pushed him and tried to steal his control. It was a game they both enjoyed. So what the hell was going on? What did she need to do so he'd drag her into bed and satisfy her needs?

She pressed the tips of her fingers into her forehead. That wasn't a very ladylike thought, but nothing about Connor made her want to act like a lady.

Men. They were more confusing than a messed up Rubik's Cube. All she wanted to do was peel off the stickers and put them back on the way they were supposed to be.

"You okay?" Connor asked.

"Yeah, great." If wearing one's sexiest dress and being barely looked at was the new definition of great.

Wow. She was officially driving herself crazy. Connor was her boss. He was here as her pretend date. End of story.

She yanked on the parking break, knowing she should have stayed back at the cottage and worked. Sitting beside Connor for two hours would either make her want to jump his bones or else think about work. And chances were it would be the latter, given all the emails she'd have to deal with when she got back to the cottage.

"I wish Hailey was here." Maya palmed her car keys, missing her eldest sister. Maybe it was knowing that Hailey was living a new life—a whirlwind one with a movie star that was already sweeping her away to new worlds where the rest of the sisters couldn't go, and couldn't relate to.

"She's in Hollywood?" Connor asked.

"Yeah, celebrating the movie's release with Finian. She's such a colossal pain in the ass, and acts as though she's solely responsible for our lives. However, she deserves the way hers is finally taking off." Now if only Maya's would, too. Maybe that was why she was so edgy tonight. It was as though she was on the verge of missing something important in life and she didn't know what it was, only that it was slipping away. "Do you have siblings?"

"Yeah, I have a brother." Connor's voice was quiet.

"So you know what it's like."

"Sure."

"You don't get along?"

"Nah, we do," he said quickly. He opened his car door, his moves tight, as though he was holding back emotion.

Very curious.

She allowed him to take her hand and lead her past the small park beside the theater, not letting go as they stood in line. She felt jittery trying to figure out what his hand-holding meant. Casually, she allowed her chest to rub his arm as she checked behind his tall build for her family. His Adam's apple bobbed as he swallowed and the tune he'd been humming faltered. Okay, so she did have an effect on him. Major relief on not being alone on that one.

Daphne, laughing and smiling, met them in line.

"Where's Shawn?" Maya asked.

"He canceled. I think he's afraid of Connor." She grinned up at Connor, who let out a laugh before apologizing.

"Where's the little munchkin?" he asked.

"Babysitter. This is an action flick."

Connor smiled, his attention distant. "Right."

What was going on with him? Why all the distance? But at the same time, he was still holding Maya's hand. Which felt great—she didn't want him to let go. Not ever.

Melanie joined them, her hair tucked in a ponytail, no contacts. "Were we supposed to bring a date?" She glanced down at her baggy shirt and paint-splattered capris.

"Um, Melanie, this is Connor MacKenzie…my boss." Maya gave her a pleading look, hoping she would let his presence slide.

"Hello." Melanie shook her head, grinning in a way that made Maya want to rattle some sense into her. He was her *boss*. Quit grinning like that! Yes, Connor was a major, totally beddable hunk, but he also had a big say in where her future went from here.

"Um, Maya?" Daphne asked tentatively.

"Hmm?"

"Weren't you going to bring Mom?"

"Say wha—*shit*!" Maya checked her watch, laid a hand on Connor's arm and said, "Wait here. I'll be back in a flash."

Melanie sighed and began walking off. "I'll go get her."

"No, I will. Besides, didn't you drive your moped?"

"It's a full motorbike."

"You're not taking Mom on that thing." Maya backed away from the group. "Really, I'll return soon! Save Mom and me seats."

Melanie, arms crossed, raised her eyebrows in amusement.

Connor strode toward Maya. "I'll come with you."

"It's okay. We might miss the beginning."

"I want to go where you go."

That sounded amazingly great. Was there time for her to lead him somewhere sexy and romantic, where clothes weren't even an option, such as her bed? Because that was where she really wanted to go.

MAYA SQUEALED HER TIRES as she pulled into the parking lot of the nursing home. There in the entry was her mother, waiting in her wheelchair. Was Maya the worst daughter in the world or what? Never mind what Connor must think of her.

She hustled up the ramp and through the automatic doors, putting on a cheerful smile. "Hi, Mom! How are you?" Without waiting for an answer, she began wheeling her outside.

"I thought you were going to be here—oh!" Catherine stared

up at Connor, who had come out of the car, handsome and welcoming.

"You must be Maya's mother, Mrs. Summer. I'm Connor MacKenzie, her boss over on Nymph Island, for the time being. You have a fine, smart daughter, Mrs. Summer."

Maya shot Connor a relieved smile as her mother grinned up at him, her mood lightening. "Call me Catherine, sugar."

Connor gave her a lopsided grin. "Sure thing, Catherine sugar."

Her mom laughed, and Maya wheeled her to the passenger side as Connor held the door for them.

"And how are you enjoying Nymph Island?" Catherine asked him.

He moved to help her into the car, while Maya quickly unlocked the chair and flipped it flat so she could put it in the trunk. He replied, "It is wonderful. Very quiet and relaxing."

"Some might say magical," her mother teased.

Maya slammed the trunk closed. "Mom, don't start." She checked Connor's reaction, hoping he didn't think her mother was off her rocker.

"I saw fairy houses," he said. "What are those about?"

Maya replied quickly, "Just a tradition. It's...it's nothing." Her mother gave her a look of understanding as Maya took the driver's seat, Connor making himself at home in the back.

There was nothing like taking your boss on a date with your mother, and talking about the mystical beings she secretly believed in.

Outside the theater, Connor gently elbowed Maya out of the way, taking care with Catherine in a way that lit her up from the inside with pleasure and adoration. Maya knew the feeling, as the man had a way about him. No wonder she'd forgotten to pick up her mom: Maya was living with the guy.

As Connor pushed the wheelchair up to the ticket window, she nudged his arm, mouthing *"Thank you."* He gave a nod, seeming almost bashful. He was so real, so present, she wanted to hug him and never let go.

Simone stepped out of the lobby before they could ask for tickets. "It's sold out. Come on, I have your tickets and Mellie saved seats."

"Thank you." Maya gave her a hug, funneling all the appreciation she felt for Connor toward her friend.

"Oof! You're welcome. I'll let you sit beside the hunk if you let go."

Laughing, Maya released her, and followed Connor, who was still pushing her mother's chair. He parked it in the dark cinema beside the row of familiar faces, and Maya let out a gasp as Finian took to the screen. He seemed so large. So real. So...so like someone Hailey should be with. Forever.

"I can't believe your sister had sex with him," Simone announced. A few people nearby laughed, having heard about the whirlwind fire-and-ice romance the two had begun only weeks prior.

"I knew Hailey would be good for him!" called a knowing voice a few rows back.

"Wilma Star, is that you?" asked their mother, peering through the dark.

"To rights it is. How are you Catherine? I told my cousin back in Blueberry Springs—"

A chorus of shushing silenced the woman who then whispered loudly, "I'll catch up with you later so we don't get thrown out for chatting."

"Come for poker night at the home, Wilma. It's Tuesdays at three."

"I hate to break it to you, honey, but that's not 'night.'" Mrs. Star laughed and the shushing got more insistent.

"This is like knowing a movie star by proxy," Connor whispered.

"You know him once removed," Maya whispered back, as she got settled in the seat beside him.

The movie was great, but the best part was how halfway through it Connor placed his arm around her shoulder, drawing her against his side.

Oh, yes. Good things were going to happen between them. Again.

CONNOR HELD THE DOOR to the cottage for Maya, then closed it behind them. He loved her perfume. How gentle and flowery it was—a complete contradiction to the woman he'd come to know and admire.

"I can't remember the last time I saw a movie in a real theater," he said as she switched on a battery-operated lantern.

"Really?" Maya turned to him in the kitchen's weak light, her body nudging up against his as they stumbled into each other. He placed his arms around her to steady them, burying his nose in her hair.

"You smell good." He inhaled the scents that had clung to her, hiding beneath her perfume. "Sunshine, lake water, sunscreen and popcorn. You are a perfect summer scent."

"You smell pretty awesome yourself, Connor."

He grinned at the compliment. "It's the aftershave."

"Power, money, and seduction."

He laughed and grasped her arms, holding her in front of him as his eyes adjusted to the light. "Money, power, and *seduction*?" This woman was going to destroy him, she was such a turn-on. How was he going to continue to resist her? How was he not going to reveal his cards? Because when she saw him unable to...

He spun her around so her back was to him. Time for a distraction. Maybe give her another orgasm, then disappear so she'd never have to know how broken he was, and how far he was from being the man she deserved.

He could have anything he wanted in the world except the one thing he craved.

Maya lowered her head to the side so he could place his lips on the spot where her neck and shoulder joined, and he skimmed her waist with his hands. She pressed into him and his touch crept higher, lightly gliding over the sides of her breasts, then up to her neck. He trailed his fingertips down the delicate bare skin, continuing as though gravity was in control, lightening his touch as it traveled over her collarbone. She shivered and he allowed his hands to explore of their own accord. Over the swell of her chest, across her hard nipples and down to her rib cage, where he gripped her, spinning her back around to face him, lowering his mouth to hers.

Her tongue licked his lips, wrestled with his own as the two of them fell against the fridge, needing its support as their bodies clicked into overdrive. Their kissing frantic, they bumped their way to the counter, Maya's hands running wild over Connor's back, his neck. Through his hair. Cupping his butt. He shoved his hips against hers and swept an arm across the countertop, knocking things off in his frustration and an unreleasable sexual buildup.

She pushed him away, toward the bedrooms.

He couldn't. He reached in front of her and closed her bedroom door before she could enter, pinning her against its solid wood panel. There was no way he could leave her like this, but no way he could expose his secret.

He placed her hands against the door frame like an officer preparing to frisk her. Moving his crotch to her ass, he ran his palms down her front, over her legs, shimmying her dress up her thighs in a move so slow he knew it would try her patience. He breathed on her neck as he explored the front of her panties, then her bare stomach, her head dropping back onto his shoulder when his caresses hit her just right.

"I want you in my bed, naked, Connor."

"Patience, Maya. It will be worth it when the time comes."

She spun in his arms. "The time is now."

"No, it's not."

He danced his fingers over her shoulders, sliding them into the neckline of her stretchy dress, letting it drop to the floor. "My terms, Maya." He skated his hands over her lingerie, loving the smooth satin, and the way he could feel the damp warmth between her legs as he petted her slowly, softly.

"What about what I want?"

"Trust me, spitfire. Our dreams will collide when the time is right."

Chapter Twelve

Maya was so sexually frustrated she could scream. Connor had got her all revved up last night, then backed off with some stupid line about her being patient, and the two of them waiting for their time. There was no "their," so how could there be a "their time?" He was such a tease!

She wanted to rip his clothes off and ravage him, but she also wanted to kick him in the nuts for turning her on, and doing nothing more than allowing her an orgasm by his hand, then his mouth. And yeah, hell yeah, his hands and mouth were magic, but he always left her craving the real thing. If they didn't get down and dirty with his hard cock between her legs really soon she was not going to be responsible for her actions.

She shook her head and contemplated diving into the lake, fully clothed, just to cool her steamy thoughts. Instead, she stepped away from the dock's edge and nervously dialed the contact Connor had given her.

"Nolan McKinley please?" she said, clearing her throat as a man answered the phone.

"Speaking."

Hot damn. She just about dropped her cell in the water. Connor had been serious about getting her a direct line to Nolan.

"Hello?"

"Yes, sorry." Maya introduced herself and explained why she was calling.

"Connor's branching out, is he?"

"Sort of. It's an experiment. I'm a summer assistant and…well, it doesn't matter. Anyway, we're having trouble with some licensing for a project he's backing. Would you be able to help us speed up the process?"

Ah, crap. She'd forgotten to do that connection stuff everyone was talking about. Oh well, time was money and she was sure he had better things to do on a Monday morning than talk about the weather. And anyway, she could still do that listen, pause, reflect thing Connor had mentioned.

"Connor's already committed?" Nolan asked.

"He has."

"And he missed the timeline for this?" There was surprise in the man's voice.

"I overlooked it."

"And you're hoping I can fix that?"

"I am."

"And you are…?"

"Maya Summer." She flipped through her mind's rolodex of memories. A bond. She needed a bond. "Mr. McKinley?"

"Yes?"

"Are you the same McKinley who was a guest seminar speaker at the U of T, let's see…three years ago? It was on…" *Come on, brain.* "…patents, I believe."

"Good memory. How'd you enjoy the class?"

"Technically, I…kind of crashed that one. Sometimes I'd sit in on seminars that sounded useful or interesting while I was waiting for my next class."

Nolan laughed. "So what did you think of my oh-so-memorable talk, Maya Summer?"

"I thought you were a very good speaker. Knew your topic and provided valuable insight, as well as—"

"Did you like my hair?"

"Your hair?" Maya shut her eyes. Thank goodness she'd checked him out online before calling. She could put a face to him as she thought back to the seminar. Mid-fifties. In fairly good shape. But he'd had a slightly scruffy look back then. "If I recall, you may have needed a cut."

Nolan laughed. "Consider me on the case. But no guarantees, Maya." His voice had a slight dry warning to it. She'd done okay, but not stellar.

"Thanks."

"And thanks for remembering an old man, kid."

"You're not that old," she protested.

"Probably not. Tell Connor I said hi, and that next time we play racquetball I'll kick his ass again."

Maya raced up the path to tell Connor the good news about Nolan helping out, but paused when she hit the veranda. Connor was standing stock-still, a chipmunk perched on his bare foot. In his damp swimming trunks, with the odd trail of water weaving down his legs, he looked hotter than ever. She refrained from moving forward, from touching his tanned skin, the surprising firmness of his stomach, the broadness of his shoulders. An amazing transformation had occurred behind her back and she wanted him more than ever. He'd filled out in all the ways she'd dreamed of.

He caught her eye and winked.

The chipmunk rose up on its back feet and stared at Maya before scurrying away.

"How cool was that?" Connor asked.

"Tigger's training is working."

"You catch Nolan?"

Maya nodded, coming closer as though she was a magnet

unable to resist him. "He said he's going to kick your ass again at racquetball next time he sees you."

Connor let out a rich laugh and patted his flat stomach. He gently placed a hand on her arm. "He doesn't know I've been working out."

Maya contemplated his lean, strong frame. Their eyes met and he lowered his face until their lips were almost touching. Maya slowly raised herself on her toes, leaning her still-tender palms against his chest so their mouths could meet. They broke the kiss and stared at each other, their bodies propped together for support.

Connor swiftly pulled her into a tight embrace, his lips locked against hers. She dipped her tongue into his mouth and hugged his neck, his damp skin cool against her chest and arms. He trailed kisses down her throat, nipping as he went. Her body responded with frightening urgency, and she began tugging at the drawstring on his trunks. His mouth was back over hers, and he drew in her bottom lip, biting it as he grabbed her ass, pulling her against his crotch, trapping her hands.

"Connor," she breathed.

He leaned back and she yanked him close again, wanting him inside her.

As if unable to sense her desire, he withdrew her hands from around his neck and kissed them. With a smile, he slipped away, saying, "Later, my Maya, later."

"Connor." She followed him a few steps, and he gave her a wink over his shoulder. The leaves on the trees rippled and showed their pale underbellies, foreshadowing a storm.

"You need to learn patience."

"For heaven's sake, Connor, you can't just kiss a girl like that and then walk away!" She picked up a cushion off a wicker chair, prepared to throw it at him.

He returned to her, purpose in his moves. She hugged the cushion and he clutched her chin in his palm, giving her a light kiss that was at once tender and desperate. "I'm going to blow your socks off, but not until I say we're ready."

She trailed a hand down his chest to his swim trunks, but before she could cup him he turned his hips away.

"Anticipation makes it all the better, Maya." His damp hair cooled her skin as he inhaled her neck, his lips grazing her as he spoke. "When you think I've forgotten you, I will slip into your bed and make you come so hard you'll forget your own name. I promise you that, spitfire."

He turned, leaving her swaying on weak legs, with shuddering breath. That man had better stay true to his promise. And she'd better start sleeping with her bedroom door unlocked.

MAYA PACED THE LIVING room of the cottage, hating the way Connor was staring at her, eyes narrowed as he stood with his back to the fire. Only hours earlier she'd wanted him to touch her all over. Wanted to run her mouth down his chest and see where the fine trail of chest hair led her. Now she almost wanted to shove him into the burning logs.

He cocked his head, assessing her.

She repeated herself slowly, trying to quell her anger and the way her chest was starting to heave from holding it all in. "I think James is up to something that could lose your company a lot of money."

"Why would he do that?"

"I don't know, but he's blocking me. And he's blocking Em, too."

"Maybe because you are butting into his business? You know

you are an assistant, and that he's put a lot of time and thought into this deal?"

Maya tried not to react to the dig about her position in the company, and that his comment could easily imply she didn't have a brain. He was playing power games today, and it made her want to rake her claws down him—and not in a good way.

"But you're paying too much for it, and you're not going to make that money back!"

"James is a savvy businessman."

"That's what I'm afraid of."

Connor came closer, his size alone making her want to shrink back.

"Ever think that maybe there is a reason we're purchasing this lumberyard? That maybe there are tax benefits?"

Maya crossed her arms, holding her ground. "They would have to be pretty substantial."

Connor rubbed his face and sighed. "Can you let this go, please? I trust James and his judgment. It's time to stop worrying this bone like a bulldog, Maya."

She waved the papers in front of him. "Did you even read these?"

"I think maybe you'd better read them less."

"But Connor—"

"Maya, James has been doing this for years. How long have you been out of school?"

"That is *not* relevant."

"I think it is. You are questioning and upsetting one of my most loyal advisors, which means you are also questioning me."

The wind rattled the shutters and Maya clenched her jaw, fighting for patience. "Connor, how do I make you see this?"

"Maya, I've hired good staff for a reason."

"What if he's turned on you, or is missing something?"

"Maya, stop."

"I can't work on something that is so obviously going to fail. I can't just waltz along, knowing this deal is going to cost you hundreds of thousands."

Connor crossed his own arms, brow furrowed. The shadows in his eyes were back. "Do you have evidence? Or is all of this your gut?"

"The lumberyard seems overvalued."

"And you are an expert on this?"

"I did some research."

"Maya. You know you can't value one company solely based on others, right?"

"I know." She sat in the chair by the fireplace. Maya had to win this one. She knew she was right. She just didn't know how to get Connor from point A to point B.

He tossed her papers on the coffee table and leaned over her chair, trapping her with a hand on each armrest. "You know arranged marriages?" He waited for her to nod. "Do you know the owner of that lumberyard? Not his name, but who he is?"

Maya shook her head.

"Exactly." Connor stepped back, crossing his arms again. "Arranged marriages still happen in the business world. Maybe James can see long-term value in this short-term loss."

"So you're going to lose half a million dollars just so you can get in this guy's pants? He must have something pretty special hiding in there."

"Maya, just do your job, and keep your nose out of James's way. I trust him."

"Do you trust me?"

"James and I have made many lucrative deals together. How long have you and I known each other?"

"Maybe he's making a deal on his own."

"Maya," Connor roared. "This has got to stop. If you continue to get in the way of my business partners I will have to terminate our connection. Do you understand?"

She stood, going toe to toe with him, looking for a crack to wiggle into so she could show him what she saw—that James was up to no good and would take down Connor, and his company, if left to his own devices. "You are a stubborn old donkey, Connor MacKenzie. I can't believe you won't investigate this enough to tell me I'm wrong. And if you can't see that this whole deal is faulty, then what will it take?"

"Who is being the stubborn ass here? I've told you to stand down."

Maya raised her voice, anger tightening her muscles as she prepared for a fight to the finish. "Why is he giving Em a hard time? Because she agrees with me. And James knows I'm right. He's up to no good, and that's why he wants me out. Everyone is pushing this through because they know you're completely out of it!"

"Maybe it's because you're a pain in the neck who thinks she knows everything."

Maya closed her mouth, hot tears pricking her eyes. "If you want to fail, then fine." She turned away, throwing another log on the fire to ward off the chill that had seeped into the cottage. "Stick your head in the sand. Ignore the smoke signals, and while you're at it, shoot the messenger."

Connor spun her around, and for a second she thought he was going to make his alpha sexy moves on her and finally take her in front of the fireplace.

"Maya, are you going to drop this?"

"No, I am not."

He drew away from her, regret flashing across his face. "Then," he said, his voice low, "I have to let you go. I am no longer in need of your services. You are getting in the way of James doing his job, and you refuse to listen to my warnings. That is not acceptable."

Maya ground her teeth and slammed out of the cottage, running up the hill out back, the cold wind slicing through her clothing. Leaves tore off the trees as she held her phone up to the darkening sky, searching for service.

Her phone dinged with a voice mail. A call from Nolan.

"It's not looking good, Maya. You might want to check other avenues."

Maya deleted the message and, sniffing back tears, listened to the next message.

"Maya. It's Em. No news. James is shutting me out and has hired a temp for all work on the lumberyard stuff." Her voice sounded tight. "I'll call again tomorrow. Don't send emails."

Maya stared at the peak of the cottage roof, visible through the swaying trees. Everything was coming down. Fired. She'd been fired. Was playing the business world's games really that important?

She was going to have to go back to her old job, begging. She sat heavily on a rock, letting the wind whip through her hair as she let out a sob. Her phone dinged. Another voice mail. Great, who else was calling to inform her that the world sucked right now? Hoping for something good, she dialed back into the system and listened to her new message.

It was her sister Melanie. Maya looked to the sky, hoping her sister was calling to see if she'd be free to go out for a few drinks, because her week had certainly just opened up.

"Hey, Maya, Mom had a fall. She's okay, but they've moved her over to the hospital in Bracebridge. We're all going over there now. I'll call with more info as I get it. There's a storm coming, so you might want to sit tight until morning."

Maya nearly dropped her cell as she tried to shove it in her pocket. Rain began to sprinkle as she tore down the hill, her breath catching in her chest along with unreleased sobs. She raced into the cottage, ignoring Connor, her ex-boss, as she grabbed the key for the boat, planning to leave him stranded on the island. If he didn't want to listen to the truth, then he could sit here and rot. She wasn't making him breakfast one more time.

CONNOR GINGERLY CLOSED the cottage's glass doors, which covered the screen doors from the inside, battening down the hatches. Maya had stormed out, jumped into the boat and torn off across the lake, into what looked like some pretty nasty incoming weather.

He honestly hadn't thought she'd take getting fired that badly. He'd warned her that she was treading on dangerous ground, but she'd ignored him. He probably should have handled her more carefully, especially because of their past and the way he'd left her satiated yet frustrated last night.

If he'd been thinking straight, he should have eased off after his warning and given her time to cool her heels. But she hadn't backed down and had promptly gotten under his skin, leading him to fear he wouldn't be able to shut her down. Nobody wanted a loose cannon at work, one they couldn't control.

Sighing, he gazed out the window, watching the tops of the trees fold in the wind. No wonder most HR departments had no-dating policies between employees.

But if James was upset, then it was obvious what the problem was. Connor just wished Maya could have taken all that vim and vigor, redirected it and stood down for once. He was too damn tired for drama and theatrics. He knew who James was, but honestly, did he really know Maya that well?

Connor walked through the large cottage, checking the windows in each room, wondering if he should be worried about Maya. Although maybe he should be more worried about a tree falling on him or the wind ripping the plastic off the broken windows Shawn had yet to replace as promised.

Maya's laptop whirred on the table in the living room, and he tapped the touch pad, expecting the screen to be locked. Instead, he saw the digital version of the papers she'd been waving about earlier. Drawing up a chair, he read through her notes left in the open document. The familiar tightening in his chest began the more he read. This girl had a healthy dose of conspiracy theory in her. And while she had valid points, she had to be missing the full picture. James wouldn't do something this blatantly stupid and obvious unless he thought Connor had lost his marbles.

His mind flashed to the scene just before he'd left his office for the ER. James had seemed concerned, but relieved. What was that about? Was it a business partner wishing the best for a friend? Or was he concerned Connor would take a break, come back and figure out what he'd done?

Connor glanced around the table for a phone before remembering he'd need a cell and have to go out in the storm if he wanted to contact James to double-check his gut reaction on firing Maya. Connor had noticed his BlackBerry at the bottom of his bag a few days ago, but the battery would definitely be dead by now. He searched Maya's computer for Skype, feeling out of line for snooping through her applications, and began punching in James's number. Then he paused. He should probably start the generator to ensure the battery used to power the place was charged so he didn't drop out midcall.

Rain was slanting sideways through the sky, and he'd need a raincoat to go out there or he'd be soaked in seconds. He lifted a stack of old Muskoka Lakes Association yearbooks off a steamer trunk by the door and peeked inside, hoping for an umbrella. Nothing but old letters and photographs, yellowed and damp smelling. He closed the trunk, rethinking his plan. This conversation was probably best held face-to-face in Toronto, because what if Maya was right? He'd want to see every tell in James's body language.

Rubbing the tight spot between his ribs, Connor ignored the strange feelings of betrayal, and slammed the laptop shut. James was reliable. Trustworthy. Maya was the one who had left him hanging. She'd found her way under his skin, and had begun to make her conspiracy theory against James feel valid, that was all.

Cupping his chin, he paced the living room. He didn't need this crap. He needed people who took care of things and let him get much-required rest. He had only a few more days of vacation and he still wasn't feeling completely human.

Connor drifted back to the table and poked through the papers beside Maya's computer, stopping to read through the entrepreneur deal. He smiled, liking how detailed her notes were. She didn't let her own enthusiasm keep her from seeing potential barriers and stumbling blocks. The woman had good instincts when she wasn't barking up the wrong tree, and she would do okay without him and his job. She'd bounce back. How could a spitfire like her not bounce back even better after a tribulation like this?

Cracking his knuckles, Connor wrote a quick reference for Maya, focusing on her willingness to work hard and take initiative. He saved it on her desktop, so she'd see it, and closed the computer.

Then he went out in the storm, started the generator and typed a new phone number into Maya's computer.

MAYA CLUTCHED HER MOTHER'S hand as Catherine dozed in her hospital bed. She appeared so frail and weak. How had she aged so suddenly? She was only in her fifties, but here in the ER, she seemed so close to—

Don't think about it.

"You okay?" Hailey tugged a blanket up around Maya's damp shoulders. It was pouring outside in what their mom would call a gully-washer, and while Maya had just managed to miss the deluge, she'd still gotten soaked through by driving the boat in the rain.

"Aren't you supposed to be in Hollywood?"

"I got in a few hours ago. I'm back for a few days before I go to New York. I can postpone, though."

"Is it that bad?" Maya's attention was drawn back to their mother.

"The doctor says she's okay. A concussion and a few bruises is all, but they want to keep her overnight for observation. Until the effects of the concussion have passed, she's at risk of another fall." Her sister's voice cracked and Maya leaned her head on Hailey's hand, which still rested on her shoulder. "She's just so…"

"I know," Maya said grimly. "It's hard."

Hailey nodded, unable to speak.

"You know we'll call you if anything happens. You should still go to New York."

"It's only work, Maya. This is…this feels like…"

"Let us take care of Mom. We've been holding you back for too long."

"You guys haven't been holding me back."

"Yeah? Then why didn't you go to that arts college for photography after you graduated from high school? I know you were accepted." Hailey's head turned so fast, Maya feared her sister would get whiplash. "You stayed to help us. And while we appreciate it, it's your time to follow your dreams. It's our turn to stay close and take care of each other. You know we'll keep you in the loop." She gave her sister's hand a squeeze. "It's okay, Hailey."

"I'd never forgive myself if…" She swallowed hard.

"Don't think that way. She only fell down. It's not like she had another stroke. And anyway, by the time you have to go she'll be back to her old self."

Hailey nodded reluctantly. "I think Mellie Melon's waiting to come in. She didn't want to crowd you, since you were the last to arrive."

Maya nodded, trying to untangle her wet hair. Her curls were a crazy mess.

Hailey left and a few moments later Melanie entered, taking the chair across the bed.

"Thanks for calling," Maya said.

"I'm glad you checked your messages in time to beat the worst of the storm."

The sisters stared at their mother for a while, saying nothing.

"How's it going out there?" Melanie asked, pushing her glasses up her nose.

Maya blinked back unexpected tears.

"What's wrong?"

"Nothing." She heaved a sigh. "I got fired."

"Fired? I thought you quit the restaurant."

"No, I mean…"

"Connor MacKenzie fired you?" Melanie lowered her voice as their mother stirred. "What did you do?"

"Why do you think it was something I did?"

"You were *fired*."

"Fine. Connor's advisor is putting through a deal with a lumberyard that doesn't appear profitable for the company. Connor says it's for tax reasons and diversifying his portfolio, but

I can't see how he's going to come out ahead. Things seem shady, but I have no evidence of intentional wrongdoing."

"You brought this up with him?"

"Yeah."

"Of course you did. You have no sense of self-preservation. Why did I even ask?" Melanie leaned back, her lips pursed. "Did it ever occur to you that maybe Connor *knows* it is shady, and that's why he fired you?"

"What?" Maya sat back. "No."

"Why not? You said he's on top of his game. Half of Bay Street's success is probably shady. Why should he be different?"

"He's not involved."

"How do you know?"

"He looked…surprised. Slightly doubtful."

"Maybe he's a good actor. Or amazed that you figured it out."

"His advisor in charge of the project is shutting out anyone who questions it. I think he's… It doesn't matter." She waved away her thoughts. "He trusts his advisor, not me." Maya stretched, releasing their mother's hand. "It's for the best, anyway. I couldn't work on a project I knew was going to bomb. I couldn't stand sitting there, letting it fail. If he's too stupid to see it, then he deserves it."

The problem was she didn't believe her own words. She felt as though it was up to her to save Connor, protect him. He was severely burned out, and she could see just how bad it had been, now that he was starting to come alive again. He was returning to the man she'd admired and wanted to emulate.

She didn't doubt there was something about the deal that would result in good things for James. Nobody in the business world was that loyal forever, especially when their boss was being called the king of Toronto and you were just his hardworking, behind-the-scenes peon whose ego was being continuously bashed in.

Maya rolled her shoulders, and remembering that she was sitting across from a lawyer, sat straighter. "Mel?"

"Yeah?"

"If I initiated a side project with Connor, am I still fired from that?"

"What do you mean?"

"Legally, do I still have a claim? I'm the lead and he's the backer. We are to split the profits." Maya batted at the air, dismissing her line of thought. "Never mind. That thing isn't going to fly, anyway." She let out a sigh. "Not unless you know someone who can get licensing for a medical device. Kind of in a time crunch."

"Have you tried expedited licensing?"

"How do I do that?"

"You can request it in certain situations. You might qualify."

"How do you know about this?"

"I took a business law course when I thought I wanted to be a corporate lawyer."

"I could seriously hug you right now."

Melanie smiled. "I'll send you the link."

"Do you think I should keep digging on the advisor thing?"

"You were fired, Maya."

"I know, but…"

"You know Officer Cranks?"

It had been years since the man had played poker at their house with their late father, but he was hard to forget. Especially since he'd forgiven a few of Maya's speeding tickets.

"Wow, you play for keeps."

Melanie smirked. "I'm not talking about arresting anyone. His son, Jamie—you know, from the bar? He's dating someone who knows about licensing, if you need more help."

"How do you know all this stuff?"

"I talk to people," her sister said with a frown. "How do you *not* know all this stuff?"

Maya focused on their mother's pale face. Right. That whole connect-with-people thing she kept failing at.

She let out a sigh. She couldn't seem to do anything right these days.

Chapter Thirteen

Maya walked up the wet path, cool sprinkles of leftover rain dropping from the leaves above. She paused to take in the cottage, basking in an early morning sunbeam. Waking up with a crick in her neck from sleeping beside her mother's bedside, she'd realized she'd better at least come back to the cottage and haul Connor to the mainland.

She continued up the path, on the lookout for fallen trees. So far it seemed as though the island had weathered the storm well, other than the odd tree hanging farther out over the water. The damn waves were eroding the shore little by little. Too bad the tax department wasn't going to come out and remeasure their shoreline and thus adjust their applicable land taxes down a tad each time a storm shrunk their frontage.

"Hello?" called a voice.

Maya turned, to find a man on the dock—a man looking out of place in a suit. She frowned and hurried back down. She hadn't heard a boat pull up. As she got closer, she recognized the man, and alongside the dock, the rowboat from the other day. It was tied in a way that if a large swell came along it would damage the boat as well as the dock. Dumbass.

Aaron from Rubicore Developments. What on earth was he doing here?

"Hello." He hurried forward and shook her hand. "Aaron again. From Rubicore Developments?"

"Yes, I remember."

"I dropped off an offer with you?"

"Yes."

"I was wondering if you had come to a conclusion?"

Maya wondered if he meant to sound as though he was playing that kids' game where you had to make every sentence a question or else you lost and had to suffer a knuckle rap from your siblings. She supposed he was feeling her out and attempting to be nonthreatening so he could get what he wanted. A typical man, in other words. "The offer is valid until mid-August, according to the papers."

"Yes, yes. It is. I was just checking to see if you had any questions or concerns." He passed her a business card, seemingly having broken out of his game.

"Why do you want our island?"

"We're developing across the water."

"What are you doing over there, anyway?"

"Spiffing up the place."

"That I can see." There were permit signs posted all over the place and every stitch of heritage was being striped away as if a pile of termites had been dumped on a woodpile.

"Do the Fredericksons still own the blue cottage? I thought I saw them on the dock the other day."

"The holdouts?" Aaron cleared his throat, pressing a fist over his mouth. "The Fredericksons, yes. Yes, still there."

"Hmm. What do they think of all the construction you're doing?"

"Did you have any questions about the offer?"

"Your offer is a bit of a lowball. I doubt my partners will go for it. This island has been in the family for over a century."

Aaron's jaw tightened and he stared up at the green building behind her. "I see."

"Maybe if you added a few tens of thousands, we might get a little more serious about discussing the offer."

"Your structure needs quite a lot of work."

"And how would you know that?"

"It's quite old. It looks original."

"How do you know we haven't kept it like new?"

He swallowed and stole a glance at the leaning boathouse. It was rather obvious they hadn't, but his assumptions were starting to annoy her. A man like Aaron wanted their cottage only to destroy it.

"I think it is a fair offer," he said.

"Well then, we'll be sure to let you know whether we agree by the deadline." Maya turned to walk up the path.

"You could make a counteroffer."

She gave a shrug as though considering it. "Maybe. We'll see."

The man straightened his suit jacket and stepped into his rowboat, windmilling his arms to regain his balance when the boat jerked and rocked on its tether.

Maya rolled her eyes and continued up the path, hoping he'd fall in.

CONNOR STROLLED DOWN the old Milan cobblestone street, miles from the Teatro Alla Scala where he would enjoy *Don Chisciotte* that evening. Everything from the locals' laid-back manner to the fountains reminded him how much he missed Muskoka and his daily swim. The smiles of the women made him think of Maya, particularly when their gazes strayed down his physique in blatant appreciation.

And yet he was in Italy. Alone.

If he was honest with himself, he'd admit he hadn't come here to finally see an opera, but to try and outrun the voices in his head that were arguing Maya's case. She'd brought up a lot of seemingly good points against James, and Connor was finding many reasons why she should still have a job despite everything.

He wandered past a café that smelled heavenly. Coffee? Pastries?

Connor glanced down at his gut. Maya had helped fill him out a bit. He felt good, stronger. He'd enjoyed being able to walk all afternoon despite the jet lag. But would adding a stimulant and sugar set him back, or was he being too hard on himself? How often did he get to enjoy a real espresso in a little Italian café? Coming here was one of the promises to himself that he'd never honored, and the aromas were seriously tempting his senses.

Should he do it?

He sat on a stone bench and watched children splashing in an ancient fountain while he waited for the urge to break his new habits to pass. Did any of his resolutions matter if he wasn't going to get the girl?

He'd changed while in Muskoka, though, and he still hadn't quite figured out what it meant. All he knew was that the old Connor would have listened, checked into Maya's issue, resolved it and carried on even stronger than before.

Maybe he needed purpose. Something that would perk him up, like Maya's side project had done to her. It had boosted her drive in a way that was sexy as all get-out. He remembered that feeling of having a new project that was so exciting and thrilling you couldn't help but smile. He'd had that years ago, but had since lost it somewhere.

Maybe that was what he was missing. Not balance, but purpose. Back when he'd started his business, his goal had been to earn enough money to float a small country. He'd done it. He'd climbed to the top and shouted *"I'm the king of the castle."*

In hindsight, he could see that that was when he'd begun to

falter. There had been nowhere else to go from the top but down. Without another purpose, he'd blindly flailed on, struggling to maintain his position. The only thing that had been driving him forward was a fear of failure, and of a dirty rascal knocking him off his mountain.

Connor rubbed his arms, shivering. The day had grown cold and the old-fashioned streetlights were coming on, twinkling off the worn cobblestones. The children who'd been playing in the fountain were gone, leaving the square silent and empty. He turned up the street, stumbling on the stones as he made his way back to his quiet, lonely room.

Making a change in his life felt harder and riskier than it had when he'd had nothing. Now, he had everything to lose, but was slowly realizing that none of it had been worth a thing to begin with.

WHERE THE HELL WAS Connor? Had he left the island? There was stuff strewn about his room, but it appeared as though his bag might be gone. Did he drown while swimming around the island? Had something happened to him in the storm? Or was he gone?

Maya climbed the slippery, lichen-covered rocks behind the cottage to call Em.

"Maya? What happened?"

"Do you know where Connor is?"

"He's off to Italy—or rather, there already. He said he fired you?"

"He went to Italy?" Relief and anger scorched Maya's gut. "Well, I guess that saves me from having the lake dredged."

"He didn't tell you he was leaving?"

"Why should he? He fired me." The bitterness in her own voice almost brought her to tears. She'd always been one to let bad stuff roll off her back, making her stronger for the next time. But this...this was hitting her hard. "Did he say anything about a refund?"

"For what?"

"The rental and, uh, me. My assistant services."

"No. Did you tell him about the lumberyard?"

"Yeah."

"Oh. Well, don't take it personally, Maya. He's in a weird space right now."

"I thought he was the kind of man who would at least hear me out."

Em made a sympathetic noise, then paused before lifting her voice in triumph. "You will never believe the info I discovered at a function last night."

Maya ran a finger over her thumbnail, her interest piqued even though she wouldn't mind a tad more sympathy from Em.

"James," she continued, "is a nephew of the financial officer who is in charge of the lumberyard's accounts. And it seems as though this guy is the true owner, too. I'm looking into it, but get this." She stopped sharply, and Maya wondered if underneath her excitement Em was actually pissed off. "The guy who did the evaluation on the lumberyard's worth is a *friend* of James from way back."

"You're kidding!" Maya sat down hard on a rock, her tailbone protesting the poor treatment. "These can't be coincidences. How did you discover this?" She stared at the sparkling flecks of mica in the rock under her, unable to wrap her mind around the new information. James wouldn't be so ballsy or dumb as to think he could get away with something so obvious, could he? Yet these two connections were in the very places she'd been unable to make the math work.

"A little eavesdropping," Em said, "a copy of the guest list, a few files from the temp, and a bit of searching the net."

"Damn, girl. You're a regular James Bond."

Em let out a pleased laugh. "So? What should we do now?"

"I got fired, Em. I'm out. Connor doesn't want to hear it."

"Pshaw! The Maya I know isn't giving up already."

"Connor didn't want to hear what I had to say about my suspicions. He trusts James, not me. How do we even know Connor isn't involved in the whole shebang?"

"He's not."

"How do you know?"

"I've worked for him since he started."

"So? People change."

"I know Connor."

"So?"

"He's burned out. He's always wanted someone to pick up the reins on a project—more than Bill and James have in the past—and so now that James is finally stepping up to bring in some profit, I think Connor's reluctant to focus on how he's doing it."

Listen. Pause. Reflect. Connor wasn't following his own advice.

"We need to get him to reflect on what I said about James," Maya mused. The stubborn man was refusing to deal with anything business-related these days. How was she supposed to get him to reflect?

Connect.

She needed to connect the dots for him.

"We need a tight, incriminating package that will help Connor connect the dots, Em."

"Well, then maybe I have something that will help with that. I did some research at the land titles office, too. I have an old roommate who works there." She paused, as though waiting for praise from Maya. "Not a lot of lumberyards have been sold over the past few decades, but accounting for its size and inflation, I'm guessing this business was overvalued by about four hundred thousand dollars—which was exactly your guesstimate, based on your own research. Maybe we could use this to help him see what we see?"

Maya rubbed her forehead. "This isn't good, Em."

"I thought this was the kind of thing we were looking for?"

"I mean it's not good for Connor."

"I've got more."

"Are you freaking kidding?" Maya bit her tongue to keep from swearing at the injustice of Em's timing with this info. A day sooner and it might have kept Maya from being canned.

"I know. Sorry. Yesterday was just a really good day."

"No, it's okay." Maya tried to strip the emotion from her voice. "Keep going."

"At that function last night I saw James and his wife, so I started chatting her up. Turns out they just bought a second home, in Florida."

"Florida?"

"Apparently he's been getting bonuses lately." She paused, her voice became low, sending an eerie vibe through Maya. "He hasn't, Maya. Not from CME. Nobody has. I asked Accounting."

"You're serious?"

"I know this feels like a ton of evidence, and to us it seems pretty incriminating. But I'm thinking if Connor blew you off, we're going to need the smoking gun *and* James's confession, because if you look at it from the other side, there are possible explanations for everything. People do business with relatives all the time, so maybe this uncle being the financial officer, CEO guy isn't a big deal. As for the appraiser, a lot of people are on summer holidays. Maybe our usual appraiser is gone, so James called in a favor with his buddy. Maybe the overvaluation is accurate—

maybe land is included, or something valuable that we don't know about. Maybe James has been doing consulting on the side, which explains the bonuses. It can all be explained away."

"He's got to be screwing over CME, though, Em. There are too many maybes, and this deal isn't Connor." Maya ducked when she flushed a flock of birds out the trees as she began walking the path at the top of the hill to burn off some of her energy.

"Let's eliminate the excuses, then."

"Do you have time for all of this?"

"If I lose my job I will be regretting not taking a few hours to snoop things out, now won't I?" Em replied in an all-business tone. "We need a solid plan and some good ammo before we talk to anyone—anyone, okay? Be patient."

Be patient. Be patient. That's all everyone ever seemed to tell her these days, and nothing good ever seemed to come from being patient.

"Once we have more info," Maya said, "promise me we can lynch James."

There was silence.

"Why do you care so much? Connor fired you," Em said finally.

"I guess…well, because Connor trusted James, and Connor is a good guy. He deserves to have someone good on his team, someone trustworthy who he can count on when the chips are down and he isn't well."

Em sighed. "I keep hoping James isn't doing anything wrong, but the more I find out, the more it seems like…" She let out another sigh.

"I know. Say, do you know anything about licensing?"

"What do you mean?"

"Patents and all that kind of new product stuff."

"No, but Connor's buddy Nolan McKinley would. I gave you his number, didn't I?"

"Already tried him."

"Did you play nice and ask him about his wife first?"

"What do you mean?"

"Maya, I know you want to make it in this world, but there is a game you have to play. You have to act as if you care about the personal and not just the business."

"I care."

Em laughed and Maya couldn't help but join her. "I know. I'm sorry. I'm trying. Really I am. I just want to get down to business."

"Umm-hmm."

"So?" Maya asked, trying to think of something conversational. "Do you have a cat?"

"Maya, shut up."

"I need practice?"

"A lot of practice."

"Do you have a dog then?"

"What is this? Go Fish? Get off the phone so I can do some more snooping around. And don't forget—play the game."

Maya sighed and clicked off her phone. Connections. Right. She could work on that. But being patient was going to do her in.

MAYA PLUNKED HERSELF in the chair beside her mother's bed. Her mom gave her a thin smile.

"You look tired," Catherine said.

"I am."

"I love you, kiddo."

Maya, feeling teary, reached for her hand and gave it a squeeze, hoping her mother would know she felt the same even though she couldn't say the words for fear of bawling.

Her mom gave Maya's hand a light shake.

"How are you feeling?" Maya asked when the lump in her throat had been successfully swallowed.

"Not bad. Mild headache is all." She gave her a wink from her good side.

"I love you." Maya said it quickly, before the emotions could come flooding out.

"I know."

"Can I get you anything?" She needed to do something, needed to move. Standing, she straightened the flowers on the windowsill and checked them all for water. Obviously, Hailey had been by already, as everything was fine.

"I'm good. Hailey was here earlier. I have my Twix chocolate bar."

Maya kept her attention on the flowers. "I did something stupid, Mom." She turned to face her. "I got fired. My shot at trying to help the cottage didn't work out very well. Although Mr. MacKenzie hasn't asked for a refund for unused days."

"The cottage's destiny…"

"I know. Destiny keeps it in our hands. Or not." Maya gave her a wry smile. "We got an offer from a developer across the water. I don't know, though. It doesn't feel right. You know I don't really go for all that heritage stuff, but they're knocking everything down over there and changing it." She gave a laugh. "Who would have guessed? I don't like it."

Her mother had a peaceful glow about her, as though the world was unfolding as she felt it should.

"When will I learn to keep my mouth shut, Mom?"

"You need to work someplace where you can talk. A lot. That's all." Catherine smiled with fondness.

"Yeah. As an auctioneer, maybe?"

Her mother let out a light chuckle.

"I thought Connor's advisor was crooked. And I still think he is, but Connor... Oh, I don't know. I'm confused." Her mother remained silent, allowing Maya to continue when she was ready. "There are arguments that the advisor might be on track, but my gut is telling me he isn't, that he's corrupt. But I don't have enough facts, and it's frustrating. Connor's supposed to be signing this deal in a matter of days, and I want to help, but he fired me. He didn't want to hear about James."

Maya bowed her head. "And to top it all, I think I'm about to lose forty thousand dollars of his—I mean, I might get it back, but I dropped the ball with licensing stuff because I didn't know enough. How could I graduate at the top of my class and still know nothing?"

Her mother was fighting off sleep, her eyelids drifting shut.

"I'm sorry. I'm nattering on like crazy, and you're tired." Maya tucked the blanket up around her mother's chin. "I'll come by again tomorrow. I'll know what to do by then."

"You always do, Snap." Catherine smiled, her eyes closing. "You always do."

Maya pressed her lips together. She wasn't Snap any longer. That confident gal was gone. There were no snap decisions to be made, and no way for her to snap out of her funky mood.

She sniffed back tears and, picking up the city's classifieds, dropped them in the recycling bin on her way out. Toronto seemed farther away than ever.

CONNOR STARED AT HIS untouched cappuccino and straightened his bow tie. Women in fancy evening wear chattered as they wove past his spot at the opera's standing bar, their heavily adorned fingers weighted down with precious gems. He used to love events like this because he felt as though he had finally made it. But over time the people and their perceived problems had begun to bore him.

He'd always wanted to see an opera live in Italy, thinking that was the pinnacle for someone with his musical tastes. But the first half of the performance had bored him. He was alone and didn't speak the language. His bow tie felt too tight. The sound was amazing, the voices incredible. But...something was missing.

Maya.

Which was silly. She wouldn't be able to sit through an opera. Why was he even thinking of her? She was meddling in his affairs, sticking her nose where it didn't belong. She didn't even trust his most loyal advisor, a man who had been working at his side for ages.

"Signore?"

"Yes?" The lobby bar had emptied, the opera ready to resume, and an usher dressed in a tux stood smiling, his hands clasped lightly behind his back.

"The opera is beginning."

"Thank you. I won't be going in."

"It is not to your tastes?"

"It is. Very nice. Jet lag."

"Ah, I see." The man bowed his head and stepped away. "Have an enjoyable evening."

Enjoyable. Connor didn't even know what brought him joy any longer, other than bantering with Maya and trying to get her to call him names.

He pulled out his phone and played with the On button. Sighing, he opened his email, not sure what he'd find or why he was even checking.

There were quite a few messages, but two recent ones from Maya caught his attention. The first was about the entrepreneur deal. Details, etc. The second one was more intriguing. He touched the screen to open it, and scanned the first paragraph, trying to remind himself to stay cool and objective. It was about James. Of course.

The email was an argument against James, and his supposed corruption was outlined by several points. Number one, he'd overvalued the lumberyard by approximately half a million dollars. Number two said James was claiming to be getting bonuses. Number three, he had bought a home in Florida. Connor's fist closed and he ground his teeth. He made himself read number four. He read it again. On the other side of the doors, a clear voice sang of love, deception, and betrayal.

Connor's finger paused over the phone's Off button. He could still go in and listen to the opera. He didn't have to read this. He didn't need to add it to his list of worries.

Number four...James was related to the lumberyard's owner, who was also its financial manager, and James was a high school buddy of the appraiser he'd hired. Not exactly an impartial third party, as Connor had dictated.

Was that simply a coincidence? Or did all the pieces add up to something alarming? And if they did, how had Maya snooped it all out in a matter of days? How come Connor hadn't discovered any of this?

And what was he going to do? He was set to sign on the dotted line in less than seventy-two hours. Should he bail? Carry on? Confront James and fire him? No, sacking James would create a hole so big Connor would end up burned out almost immediately from trying to pick up the slack.

The bottom line was that Maya was right on one thing: the lumberyard didn't fit his portfolio, and what she'd found looked bad. Connor couldn't recall why James had wanted to buy the company. Was it merely for tax purposes? Was it to flesh out their portfolio and make them more stable as the economy continued to twist and turn, with dips and dives? There had to be more.

But the big question, if Maya was correct, was how much did he stand to lose? And why did she still care?

Who could he trust? Who could he turn to?

He needed more time.

Chapter Fourteen

Maya balled her hands into fists and stared down James outside his office. She knew the two of them were gathering a crowd in the open area, but she didn't care. Not one bit. Connor was due to sign the lumberyard purchase agreement in less than twenty-four hours, and he hadn't replied to her email about James. As far as Em knew, he was still in Italy. It was time to deal with things, patience and all that bull crap be damned. Maya had given her ex-boss time to reflect. Now it was time to act.

"I don't think you have Connor's best interests at heart," she announced, ensuring her voice could be heard by all the eavesdroppers who had suddenly found this area of the seventy-second floor incredibly interesting.

Em shot her a look of warning from her desk near Connor's office. She was half out of her chair, uncertain whether to intervene or not.

"What do you know about business? You're just some lowly assistant," James replied, his face tight with anger.

A faint gasp rose from the eavesdroppers—mostly female assistants. Maya caught flashes of righteous anger before she returned her attention to the well-dressed businessman.

"I know when someone is using nepotism for his personal advantage, and selling out his boss." She dropped her hands onto her hips and watched him consider running away. Nope. He had too much at stake to turn tail. Good.

James strode to the nearest desk, where a secretary cowered, her eyes round. She leaned away as he snatched her phone and punched in two numbers. "Security. Floor seventy-two. I need someone removed. Now."

Maya smiled. "Thank you for confirming my suspicions, Mr. Culver."

James paused, the phone halfway to its cradle. "What suspicions?"

"That you are corrupt."

James slammed down the phone and pointed at her. "You were fired by Mr. MacKenzie. Do you really believe you are one to judge?"

Out of the corner of her eye, Maya spotted Connor's second advisor, Bill Hatfield, appear in his office doorway. He took in the scene, then gently closed his door again.

She turned to the cluster of employees. "It's true. I was fired." She turned back to James. "Because of you."

"I had nothing to do with it. You were causing a disturbance with your conspiracy theories." Red crept up James's neck. "It is time for you to leave."

"Sure, but before I go, I think the staff might find it interesting that you bought a house in Florida based on a bonus you got from Connor." She turned to address the workers, who were leaning forward awkwardly, straining to hear what was being said over the loud rain that had begun drumming on the large office windows. "Anyone else here get a bonus?" People shook their heads, their attention drifting to James. "Funny, because according to Accounting, neither did Mr. Culver."

Whispers riffled through the room and James shifted

uncomfortably. "I don't know what you are trying to prove, Miss Summer, but you are not welcome here. You are bad for morale."

"And you're bad for CME's bottom line. Why else would you convince Connor to purchase a *sawmill*? There is no profitable reason for him to buy a primary industry—especially one that has lost money for almost a decade." She casually leaned against a nearby desk. "Well, unless, of course, you were trying to do a favor for someone in your family. Maybe an uncle who owned the failing lumberyard and was wanting to retire? Maybe promise him a secure future at Connor's expense, through a little something called a finder's fee? Smaller, of course, than your own kickback—sorry, *bonus*."

"Are you trying to accuse me of something?" James asked, his nostrils flaring.

"It must be hard being you." The man's jaw clenched, and she could tell he was itching for her to explain why. "I know how hard you have been working lately. Connor has been leaving more details to you." She glanced around at the eavesdroppers. "To everyone, really. But being the man who never gets any credit from the public as to your role in the company's success... It must be hard to take."

"I don't need credit."

"That's good. Because I doubt you'd want to be the one named for losing Connor's company over four hundred thousand dollars."

"I never!" James swung his fist down as though searching for something to slam.

"The overvaluation, though? It's by over 400 K, James. I've done a lot of research, and it seems very odd that someone with so much experience in the business, such as your old high school pal, Peter Stoker, would make such a large error when determining the value of your uncle's lumberyard."

James licked his lips and swallowed, his Adam's apple bobbing. His eyes were shifting from side to side and Maya knew she had him.

"Well, unless Peter was also doing someone a favor. Say, in exchange for a brand-new SUV for his wife? How's she liking it, by the way? Is it nice? I hear she got a lot of upgrades."

"That's a coincidence! You don't understand the complexities of purchasing another company, and are jumping to unreasonable conclusions. There are tax benefits—"

"That come nowhere near covering the loss that Connor is going to take on this." Maya spread her arms out. "That everyone in this company is going to take."

She saw the fear in staffers' faces as they turned nervously to James.

"This is utterly ridiculous," he spat.

"No!" Maya shouted, her patience gone. "*You* are utterly ridiculous! The fact that you would do this to the man you work for. The man who taught you everything you know. To betray him so deeply..." Her voice shook with emotion. "Don't you get it? Don't you get who you have become? Don't you get what you are asking these innocent employees to be a part of?" The crowd behind her rustled nervously. "Who would hire a man who has a history of being fined for taking kickbacks when overvaluing companies? Do you know how bad this is going to look in the courts?"

A heavy hand landed on Maya's shoulder, and James's expression changed. She turned to face Connor, who was decked out in a suit and looking very sexy and in charge.

"Thank goodness you are here," she said quietly. Now he could finally see what she'd been saying all along, and make it right again.

"That'll be enough, Miss Summer," Connor said, his voice flat, the dark lines that had been under his eyes when they'd first met seemingly tracking across again as she watched.

She smiled in relief when he gave James a stern look. Her work here was done. That corrupt man was going to be packing so fast it wouldn't even make it onto Facebook before he was long gone.

She glanced back at Connor, ready to reap her reward, but his shadowed jaw was set, his cheeks flushed, and he was staring at her in a way that made her hesitate. It was almost as though he didn't think James was in the wrong. That maybe she was.

"Please come with me," he said.

James gloated, crossing his arms and leaning back on his heels, as though he was a bouncer and she was about to be bounced.

How could Connor be so blind?

Maya pulled her shoulder out from under Connor's grasp as two security guards rounded the corner.

Em stepped to Connor's side, wringing her hands. "Mr. MacKenzie?" she squeaked.

"I've heard enough, Em," he told her.

She nodded and stepped back as he addressed the security guards. "I'll see that Miss Summer is seen out of the building." He placed a hand on Maya's lower back. Over his shoulder he said, "James, carry on taking care of things for me, please."

The man grinned smugly. "Like it was my own company, Connor."

"Excellent. That's exactly what I need to hear."

Maya shook off Connor's hand. "I will let myself out." As she headed toward the elevator, she addressed the room. "I know I'm not the only one who sees that James is about to lose this company hundreds of thousands of dollars. Why are you too chicken to say anything?"

Gazes flicked away as she tried to make eye contact with people as she passed.

"That'll be enough," Connor said quietly. He began moving them faster, his palm once again an insistent force on her back.

Outside the building moments later, he trailed her onto the wet sidewalk, where she wanted to run from the humiliation and never look back. Her heart felt as though it had been stung by a thousand stingrays, and her eyes were burning with held back emotion.

As he reached for her arm, she dodged him, pulling her jacket tighter around her shaking body. If he couldn't come to the conclusion that James had to go, then it could only mean one thing. Connor was in on it.

"Maya."

"I held you on a pedestal you never deserved."

"Trust me, Maya."

"You know what? You can run your company however you want, but I thought you were someone else. Someone I wanted to emulate."

His body rocked as if he'd been hit. His eyes were dark and tired. "Trust me…" He reached out and grasped her arm, staring at her as though he wanted to say something else. Finally, with drizzle hazing the air between them, he whispered, "Thank you."

"For what?" she spat.

"For seeing things."

"If you are talking about what just went on up there, you need glasses, because you don't know what the hell you're even talking about."

He lowered his voice. "Maya, patience."

"You are such a goddamn tease! I don't know what kind of power trip you're on, but I hate you, okay? I officially hate you. Send that out in an office memo." She waved a hand across the sky. "This just in—Maya Summer hates Connor MacKenzie because he is a duplicitous, corrupt, jerk-faced ass." Her chest burned with anger and betrayal. "You're about to sign a deal that will lose you a ton of money, and you think it's funny to tell me to have patience? You're an asshole, Connor MacKenzie. Ass. Hole." She blinked and turned away from a woman who had stopped to gawk at her outburst.

She turned back and whispered harshly, "I thought you had a sense of honor and I'm *embarrassed* to have worked for you. I will *never* use that worthlessly vague reference you saved on my computer. I'm not a toy you can use in your games, Connor. I am a woman, and I hate the way you've treated me."

He reached out a hand, his brow arced in pain. "Maya, our time at the cottage wasn't like that."

"I'm talking about what went on in *there!*" She shoved a finger in the direction of the skyscraper. "It's like Arlene Dickinson said, it's not about being the best. It's about doing your best. And you failed, Connor. Big time."

"I'm not who you think I am."

"That's for damn sure."

He gripped her shoulders, drawing her closer. "Why do you care so much, Maya?" When she didn't answer, he gave her a slight shake. "Why, Maya? Why?"

Her bottom lip trembling, she broke free of his hold. She felt shattered. This was worse than any heartbreak she'd ever experienced. And all for a man she'd never even had. A man who'd never been truly real with her.

"You wouldn't understand," she whispered as she walked away.

THE RAIN CONTINUED to drizzle outside the cottage, and Maya and her sisters sat around the fireplace, enjoying the blaze. "I can't believe he didn't *care*. That he was such a—a…" Maya downed the rest of her hot toddy.

"Whoa, girl. You're going to end up hurling if you keep drinking that fast." Hailey gently pried the empty cup out of her hand.

"I like my drinks to go down fast and easy. And we're finally drinking something that doesn't give me brain freeze." Maya turned to Hailey, taking in her jeans and sweater. "Don't you have a flight to catch to New York or something?"

"I booked the red-eye. Tell us more about this thing with Connor. You really think his advisor is up to something, and that he might be in on it?"

Maya nodded, her head throbbing with held back emotion. "It's the only explanation."

"Are you sure?" Melanie asked, hesitation in her voice. "It doesn't quite fit right in my mind."

"Neither does him showing her out of the building and not James," snapped Daphne, with enough indignation it could have been her in Maya's shoes. Daphne was usually so "let it go" that Maya briefly wondered if something else was going on with her kid sister.

Maya pushed herself deeper into the cushions of her chair, the heels of her hands against her cheeks. "I don't know anymore. Nothing is a snap. He was so calm, but he had this haunted look." She reached for her cup to refill it. "Can we talk about something else?"

"Did you sort out that licensing thing?" Melanie asked.

"I meant something not me-related."

"No luck?"

"Jamie's girlfriend said she'd try. Everyone says they'll try, but nobody is on my side. Nobody cares."

"Yeah, go eat worms, would you?" Hailey snorted, tugging the filled cup away from Maya. She began singing softly, "Nobody likes me, everybody hates me…"

"I know, okay? I suck at making connections in the business world. I know, I know, I know. I'm too impatient. I want to get stuff done and people want to bond. You don't have to say it, the universe is already saying it loud and clear."

The sisters joined Hailey's song, singing about eating worms because of not being liked, and Maya broke into giggles at the silliness of it all. "You guys suck."

"Aw, Snappy, Snap, Snap," Daphne cooed, making kissy faces as she pulled Maya close.

Maya laughed and pushed her away. "I hate you guys. I'm being serious."

"So then?" Melanie asked. "What are you going to do?"

"I'm going to walk away."

"But…" Hailey looked to her sisters for support.

"Maya, that's not what you do," Melanie said carefully.

"Yeah? And you guys have better ideas?"

Listen. Pause. Reflect. Connect. That was what she was supposed to be doing. Too bad that advice sucked.

"I have to get Tigger," Daphne said, fiddling with her knit pullover as she stood. "The party she's at ends soon."

"Yeah, we should all go. Are you coming, Maya?"

"I'm going to stay here a few days. I need to get over this, and send out some more résumés. I may as well do it here without distractions. I might paint the screen frames, too."

"Are we keeping the place?" Daphne asked, her forehead furrowing.

Maya shrugged. "We have paint, I have time."

"Because, um, I have news."

The sisters turned to her. The last time Daphne had had news and used that hesitant, the-world-might-end tone of voice was over five years ago, when she'd announced she was unexpectedly expecting Tigger.

"I was at the planning office for the protest I'm doing in Bala against the big development there." She paused, inhaling in a way that made her chest heave.

Maya began planning out the rest of her evening in her mind, as Daphne, no doubt, was about to launch into the tale of another atrocity that needed desperately to be stopped. There was one every month, it seemed. Maybe after her sisters left Maya would check out head hunters to see if they could find her a job. And of course, finish off the last of the hot toddies. And maybe plot the demise of Connor, seeing as she couldn't seem to stop thinking about him.

Daphne mentioned Baby Horseshoe Island and Maya perked up. "Sorry, can you repeat that?"

Her sister's face pinched with worry as she said, "Rubicore Developments has bought out most of Baby Horseshoe Island and has plans to create a private resort complete with an airstrip, boating and wake boarding school, golf course, staff housing, mini marina, and hotel cabins."

"What?"

"I know." Daphne's voice shook.

"When?"

"The plans are still a proposal. We need to go to the next town meeting. The environmental implications alone are horrific."

"If we group together on this we can kick them right off that island," Melanie said, swinging her fist through the air. "I'll go to that meeting and show them exactly who they are messing with."

Daphne shot her a grateful smile.

"But if they've bought most of Baby Horseshoe they're not going to just roll over." Maya shook her head, adding up the pieces. "Aaron referred to the Fredericksons as the holdouts when he stopped by the other day. Are they the last owners?"

Daphne nodded.

"They've even bought out JoHoBo—I mean, Missy's Getaway?" No wonder the renovated cottage had been empty all summer. It was a miracle the place was still standing, seeing as at its core it was a hundred-ten-year-old cottage such as theirs.

Another nod from Daphne.

"And they offered to buy our island?" Hailey asked. "What does that mean?"

"It means they don't want the hassle of us over here complaining." Maya crossed her arms. "Daphne's right. We need to do something. And we need to not lose Trixie Hollow."

"We're going to need more people on our side." Melanie tapped her chin thoughtfully. "We need...a developer on our side. Someone who knows how these guys are going to duck and dive, so we can block them before they try anything sneaky."

"Do you think they're going to bribe council?" Maya asked.

"They probably already have," Daphne said, blinking back what appeared to be several cubic meters of panic.

"We'll figure something out," Maya assured them all. "But in the meantime, we need to get our butts in gear and save our cottage, so it doesn't fall into their hands." She rolled her shoulders, trying to force herself to chill out. At least Connor hadn't asked for a refund. That was something helping them in the right direction. Too bad she didn't have much to live on, much less help pay the back taxes.

She walked her sisters down to the dock, their mood somber. Visibility was diminished due to the light rain and it was a nice break from the heat of last week. Plus, Maya thought ruefully, it matched everyone's frame of mind.

As Maya watched her sisters' boat disappear into the mist, another boat pulled up. She couldn't make out who was under the yellow rain hat. Was it Connor? Did he decide that she was right?

Had he realized they were an amazing team, and that he missed her?

She loathed the part of herself that missed him, and the way her hope turned into a disappointment so deep it seared her lungs when she discovered it wasn't him in the other boat. She fought back the tidal wave of emotion. Maya Summer did not cry. Damn him.

The boat pulled up alongside the dock, the captain tossing her a line as he peeked out from under his yellow slicker.

"Jamie?"

"Girlfriend asked me to drop this off—I heard you were out here." He passed her an envelope sealed in a blue plastic bag.

"What is it?"

"Some licensing thing she said was important."

"Really?"

"Yep."

Maya clutched the envelope to her chest. "Did she get it to go through?"

He grinned. "It's all there in black-and-white."

As Jamie motored away, Maya stood under the protective eaves of the boathouse, reading the papers. Then she pumped the air with a fist and grinned. Maybe destiny wasn't such a bitch, after all. Maybe she was just being tested.

CONNOR SAT AT THE HEAD table of the wedding party, a warm tropical breeze ruffling his hair, which was in need of a cut. He smiled at his brother's delirious joy, having to admit the kid looked pretty good in a tuxedo.

"Having fun?" Curtis asked.

Connor nodded. Surprisingly, he was. He gazed out across the sandy Tahitian shores to the rolling ocean. What a view. If he ever got married, something like this would do the trick. Would Maya want a destination wedding? She seemed like a no-fuss, no-muss kind of woman. Despite her desire for everything big and important, she'd probably love a low-key event in a setting similar to this.

He stretched his hands, which had closed into fists. Why was he even thinking of her? She hated him. He'd lost out. He pushed his fingers through his hair, glad for the breeze slapping the large canopy above him. He'd ruined it completely, but he couldn't let her in. He wasn't ready, wasn't there yet. And this was too big. Nobody could know. Not yet.

"I expected you to be on your phone all night." His brother's voice lowered with emotion as he clapped Connor on the shoulder. "Thanks, man."

"For not being on my phone?"

"For being here. Really being here."

Connor nodded, unable to speak. He'd become that guy who was never around. If he had a wife, she'd be doing everyone on the side in a quest for love and attention.

"Connor, you look fantastic," Roberta said, leaning around her new husband. Her cheeks were flushed and her hair was done up in curls that kept falling in her face in a way that reminded him of Maya. It seemed he couldn't get away from thoughts of that woman. "We're so glad you came."

Connor nodded, his heart sinking. They had truly believed he wouldn't take time to come to the wedding. He thought back to who he'd been two and a half weeks ago. Chances were he would have missed the flight, cramming one more thing into his day. Then he would have come on a red-eye and barely made it to everything on time, his mind still stuck behind his desk in Toronto.

"Have you been working out?" Roberta asked.

He nodded. "A bit. I took some time off."

"Well, it's good for you. You look less like death warmed up and served on dry toast. I was starting to worry about you." She gave him an affectionate tap on the arm and turned her attention to one of her bridesmaids, who was whispering something in Roberta's ear, assessing Connor. They were talking about him.

He fidgeted with the flute of champagne in front of him. Roberta wasn't the only one who'd been worried about him. He'd met with his doctor yesterday before catching his flight, and while he had permission to go back part-time, Connor knew he wasn't out of the woods. If he returned to CME he'd get sucked back into it all, and in a matter of weeks he'd be back in that ER. But without CM Enterprises, who was he? What would he do with his days? What could he do so he didn't keel over?

Curtis swept his new wife onto the dance floor and Connor watched as they smiled and kissed, wrapped up in each other's world. That's what was missing from his life. That was what he needed. Someone like Maya to be his other half and lighten his life. She gave him hell all the time and was pushy, but he liked it. She knew what she wanted, and wasn't going to turn into some vapid trophy wife just because of who he was. She'd do things that mattered and keep him on his toes, forcing him continually to be a better man.

The bridesmaid moved to sit beside him, her eyelids doing some strange batting thing that he figured was supposed to make him randy. He gave her a tight smile and focused on the dancers.

She walked her fingers up his arm. "Wanna dance?" She gave him an expectant look and he knew he'd be rude not to accept. But if he did it would lead to her being all over him for the rest of the night, and he really wasn't in the right headspace for that kind of company. Unless it was Maya.

Damn her. How did she get to him so easily?

"I'm sorry, I don't think my girlfriend would appreciate that."

The woman glanced over Connor's shoulder. "She's not here, though, is she?"

"She is not."

The bridesmaid pulled on his hand. "Then what she doesn't know won't hurt her."

"No, but it might hurt me." He offered her his untouched glass of champagne, and she accepted it with disappointment. Connor scanned the room and finally pointed to a man near the back who was watching them. "I think there is someone over there hoping you will notice him."

"Who?" She turned, her eyes round with curiosity.

"He's been eyeing you."

She spun abruptly, putting her back to the man. "Really? Do you know his name?"

"Drink up and go find out for yourself."

She did as he suggested, her dress flouncing in a way that reminded Connor of Maya's niece. Saving her from the falling tree felt like forever ago. His mind drifted to the cottage bathroom, where he'd helped Maya doctor herself. He'd been such a broken husk. But was he any different now? Had he changed enough that he could finally be the man she deserved?

Sighing, he realized she probably wouldn't see it that way, and that woman saw everything.

He laughed as his brother swept Roberta into a deep dip, pretending to drop her. Connor missed this—being able to be present at an event without feeling as though he was about to lose his company if he didn't go check his email or texts. He missed *people*. Not everything needed to be about work all the time. But he still needed something the business world could give him. Something only James could deliver.

CONNOR SAT AT THE LARGE conference table and clasped his hands together. As long as James played his right cards, Connor was going to walk away a free and happy man.

Em, her moves edgy, offered the two men coffee. Connor waved her away, but James, bags under his eyes, accepted.

"Do you want me to stay and take notes?" Em asked Connor.

"No, that's fine. I just wanted to chat with James and get up to speed."

James and Em frowned. The conference room was considered neutral turf, and the only time Connor met with an employee for a "chat" in here, it led to either a pink slip or a severe reprimand. The fact that Connor's second advisor, Bill, was not present made it more clear something was about to go down.

"How's…" Connor snapped his fingers as though he was still burned out, and unable to pull up his other assistant's name. "Stella?"

"Fine," Em replied. "She can come back to work on Wednesday."

"I had Accounting send her a bonus this morning. Can you be sure she gets it?"

"Yes, sir."

"You'll get one, too. I appreciate all you do around here."

Em blushed as she nodded, whispering a "thanks" as she exited the room.

Connor, making sure his shoulders seemed weighted by fatigue, returned his attention to James, who was sitting at the other end of the table looking unsure, but also expectant.

"I want to thank you for taking care of the place while I was gone, James. I know it couldn't have been easy, with me pulling the plug on myself in the middle of a deal."

James cleared his throat and shook his head with vigor. "It was no problem, really."

"Well, I want you to know that I appreciate it. And this latest deal with the lumberyard, which you managed to close yesterday, was a good idea. I was looking at the papers and how much it increased the valuation of CM Enterprises."

James smiled, pleased.

"You've done a lot for me over the past year, in particular." When his advisor nodded, his chest expanding, Connor added, "And so I would like to make you an offer."

James leaned forward, hungry for details.

"I know you've been interested in having a larger stake in the company for some time."

"Yes, yes I have. I think I would do an amazing job with more control."

"How much would you like?"

James's greed practically turned him green. "As much as you are comfortable giving."

"I was thinking fifty percent."

He grinned and leaned back like a fat cat. "That would be fantastic."

"Or maybe you'd prefer to have majority control here?"

"What do you mean?" James's voice was breathless.

"Buy the company." Connor leaned back, hands folded behind his head.

"*Buy* the company?"

"Outright. You've done an amazing job, and your projections show that within five years you'll be rolling in it. It's a good time to buy."

"Why are you selling?" James licked his lips twice, a tell that he was nervous.

Connor laughed. "Have you seen me this past month? I can't even remember my own name. I'm not the king any longer and it's burning me out trying to be. I'm done, man. I'm *tired*. You do a much better job of balancing things. That's why I thought of you first. You are truly the new, uncrowned, king."

James swallowed hard, sitting a little straighter with the compliment and the hint that Connor might sell to someone else if he didn't grab the opportunity. "And what is the offer, exactly?"

"Purchase outright at your recent valuation."

"My recent…" James cleared his throat. He blinked, licked his lips.

"Yes. I trust your valuation. If the past is any indicator, it's probably conservative. Since it is your valuation, you know exactly what you are getting and, man…" Connor smiled and shook his head. "I can't believe I am even thinking of selling this place. It's been my everything for so long." He spread his palms flat on the table, rounding his shoulders as though in resignation. "But I can see how I'm in your way. You are the new king and it's time for me to step aside and let you shine."

James grew in his chair, shoulders straightening. "Yeah. Yeah, maybe."

"You in full control. Look out, world. Corner office. *Fortune* magazine calling you. Hell, I must be crazy." Connor shook his head as though he couldn't believe it. He gave James a moment to imagine it all, then leaned forward. "So? What do you say? Are you in?"

James nodded hesitantly, his eyes drifting to the large windows along the wall. "I'm not sure about the value…"

"Why? Is something wrong?" Connor made himself tamp his anger under a large weight, knowing one false move and he'd be stuck, not James, the man who needed to pay for his betrayal out of his own wallet.

Connor had checked the paperwork when he got back from Curtis's wedding, and James had come out ahead on the past three deals, whereas CM Enterprises had not. James was the real reason Connor was so burned out. He'd been paddling a ship his advisor had been poking holes into. Now it was time for James to buy the damaged ship.

Connor grinned internally. Either way, James was caught. He couldn't turn down the offer without showing how he'd become corrupt, and if he bought it, he was stuck with his own bad deals. Thank goodness for Maya and her threat to take James to court. No matter which way he moved he was screwed. Connor just hoped the man's pride made him move in Connor's favor for once.

"No, nothing is wrong." His advisor stared at the shiny tabletop.

"Is it a fair price?" Connor asked. "Should we investigate it further? Maybe there's something that has been overlooked?" He reached for the phone sitting in the middle of the table.

Anger radiated off James. But he stood and clenched Connor's hand, shaking it as he practically growled, "We have a deal, Connor."

"Legal has the contract ready for you to sign. Shall we go over there now?"

Connor made James be the one to break eye contact and pull his hand away first, as well as exit the room.

Oh, yes. Connor was still king.

MAYA BASKED ON A ROCK on the top of the island, the morning sun warming her bones. It had been a cool night in the cottage and now the sun was out to show her it was still summer.

Her phone rang and she answered it. The entrepreneurs.

"Maya, we've run into a glitch."

"Are you freaking kidding me?" How many fires did she have to put out with this stupid project?

"The licensing is fine. It's all set, thank you. But the distributor we wanted to use experienced a major flood, and it's looking like everything is going to be delayed by months. They said they'd let us out of our contract, but time is so short and—"

"I get the picture. I can tell you're feeling a bit anxious and stressed, but we'll figure this out, okay?" Connect, connect, connect.

Son of a…

How the hell were they going to sort this out? She was going to have to call in favors from people she didn't even know. Again. And lately, it felt as though every time she turned around she was asking someone to cover her butt and make it happen, because she'd messed up somewhere. How did she ever think she could get this device out into the real world?

"You know what?" she said. "I might know somebody. It's a long shot. Really long, but I can ask."

"Maya. You are a godsend."

"I'll call you back, okay?"

She hung up and rang Steve from Roundhouse Distributions, hoping he'd recall who she was.

"Hi, Steve? It's Maya Summer, the girl with the taxi in Toronto."

"Wow. How'd you know I needed a ride downtown?"

Maya laughed. "Sorry, I'm unable to take a fare right now, but I actually had a distribution question for you. Do you have a moment?"

"Sure."

Maya explained what she needed. "So, I'm not certain if you can help, or point me in the right direction? We've ended up in a bit of a time crunch."

"I'm actually heading to a meeting right now with a distributor who might be able to help you out. I can ask."

Maya stared at her phone. If this was what everyone was talking about with the whole connections thing, then hot damn, it was the coolest thing ever.

"That would be amazing. Thank you."

"No problem. Loving the Twitter jokes, by the way."

"I'm glad." Maya grinned at the sky. The Twitter jokes. She'd forgotten about the odd joke she'd been tweeting to him here and there. She had been connecting and maintaining their link without even realizing it. "Thanks, Steve. So much, really. I appreciate it."

He let out a laugh. "I only said I'd ask. I can't promise what they'll say."

"I know, but thank you just the same."

She happily lowered her phone, feeling more hope than she had in ages. Listen, pause, reflect and connect. She and Connor could write a business book, because Snap was officially back in business. Too bad Connor was more interested in being a corrupt jerk, because she had a feeling they could make a lot of money as a team.

Chapter Fifteen

Connor rolled over, bed sheets tangling around his legs as he scratched his crotch. Hmm. Something interesting was happening there. He stroked his morning wood and grinned. He was back. Connor the King MacKenzie was back.

Jumping out of bed, he dressed quickly and shot out the door of his penthouse to finalize the papers with James. Two more hours and he'd be free.

He sent a quick text to Tristen in Muskoka, giving him the go-ahead on a project they'd been working on. Today was the first day of the rest of Connor's life. A real life.

He strolled into his building—his for only another few hours, as he'd ensured James would take immediate possession. If James was going to have a bit of financial suffering, then the least Connor could do was expedite it.

Dappled light filtered in through the lobby's dusty side windows, and he couldn't wait to get out of the city.

A few hours later, he hurried back through the lobby, the few things he wanted to take with him tucked under one arm, Daphne's sunflower painting in the other.

The security guard glanced up and, recognizing him, shouted a hello. "Hey! Is it true you're selling the place?"

"Already did it. I'm a free man." If he didn't have full arms, Connor would have spread them out to do a spin in the middle of the lobby. Within hours the money would be in his account and he'd be rich. Dirty, filthy stinkin' rich. Well, until he completed the projects he had lined up with Tristen. That was going to skim a little off the top of his nest egg, but it would be well worth it.

Climbing into his Lexus, he headed toward Muskoka. He wondered how Maya's entrepreneur project was going. Had she given up when Nolan hadn't been able to deliver? Had she carried on by finding another way? Seeing as his name was on the contract, Connor should probably check in with her. Plus it was a very good excuse to see the woman who had been haunting his dreams.

Tapping the steering wheel, he sang along to the radio, knowing he could finally love Maya in all the ways he'd wanted to since the night in the boathouse. Only two steps away from happiness, and the man he was meant to be.

CONNOR STOOD ON NYMPH Island's dock and stared up at the large green cottage. He turned to the water taxi. "If I don't come down in ten minutes, assume you are free to go."

The man nodded, folding the bills Connor had given him.

The cottage was quiet, but that didn't mean Maya wasn't there. He climbed the path, marveling at how he had energy and even a bit of pep, and was only slightly winded by the time he stood on the veranda. Not bad. Not bad at all. This place had been good for him. Magical, even.

The cottage was open and he went inside, calling Maya's name.

No answer. He began checking rooms, including his old one. He still had stuff in there. Maya hadn't packed it up and chucked it. What did that mean?

Noticing the battery was running low for the cottage's power system, he rolled up his shirtsleeves and checked the wires from the solar panels. Something was funky with this system, judging how Maya kept fiddling with it. The wires all appeared to be in order, so he checked the battery's water levels. All good. Probably just old.

Feeling as though he should do something to ensure Maya had what she needed out here, he bent over the generator. It required that adjustment she'd been tinkering with the other week. He headed back into the cottage and grabbed the toolbox from under the sink, then returned to the generator and began fiddling with it until he had the machine running smoothly. He straightened his back and stared straight into the blue eyes that had been haunting him since the night he'd left for Italy. *Maya.*

"What are you doing?" she asked.

"Giving your generator a quick tune-up. It'll use less gas. I think you probably need a new battery, though."

She let out a "humph!" and continued past him, into the building, the door slapping behind her. He carried the tool kit over to where the hinge was coming out of the old wood frame and fixed that, too.

Maya appeared on the other side of the screen, hands on her hips. "What are you doing?"

"Fixing the door. Don't open it for a few hours. The glue needs to dry."

"When'd you become a handyman?"

"I grew up in an old house."

"Why are you here?"

"I was wondering how the entrepreneur project was coming along. I thought I should check in, but I got distracted by a few things that had been bugging me during my stay."

Maya's shoulders relaxed and she laid a hand on the screen door.

"Other exit!" He placed his own palm on his side of the door, keeping it closed, their flesh separated by nothing more than a thin slice of wood.

She stared at him for a moment, then slowly lowered her hand and turned away as though she'd been rejected. After a moment, he heard the screen door off the kitchen slam shut. There was so much to tell her that he didn't know where to start. It didn't help that she was using her poker face with him.

She came around to the wicker seating area and gestured for him to sit. He took a moment to take in her luscious curves, showcased by her tank top and shorts, before joining her.

"It looks as though we are all set to go," she said. "We should have the product ready in six weeks."

"Really? The dental device?"

"You seem surprised."

He *was* surprised. "How'd you pull it together so quickly?"

"There were a few glitches. We overcame them."

"Think we'll make money?" He loved the way she jumped straight into things. No "Hi, how are you? Are we still mad at each other? Why were you such an ass?" She could be professional even when she was pissed at him.

Another good reason to choose her.

"Yes. And I think if we could get in to talk to someone at Health Canada we'd make waves faster."

"I read the paperwork you emailed. The proposal and projections seem conservative, if anything."

She nodded, and he could tell he'd reminded her of the other email she'd sent the same day as the proposal. The email about James. *In time, Maya. Have patience.*

Although the way she wasn't asking about it right off the bat told him he wasn't the only one who had changed.

"I know someone," he said.

"Of course you do." There was a bitterness in her voice.

"I think we could be a good team, Maya."

"Maybe if you listened to me and were an honest, up front... and not a—a..."

He'd never seen her at a loss for words before and knowing he was the reason for all that emotion blocking her ability to express herself, he felt horrible.

"I do listen," he said gently, "and I did. In fact, I took action based on what you told me. I'm sorry that I fired you. I should have handled things better."

Maya shifted farther away from him, her arms crossing over her chest.

"I sold CM Enterprises, Maya."

"What?"

"It'll be in the news later today."

She leaned forward, her eyes locked on his. "You're kidding."

"I'm not. What better way to ensure James got what he deserved than to leave him holding the bag?" Connor grinned. This was still too good to be true. The only downside was the way he'd had to treat Maya and still not knowing who held Bill's allegiance—him or James—and whether he'd burned a good man.

"How did you manage to convince him to buy the company he was ruining?"

"He's a proud man and would have had a lot of explaining to do if he refused to purchase the firm he's always wanted. In fact, it probably would have sounded a lot like a confession. Thanks for throwing in that legal threat during your tirade back at the office, by the way. It really helped me out."

Maya frowned, then her face slowly began to soften. He watched her expressions change, unsure whether she disapproved or not. It made him want to kiss her just to make her smile.

"It's not so bad that he can't turn it around," Connor said. "And now that he owns the place, I'm sure he will. I wish him nothing but good things."

Maya finally smiled, the tension drifting out of her pose.

Connor's phone chirped and he held it up in bafflement. "You get cell service now?"

"They put in a cell booster across the water. It seems to help us a bit. It's spotty, though."

He lifted the phone to his ear. "Connor here."

"The money went through," said his lawyer. "You are out, Mr. MacKenzie."

Connor thanked him and smiled at Maya. He set down his phone and dusted his hands together. "Transaction completed. I am officially no longer the owner of CM Enterprises, Ltd."

"Remind me to never mess with you," she said, with an admiration that stirred him up inside. He wanted to show her all he could do if given the chance, especially now that he was back on his game.

"Shall we?" he asked.

"Shall we what?"

"I'm pretty sure I can get a meeting with the man you need to see at Health Canada. Monday is a holiday, so I'd suggest we get moving. Can your people get to Ottawa on short notice?"

"You're kidding!" Maya smoothed her hair in a move that was uncertain—not typical for her. "Today?"

He pulled her to her feet, keeping her hand in his. "There are two things I never kid about, Maya Summer. Love and business."

MAYA LISTENED TO CONNOR splashing in the cottage bathroom as he shaved and got suited up to meet with his man over at Health Canada. She tried to make herself believe that she could trust Connor to stay in the business game long enough to set this thing on fire, and that he was as excited as she was. Because, really? Who sold their multimillion-dollar company that was doing well, even given James's added speed bumps? Sure, it was pretty cool the way Connor had stuck it to his corrupt advisor and all the man could do was open up and swallow it or face prosecution for misrepresentation of financial statements, bribery, having a negative impact on Connor's product development, corruption, as well as a misappropriation of funds. But the way Connor had been a shadow through the whole entrepreneur deal, and now wanted to swoop in when Maya had it in the bag, didn't quite sit right.

Then again, there was something about him today that reminded her of the old Mr. MacKenzie. A determination and focus that made her body weak with longing.

She rocked forward in her chair, hands tucked between her skirted knees, palm to palm. Then she stood and called through the bathroom door, "Why didn't you trust me? Why didn't you tell me about the deal you were making with James?"

There was silence. Finally Connor said, his voice low and tinged with regret, "I couldn't risk it, Maya. I didn't even tell Bill."

She stood, hand on the bathroom knob. She wanted to see his face.

The door opened and Connor faced her, shirtless and buff, his chin covered in shaving cream. "I'm sorry I had to let you lose face in front of everyone in the office, but I couldn't blow my position. I couldn't let on that I wasn't on James's side. Not until he'd bought the company." Connor turned to the sink to resume shaving.

"Why are you interested in this deal all of a sudden?"

"Do you not want me to go?"

"No, it's fine."

"Good, because I want to meet these people."

While Maya waited for Connor to finish up, she went over her notes one more time, trying to quell her nerves. She toyed with her necklace and wondered what was taking him so long. Shouldn't women take longer than men to get ready?

A few minutes later he appeared fully suited. She slowly took him in, her breath collapsing out of her lungs in a whoosh. He was hot. Ohmigod. So smoking hot she was amazed the smoke detector wasn't having a hissy fit. He was sexy. Powerful. Everything she'd seen in the conference he'd spoken at all those years ago, but more. There was a determination within him that stoked her internal fire. She wanted him. Badly.

He'd shaved, and his chin was a thing of male beauty. She wanted to close the distance and pull him against her and see what their bodies suggested.

He tugged his suit jacket, buttoning it. He'd toned up, and it didn't fit quite as perfectly as the man it had been tailored for, but holy... This was even better than she'd imagined. The world wouldn't know what had hit it. He'd be leaving a wake of wet panties everywhere he went today.

And he'd be on her arm as her business partner.

She picked up her purse and the boat key. "Shall we?"

Connor strode to her side, giving her a peck on the cheek. She nearly swooned. The scent of his cologne. So corporate. Powerful. Expensive.

Yes, this was the life she had been dreaming about.

Connor adjusted his suit. "This feels good. Like putting on a comfortable old skin."

She *knew* it. He may have sold his business, but he was still in the game. She led them down to the dock and gestured for him to get into the old Boston Whaler.

He held out an arm to stop her. "I have other plans."

She frowned. Was he kidding? If they didn't leave now they'd be late.

A seaplane roared in low, drowning out the rest of what he was saying. Damn Rubicore. Daphne was right to stop developments over there. It was disruptive, having richie-rich neighbors next door.

Connor pointed to the plane, which had landed and was motoring toward them. "Our ride awaits."

"A plane is going to take as long as boating to the car." Silly men. Always looking to show off.

"It's taking us to Ottawa. We can land a block from the meeting."

"What?" They were going to arrive by plane? She tore across the dock, eager to get on the aircraft.

Connor laughed. "I thought you might like that."

Maya climbed into the seaplane and grinned at Connor. Without thinking, she grasped his face and drew his mouth to hers. Connor braced himself against the small plane's frame and leaned into her kiss, offering more than he ever had before. His free hand went to her waist as he deepened the kiss.

"I've missed you, spitfire."

"My family calls me Snap," she whispered, her lips barely away from his.

"Why's that?" He gave her another warm, moist kiss.

"Snap decisions."

"Not because you snap at people?"

"Only when they deserve it." She flashed him a wicked grin and his eyelids lowered, his face nudging closer to hers. She inhaled his minty fresh breath and waited for him to kiss her again.

"You've learned patience, I see?"

"Shut up and kiss me. There's a time and place for everything."

"Ottawa?" the pilot asked.

"You know the place," Connor replied. He turned his attention back to Maya. "Buckle up. We have some people to woo."

HE'D DONE IT. Maya could barely believe it. Connor had come in all smiles and information, and drawn everyone in the meeting into one big happy, collaborative family. It was incredible. If there had ever been any doubt in her mind why he was the king, this meeting had definitively squashed it.

Connor helped Maya out of the bobbing aircraft back at Nymph Island.

"So?" he asked. "Did you like traveling in style?"

"Hell, yeah."

"Want to keep doing it?"

Maya turned, her long skirt swishing against her legs. "What do you mean?"

Connor's hand drifted to hers, and he linked their fingers lightly. "I mean, do you want to become business partners? On more than just this project."

"Say what?" She couldn't have heard that correctly, because her brain was definitely incapable of computing the idea of the two of them as business partners, and it could compute plenty.

Connor slipped closer, his expression serious. "You have amazing instincts. I ignored requests for backing for years, and never once considered venture capitalism. But maybe you and I, together, could help people achieve their dreams."

Maya bit her bottom lip. She knew *he* could help people, but what if she couldn't? What if the dental device flopped? It had barely even happened in the first place, because she knew diddly-squat about the real world and timelines, who to talk to, where to go for help and even how long things took. The idea of screwing up all these details again nearly made her hyperventilate.

Connor, with a featherlight touch, tipped up her chin. "You're freaking out in there, aren't you?"

"There's a lot to these deals, you know."

"Um-hmm."

"And a lot of stress."

"Um-hmm."

"And I don't have money."

"There is a place for everyone. You won't have to do everything like you did on this deal. Em agreed to leave CME—man, James is going to want to rename that place—and so has Stella. I gave them bonuses just before I sold." Connor sent Maya a sly grin.

"You're kidding!"

"Not at all. They are most favorably on my side." He angled his head in thought. "Although I'm pretty sure they were even before the bonuses."

"Oh, they totally were. Are," Maya said quickly. "Em was amazing with all of this."

"So, they can take care of details. You can vet the masses. I can be the backer."

"Not silent, though? You'll also be the expertise?"

Connor linked his hands through hers again, his suit jacket brushing her chest. "I happen to think that is where you and I will shine together, Maya."

She squeezed their linked fingers, Connor's hips brushing hers. "Why aren't you running away?"

Her man slid their entwined hands behind her back, releasing her fingers so he could embrace her properly. "I think you're pretty special, you know that?" He shuffled closer, bringing his body flush to hers. "I always have."

"But you..." All those times he'd pushed her away. "You fell asleep while going down on me!"

"I promise I won't ever again."

She took a step back, breaking his hold as she raised an eyebrow. "Maybe that will be an easy promise to keep, seeing as I don't mix business and pleasure."

Connor gave her a mischievous smile, his eyes darkening with desire as he drew her tight again, making her lean back in order to see his face. "Then I guess, sweet Maya, you will have to make a choice or change your mind, because I happen to know you find business pleasurable, and I want to make your pleasure my business."

His breath created light breezes on her exposed neck, making her skin tingle, and she knew she was going to cave if she didn't get away from him. Maya guessed she would just have to grab it all and say to hell with any possible consequences.

"Shall I show you?" he asked. "Give you a taste of what you are choosing between?"

Oh, yes. Most definitely.

MAYA'S LIPS WERE SWEETER than he remembered. Her curves. Her breasts. He was a very lucky man. A lucky man about to make good use of what nature had given him.

As he laid her on the bed in his room, he shook his head and stared down at her. She sat up impatiently and ripped her blouse over her head, not bothering with the buttons and sending her necklace skittering across the floor. He laughed and watched her scramble toward him, ditching her long skirt when it got in the way, her desperation to have him unleashed.

Grabbing his belt, she hauled him closer, working his pants down low. He could feel her hot breath through his boxers, and his erection jumped, trying to get closer to her. He gripped her head, bringing her face to his. She moaned as he worked his tongue over her lips, then nibbled her bottom lip.

She pushed him away, her face scrunched in thought. "Wait."

"It's okay, I have protection in my bag."

"No, I mean…are we going to set up business in Toronto?" She blinked hopefully.

"You're talking as though this is going to happen." He palmed her breast, then ran his fingers over her hard nipples, reminding her why they had moved to the bedroom. "I thought you hadn't chosen yet."

Her eyes fluttered shut and her breathing hiccupped as he continued to caress her breast, ignoring the nipple now, doing everything but touch it.

"Damn you, Connor. Don't tease me."

He laughed. "I think you like it when I tease you." He ran a hand inside her panties, stroking her clit. Her back arched away from him, her fingers digging into his shoulder as he ran a finger over her with agonizing slowness. He loved pushing her buttons. Her body responded with a shudder and he bit her bare skin, making her cry out.

"Don't tell me to be patient, Connor," she said, her voice rough with desire. "I need you to pick up the pace."

"Not yet. We're talking, remember."

He ground his erection against her, wanting nothing more than to be inside her warmth.

Maya smoothed her hands up his chest with a desperation that made him want to pin her to the bed and drive himself into her until she screamed his name in pleasure. "I want to live in Toronto," she said.

"Then live in Toronto. I already bought myself a place here. I'll fly into the city for any meetings."

"Wait...what?"

"You heard me." He nibbled on her earlobe, and she drew his body closer. "I just bought a place outside Port Carling, near Tristen's. I thought it would be good for me to get away from the rat race." He squeezed her ass, then ran his fingers along her inner thigh, loving the way she quaked with the effort of holding herself back, trying to mask her need for him. Oh yeah. It was going to be an all-nighter with his gal Maya.

"But..." She drew Connor's hand away so she could think. "I want Toronto."

"So move."

"Toronto feels like such an uphill battle," she moaned.

"Can't you have what you want here?"

She sighed and tipped her head back, giving in. Her shoulders dropped slightly. "I've always wanted out of here. But I think that was because I wanted to be a part of something big. Bigger. You know?"

"I do."

"Do you?" Her eyes on his, she slowly drew his ring finger into her mouth, sucking hard enough to make his cock bounce in jealousy.

He sucked in a shaky breath. She was doing him in. He needed her. Now. He yanked down his boxers, nudging her folds through her damp panties. "Come here, spitfire. No more thinking."

Kneeling on the bed, she wrapped his tie around her hand and shook her head. "I don't think so. You come to me." With a tug, she had him following her onto the mattress.

His mouth trailed goose bumps down her flesh, her skin sweet under his lips. She wrapped her arms around him and pulled his face to hers.

"Patience," he said, backing away.

"Next time. I've already been waiting weeks for this."

"Only weeks?" He gripped her wrists, pinning them to the bed.

"Yes."

"Then pull down your panties and prove it."

"Let go and I will." She raised an eyebrow in a dare, and he knew things would only get better for Connor MacKenzie.

MAYA OPENED AN EYE, her arm slung around a naked, strong male body. She propped herself up, drawing circles on Connor's bare chest. The best wake-up in the history of her universe. Connor MacKenzie in her bed. *The* Connor MacKenzie. And he was the king. The king of her bedroom, her destiny, her future.

"Hey," she said as he awoke. "Good morning."

"It is," he confirmed, his hand under the sheets. He smiled and gripped her bare thigh. "Always sleep in the nude, Miss Summer?"

"Only when there is a man to wrap myself around."

"And that happens frequently?"

"Not as often as I'd like, but I'm interviewing new partners and think I've found someone with potential. He's got the asset mix I've been looking for. A real go-getter, with experience."

"Are you calling me a man-whore?"

"Does that shoe fit, Cinderella?" She rolled overtop of him, trapping his body beneath hers.

"You calling me a princess? Because I'll have you know a princess can't do this." He nudged her inner thigh with his morning wood, and she swung her legs down on either side of his hips, hoping for more.

He placed her hand between their bodies, using it to stroke himself. "This is all because of you, you know."

"Sure it's not just a morning erection?"

"I'm sure." His steady gaze held something that made her

insides go gooey. As though she mattered. As though he cared about her. And a bit as though she was responsible for the way he'd turned his world around. The way his smiles lit up his face and made her want to make him smile every day for the rest of their lives.

Yes, *their* lives. She'd made up her mind. Partners. All the way, and in every sense of the word.

"For future reference, that shoe does not fit. I'm a one-gal kind of guy."

"Good to know."

"So, Maya Summer. Have you decided what you'd like to do with your future?"

"You know..." She sat up. "I think I want to try mixing business and pleasure. If that offer is still on the table."

He smiled as though she'd given him the best news of his life, and she fell a little bit further in love.

"Damn right it is," he said.

"Good, because I might even like you."

His fingers dug into her hips. "Good, because I love my spitfire. And not just because of her grit and resiliency and bulldog attitude in the business world. You get me, and I get you, Maya. You make me laugh and want to be a better man. You fix my wounds and help me find purpose in my life."

Maya's heart skipped and stuttered. Did he just say...

"I said it too soon, didn't I?"

She nodded hesitantly.

"You feel right, Maya Summer. And while my own patience isn't particularly great, when my instincts tell me something is a good deal, I tend to move fast."

"Snap decisions."

"Is that going to be a problem?"

"Have you forgotten who is naked and straddling you?" She dropped a kiss onto his lips. "Besides, gut instincts never lie."

"Listen to me and we'll go places, baby."

"I think we already are," she replied. "We have the right asset mix to make it long-term."

"Even through an economic bounce."

"Downturns in the economy."

"A bull market." He nudged her with his erection.

"I love you when you talk dirty."

"Do you, Maya?" He was serious.

"Love you?" she asked, playing for time. Could she tell him how she felt, just as he'd told her? Would it make things awkward or difficult if she let herself do so? Shut her eyes, let go of the rope and fall into whatever he had in mind?

Could she trust him? She was already changing her life for him. They were starting a business together here in Muskoka.

What about her plans? Her dreams? But things with him... they were the real dream, weren't they? The thing she'd never dared allow herself to believe she could have—all of it. Business and pleasure and success and love. And all with one man.

The real dream: Connor MacKenzie.

"Yes. I love you. And not just because you are willing to give me everything I've ever wanted and more, but because of the way you understand me and know how I'm going to trip myself up even before I do. You're there with the net to catch me before I hit the ground. And despite all my flaws, you are still here, willing to help me grow into the woman I really want to be. You trust me in ways I don't trust myself." Maya, her voice thick with emotion, whispered, "You make me a better person, Connor."

"Hot damn, Maya." He peppered her face with kisses and rolled her under him. "You are the lifeline I never knew I needed.

Like a lighthouse on safe shores, beckoning to me through the storm. The one place I always wanted to be."

"You'd better make me scream your name out soon, because we're getting pretty mushy, and I really hate to cry in front of men."

"Oh, don't worry, I have a lot of time before the next meeting to make you moan and thrash about in ecstasy. When is our meeting again?"

"In about a week."

"You are going to be so tired of screaming my name you're going to want to find a new project to keep me busy."

"I think that might just be my destiny."

Hello Summer Sisters Readers!

Do you enjoy reading romance?
&

Would you like to be the first to hear about new releases from Jean Oram?
&

Do you love saving money on ebooks?
&

Do you want to get in on exclusive giveaways and FREEBIES?
&

If you answered yes to any of these questions you're going to love my author newsletter.

For fast & easy online sign up go to: www.jeanoram.com/FREEBOOK

Love and Dreams Book Club Discussion Starters

1) Connor McKenzie is not a typical romance hero billionaire in that his financial success has come at a great cost his physical health as well as emotional and social wellbeing. Do you believe this makes Connor more real to the reader? Why or why not? Why do you believe the author chose to portray him this way?

2) Why do you believe Maya wants to be in control of so many things and is impatient for change in her life? What are the consequences of her behavior? What are some ways these personality traits have worked to her advantage or disadvantage?

3) Why do you think the sisters aren't willing to ask their rich boyfriends for help with the cottage's tax bill? How would their relationships be impacted if they accepted a large financial gift? Do you think they would find themselves in a similar situation again next year or a few years down the line?

4) Why do you believe the author chose to make Catherine, Maya's mother, disabled and unable to help the sisters?

5) The Summer Sisters Tame the Billionaires series touches upon a lot of issues such as taxation, heritage preservation, shoreline protection/nesting habitats, light pollution, watershed problems, large resort developments, and single parenting. What do you believe adding in such issues adds to the stories and the connection readers have the series?

6) Sense of place plays an important role in this book. Think about times when a sense of place has been relevant in your own memories and bonds with people in your family or friendship circles. Share an example with other book club members. Do you believe that the four sisters would be as close as they are without the common meeting ground of Nymph Island? Why do you believe Nymph Island and Trixie Hollow are so important to the Summers?

7) If the cottage was newer and in better condition, in which ways would that impact the story?

8) The theme of overcoming one's obstacles in order to grow and become the person we dream of becoming is threaded throughout the series. What obstacles do Maya and Connor overcome?

9) Do you think that two weeks of rest was long enough to show a change in Connor? Why or why not?

10) If the characters were real life people and you had a chance to meet them, who would you choose and why?

Did your book club enjoy this book? Consider leaving a review online.

The Summer Sisters Tame the Billionaires

One cottage. Four sisters. And four billionaires who will sweep them off their feet.

Love and Rumors ~ Love and Dreams
Love and Trust ~ Love and Danger

The Blueberry Springs Collection

Book 1: Champagne and Lemon Drops—ALSO AVAILABLE IN AUDIO
Book 2: Whiskey and Gumdrops
Book 3: Rum and Raindrops
Book 4: Eggnog and Candy Canes
Book 5: Sweet Treats
Book 6: Vodka and Chocolate Drops (Coming Summer 2015)
Book 7: Tequila and Candy Drops (Coming Winter 2015)

Do you have questions, feedback, or just want to say hi? Connect with me! I love chatting with readers.

Youtube: www.youtube.com/user/AuthorJeanOram
Facebook: www.facebook.com/JeanOramAuthor
Twitter: www.twitter.com/jeanoram
Website & Lovebug Blog: www.jeanoram.com
Email: jeanorambooks@gmail.com (I personally reply to all emails!)
Up-to-date book list: www.jeanoram.com

I'd love to hear from you.

Thanks for reading,
Jean

Jean Oram grew up in an old schoolhouse on the Canadian prairie, and spent many summers visiting family in her grandmother's 110-year-old cottage in Ontario's Muskoka region. She still loves to swim, walk to the store, and go tubing—just like she did as a kid—and hopes her own kids will love Muskoka just as she did when she was young(er).

You can discover more about Jean and her hobbies—besides writing, reading, hiking, camping, and chasing her two kids and several pets around the house and the great outdoors—on her website: www.jeanoram.com.

Made in the USA
Charleston, SC
15 May 2015